THE SAPPHIRE SMILE: THE ADVENTURES OF PETER THE BRAZEN, VOLUME 4

D1598154

THE SAPPHIRE SMILE

THE COMPLETE ADVENTURES OF PETER THE BRAZEN, VOLUME 4

LORING BRENT

ILLUSTRATED BY

ROGER B. MORRISON & JOHN R. NEILL

COVER BY

PAUL STAHR

STEEGER BOOKS • 2020

PUBLISHING HISTORY

"The Sapphire Smile" originally appeared in the February 8, 1930 issue of *Argosy* magazine (Vol. 210, No. 1). Copyright © 1930 by The Frank A. Munsey Company. Copyright renewed © 1957 and assigned to Steeger Properties, LLC. All rights reserved.

"The Man in the Jade Mask" originally appeared in the April 26, 1930 issue of *Argosy* magazine (Vol. 211, No. 6). Copyright © 1930 by The Frank A. Munsey Company. Copyright renewed © 1957 and assigned to Steeger Properties, LLC. All rights reserved.

"That Cargo of Opium" originally appeared in the June 21 & 28, 1930 issues of *Argosy* magazine (Vol. 213, Nos. 2 & 3). Copyright © 1930 by The Frank A. Munsey Company. Copyright renewed © 1957 and assigned to Steeger Properties, LLC. All rights reserved.

"The Hand of Ung" originally appeared in the November 22 & 29, 1930 issues of *Argosy* magazine (Vol. 216, No. 6–Vol. 217, No. 1). Copyright © 1930 by The Frank A. Munsey Company. Copyright renewed © 1958 and assigned to Steeger Properties, LLC. All rights reserved.

"About the Author" originally appeared in the January 25, 1930 issue of *Argosy* magazine (Vol. 209, No. 5). Copyright © 1930 by The Frank A. Munsey Company. Copyright renewed © 1957 and assigned to Steeger Properties, LLC. All rights reserved.

Visit steegerbooks.com for more books like this.

TABLE OF CONTENTS

THE SAPPHIRE SMILE

*Peter the Brazen returns to the Orient which has
been forbidden him under pain of death—and to a
shipboard adventure that pales his maddest exploits*

CHAPTER I

THE DEATH STRUGGLE

THE TALL, BLUE-EYED young man who had remained so aloof throughout the voyage was seated in a steamer chair and profoundly observing the effects of a full gale on one of the finest liners in the China service.

His brier pipe was gripped between his teeth; his cap was pulled down to his eyes; the collar of his gray trench coat was turned up to his ears, and his hands were thrust deep into the pockets.

The time was dusk. Under lowering blue-black storm clouds, mountains of water toppled and hurled themselves at the *Queen of Asia*. Spray, torn in ragged foaming white clumps from wave crests by the tremendous wind, came hurtling down the deck, pulverized to a white mistlike steam. This salt mist was ruinous to clothing, but the young man did not seem to care.

As if he were thoroughly enjoying himself, he sat there, gazing up the deck toward the bows; watching them rise until they seemed to scrape the low clouds, and fall until it seemed that they must plunge below the surface and never emerge.

It was a forbidding picture, with the great marching walls of white-streaked gray, each one a barrier to meet and overcome; the ominous dark clouds, themselves tattered and torn by the gale that bore them along; the rearing and plunging bows; the wet teak deck slanting first this way, then that, against the saw-toothed horizon. Forbidding and dismal, too. One

1

*The fellow dragged the
body toward the rail.*

wondered how long any ship could endure such battering, such pounding, such twisting and straining.

A little of it had sent every other passenger indoors and most of them to their cabins. There would be very few in the dining saloon tonight. One by one the young man had seen them driven by the gale to their berths, blanched of face, blurry of eye and greenish-blue of lip.

It had grown perceptibly rougher and wilder since the last of them had disappeared below. The pitch of the wind had gone higher. It no longer howled in the rigging; it screamed. And the lurching of the ship was certainly more violent.

A SHIP'S officer in oilskins and sou'wester came down the deck from a forward stairway. Expert sea legs were necessary. He clung to the rail with one hand, to his yellow hat with the other. Spray splashed into his face and streamed off curiously in long feathery tendrils from the point of his nose and chin.

Glittery-eyed, he went staggering aft. Once his eyes fell upon the solitary young man, but his eyes seemed not to see him.

The young man recognized him as the first officer and nodded, but the first officer did not return the nod. He looked worried, and the young man wondered what the trouble was. In a gale as heavy as this, so many things aboard a ship could go wrong.

Another figure now appeared at the forward turn of the promenade deck; the slim figure of a girl in a shiny red raincoat and a close-fitting dark blue helmet.

As she started down the deck, the deck began to rise. With the wind behind her, she climbed with as much effort as though she were negotiating the steep slope of a mountain.

Then the angle of the deck was reversed. The bows went up and the stern went down; a sharp, redly glistening hill extended from the girl to the young man.

She came toward him at a run. With the savage wind helping her, she was soon running uncontrollably, taking long, exaggerated strides. She was trying to reach the rail, but the deck was tilted also, so that her tendency was to run into the long white wall of the cabin.

The young man started up from the chair. He braced his back against the corridor wall, intending to catch the girl in his arms and cushion the shock of her interrupted runaway. But when she was within a dozen feet of him, the deck tilted the other way. She lurched to the left and away from him toward the rail.

She struck her shoulder against a rail stanchion, rebounded— or caromed—spun about twice in a swirl of red raincoat, dark-blue dress and slim legs, and would have fallen if the young man had not caught her by one hand and spun her about in the reverse direction—it all reminded him later very much of an eccentric dance—and caught her about the waist with two imprisoning arms, so that her back was against his chest, and the back of her head just under his chin.

FOR AN instant, the girl remained inert in his arms. Then, with a violent twist, she freed herself, and the young man now saw that, during that wild dance, she had dropped her pocket-book, a cobalt-blue leather affair, and its contents had spilled out over the deck.

The girl reached first for the pocketbook, but a heave of the deck sent her staggering away; so the young man, abandoning dignity, got down on hands and knees in the wet and began retrieving the pocketbook's contents.

A tiny blue-bordered handkerchief was whisked away on the wind and out to sea with such rapidity that the eye could hardly follow it.

In the following order, the young man recovered: a gold compact, a gold-backed oblong mirror, an ivory lipstick holder, a gold cigarette lighter, a gold cigarette case, a key ring containing three keys, and a small flat oblong box of white jade with gold hinges. On the lid of the white jade box was a design in sapphires—large, clear, Ceylon or Chantabon sapphires.

As the young man was curiously—or pardonably—interested in all things Chinese, he took the liberty of examining the box carefully. He did not lift the lid, but he did examine the sapphire decoration with the greatest interest, because there was no question but that it meant to represent a human smile; not the crescent of a blue moon, but a smile, tugged up at the corners and drooping in the middle—a sapphire smile.

But he was not given the opportunity to inspect it for long. As he knelt on the wet deck looking at it, a small white slender hand reached down and snatched it away from him.

With the other articles gathered together in his other hand, he got up and looked at the girl. It was not by any means the first time he had noticed her. He had, in fact, been noticing her daily since the *Queen of Asia* left San Francisco. He had noticed her in the dining saloon—unquestionably the most fashionably gowned woman aboard; in the smoking room, sipping an *apéritif* or a *liqueur* alone; on deck and even in the swimming tank when she had worn a black silk swimming suit so slight in area, so charmingly revealing, that three women missionaries had protested to the captain about it.

He had, quite by chance, run into her at Waikiki Beach, in Honolulu, having luncheon alone under a palm tree. And each time he had encountered her she had looked at him with the same air of disdain or contempt which she lavished on every one.

If he had remained aloof throughout the long voyage, she had been a downright recluse. Every friendly advance made by fellow passengers and ship's officers she had coolly repulsed.

NEVER BEFORE had the young man realized what a beauty she was. And her eyes quite overshadowed the slim aristocratic beauty of her face. They were so large that they were haunting. Their color was not blue, but deep violet, and until now he had never seen them when they were not aglow with some romantic preoccupation.

Now, he was less attracted to her than he had ever been; for it seemed to him that she was being unpardonably rude. After all, he had recovered everything that had fallen from the pocketbook except the wisp of handkerchief.

He said, casually and coldly: "It's pretty rough weather to be taking a walk on deck."

And her voice, which he had not heard before, answered: "It was good of you to rescue my things."

She spoke with a voice of fine quality, like good metal struck upon sharply; clear and rather sweet and, like the rest of her, curiously suggestive of romance. As if to atone for her rudeness, she added:

"It was awfully good of you to rescue all of us!"

"Not at all," said Peter Moore.

She opened her purse and dropped the retrieved articles into it. He did not see the white jade box with the sapphire smile. That had mysteriously vanished.

As if sensing his own aloofness, she asked: "Do you think this weather will last long?"

"It's often rough this time of year off Japan," Peter Moore said.

"Oh, you've crossed before?"

"Yes."

With the flicker of a smile that was not quite a smile, she turned and pursued her way aft. The deck lights had come on and the dusk had correspondingly grown darker. Only the white fangs of waves were now visible beyond the rail.

Peter Moore stood for a moment, hanging to the rail. The girl's rudeness had irritated him, and the mystery of her actions new piqued his curiosity.

That jade box, with its sapphire ornament, was worth a fortune. The sapphires alone were worth a fortune. Evidently she did not have much sense, or she would have had the purser lock it up in the ship's strong box.

The thing was as Oriental as sandalwood incense, as Oriental as the summer palace at Peking—and as regal. Why was the girl carrying the jade box and why was she making such a mystery of it? Why had she so rudely snatched it from his hand?

There is an old Chinese proverb to the effect that if you wish to live out your allotted span, it is folly to ride tigers. Peter Moore knew his China. He had ridden Chinese tigers, and he hankered after no more rides. He wanted no further Chinese adventures.

With his back to the wind, he tamped out the soggy dottle in his pipe and recharged it. As he stood there, swaying to the uneasy movements of the deck, he became aware that a pair of eyes not five feet away were fixed upon his profile.

He turned sharply and looked full into the eyes for a space of perhaps two seconds. They were oblique eyes, innocent of lashes or brows—or so it seemed in that murky light—and they were fixed upon him with an inscrutable stare. Cold, hard, implacable, bordered by a narrow, receding forehead above and the bridge of a nose below, they registered him—and were gone.

He had not seen anything of the Oriental face below the nose, because of the brass porthole rim.

With an uneasy feeling, Peter Moore started aft and around the after turn of the deck., He intended to go into the smoking room for a smoke and a whisky-and-soda.

As he rounded the turn, he became aware of two figures struggling against the rail in the dim light on the farther side. Their distance from him and the bad light made it impossible for Peter to make them out clearly. All he could see was that both wore dark suits and that they were locked in what might well have been a death grip.

Suddenly one of the combatants collapsed, but before he sank quite to the deck, the other picked him up, lifted him to the rail and dropped him into the sea!

CHAPTER II

A MYSTERIOUS WARNING

THE SURVIVOR OF this amazing death struggle turned from the rail, evidently saw the young man in the gray trench coat, and started up the deck at a run.

Peter hastily stuffed his pipe into a pocket and gave chase. When he reached the port side, he saw the man open a door and vanish, but not before Peter had caught a glimpse of the man's profile.

Unquestionably a Chinese, yet lacking the strong Mongoloid characteristics of the northern Chinese. Such a dark skin labeled him a southern Chinese, perhaps Tonkinese, Annamite, Cambodian.

The door opened upon a narrow thwartship corridor which gave, in turn, upon a wide fore-and-aft hall. A steward in the center of the hall was mopping up sea water that had spilled in over the wave-check under the door at the after end.

"Where did he go?" Peter gasped.

"Who, sir?"

"That Chinese who just ran through here."

The steward looked at him blankly. "Nobody came through here, sir. I've been here for ten minutes, and you're the first person I've seen, sir."

Peter returned to the corridor which ran to the deck door. It was logical to assume that the murderer had slipped into one of the four cabins which faced upon this corridor.

But he forebore knocking. He made a mental note of the stateroom numbers—117, 118, 119 and 120. There was no time to be lost if an attempt were to be made to pick up that poor devil who had gone overboard.

Peter, having sailed these seas for years, recognized the futility of turning a ship about to search for a man, lost overboard on such a night. Doubtless, he had been killed by a knife thrust before that watery doom overtook him. But Peter intended to notify the captain or the officer on the bridge immediately.

He opened the door to the deck—and found himself face to face with the girl in the red raincoat.

SHE WAS as white as a ghost. Her lips were gray. And her violet eyes were wide with terror. Peter saw the muscles in her slim white throat working convulsively. She threw out a hand toward the rail where that tragedy had so recently occurred.

"Did you—see that?"

"Did you?" Peter countered.

She was making obvious efforts to recover her self-control.

"I—I saw a man throw a bundle of old clothing overboard."

Peter gave her a hard grin. He wasn't amazed. Somehow, he wouldn't be amazed at anything this girl said or did. He was beginning to smell Chinese tigers again. Peter started to pass her.

"Where," the girl gasped, "are you going?"

"To tell the captain about that bundle of old clothing."

"But it's too late to—rescue them! They're a mile astern. They'd sink."

With her wide violet eyes she was pleading with him. Peter said:

"Do you know the Chinese who threw that—bundle of old clothing overboard?"

By her eyes he knew that she did, although her clear golden voice said: "No. But—" She hesitated.

"Well?" said Peter Moore.

"You are apt to cause a great deal of trouble if you go to the captain. I don't know who you are, but I presume you are an American. You look intelligent. I simply want to say that you aren't in America now. Take my advice and—don't interfere."

Peter smiled at that. It amused him to be mistaken for a callow young American who knew nothing of China or Chinese methods.

The girl's attitude was that of a seasoned adventuress. He was certain that she was an adventuress, and he wondered just how seasoned she was. She looked so innocent! But he had been deceived into believing in the innocence of schemers who seemed even more guileless than this girl.

She looked as if butter wouldn't melt in her mouth. Nevertheless, an inner voice whispered: "Beware! This is going to prove to be an exceptionally ugly tiger."

So he said, courteously: "Thank you for your advice."

Peter went forward, but not to the bridge. It was too late now to do anything on behalf of that poor devil who had gone overboard—like a bundle of old clothing. He went on toward the purser's office.

To be sure, he wanted the information merely to satisfy his natural curiosity: he intended, once he had obtained it, to do nothing. No, thank you, he was not going to mix into this affair, but he must know who occupied staterooms 117, 118, 119 and 120. In due course, he would lay his information before the captain.

A young clerk so seasick he could hardly stand let him into the purser's office and supplied him with the passenger list.

Peter said: "Hmmm," very thoughtfully. Staterooms 117, 118, 119 and 120 were all bracketed under one name—Tsing Gow Lou. This should make the identification of the murderer a very simple matter indeed.

"Who," Peter asked the seasick young purser's clerk, "is Mr. Tsing Gow Lou?"

"I don't know, sir," the young man said weakly. "I think he is a very rich Chinaman, a mandarin maybe."

"Does he have the exclusive use of these four cabins?"

"I believe so, sir. No other names are listed for them."

"What is Mr. Tsing's destination?"

"We have him booked as far as Hong Kong, sir."

PETER THANKED him and went out. He deliberated between going to the captain and personally investigating those four staterooms—and Mr. Tsing Gow Lou. He decided to do nothing for the present. He would wait.

He glanced at his wrist watch and made his way to the dining saloon. Aside from a very pale and uneasy-looking steward, the dining saloon was empty when Peter went in. He seated himself at the small table to which he had been assigned when the *Queen of Asia* left San Francisco.

A moment later the girl in the red raincoat came in and seated herself at her usual table across the room. She had not dressed for dinner tonight, but still wore the blue serge suit. She glanced over at Peter and met his eyes blankly, quite as though she had never seen him before, but she was paler than usual.

A deep bass voice boomed: "Well! Well! Well! So we've got a few sailors aboard, after all! You people had better join me at my table."

Peter looked around. Captain Runk had come in and was briskly rubbing his large red hands together. He was a tall, wide-shouldered man of forty with a short black beard and the most piercing blue eyes that Peter had ever seen.

Beside him stood a little old lady with white hair. She was smiling. Peter had seen her on deck at various times. She was always knitting, always smiling.

Peter arose. The girl across the dining room hesitated. Then she, too, got up and moved over the lurching floor toward the captain's table. Racks to prevent plates and silver from sliding about had been installed at the captain's table. The captain seated himself at his accustomed place and said:

"I'm afraid I don't know the names of you two young people. This lady is Miss Teasely, of Hong Kong."

"Mine is Susan O'Gilvie," the girl explained.

"Mine is Peter Moore," said Peter.

Miss Teasely and Miss O'Gilvie seated themselves on either side of Captain Runk, and Peter slipped into the chair beside Miss Teasely—of Hong Kong.

A fifth immediately appeared—a chubby round-faced Oriental, with shoe-button eyes set in folds of yellow fat. He resembled a complacent Buddha—the Buddha of Kapilivastu after the epochal discovery that abstinence from food is folly. He hesitated and sat down in the chair beside Miss O'Gilvie.

"We have just finished complimenting ourselves and introducing ourselves," Captain Runk said. "Miss Teasely, Miss O'Gilvie, Mr. Moore, this is—Mr. Tsing."

Mr. Tsing's face was wreathed in smiles, quite literally. About his rather full little mouth were wrinkles and wrinkles, and each one of them was a smile in itself. Peter examined him casually. Mr. Tsing!

"I know," said the captain, "that it won't make any difference to people who are such good sailors as the four of you, but the barometer is rising. I expect to run out of this blow long before sun-up."

IN HONOR of this merry occasion, the captain ordered champagne. Then Mr. Tsing ordered champagne. And Peter followed their example.

"There is nothing like champagne for relaxing the stomach," Captain Runk announced. "Well, who are we all, anyhow? We have proved ourselves to be five exceptional travelers. Most of my officers and crew are so sick they can't walk. Out of five hundred passengers, only four come to dinner. Miss Teasely, let's hear your story."

The little old lady sipped her champagne and smiled.

"The truth is, I'm not in the least exceptional. I run the only American ice cream parlor in Hong Kong."

"But that," Miss O'Gilvie cried, "is most exceptional. I think it's marvelous, don't you, Mr. Moore?"

"I think it's great," Peter said.

"I started in business four years ago," Miss Teasely went on. "I went to Hong Kong to look after a brother in the consular service who was drinking himself to death."

"The consular service?" Captain Runk interrupted.

"I was responsible only for my besotted brother," Miss Teasely said. "But it proved that he was beyond all human aid. He drank himself quickly into his grave. When I buried him I discovered that I loved Hong Kong. I discovered also that visiting Americans longed for ice cream soda and sundaes. So I started my shop on Queen's Road. My success amazed me."

"I can add to that story," said Mr. Tsing in his slow, careful English. "When Miss Teasely's brother died, he left behind him a great aggregation of chits, worth upwards—"

"Mr. Tsing, please!" Miss Teasely protested, but the Buddhistic Mr, Tsing went on:

"You two young people are Americans and know nothing of Chinese customs. In treaty cities, such as Shanghai, Amoy and Hong Kong, a white man can sign little slips of paper in almost any amount for almost anything he wishes. These are accepted by the Chinese at their face value and are used practically as currency. If you wish a new suit, you sign a chit. If you wish to buy a little Chinese girl, you sign a chit. But you cannot leave China until these chits are paid. Miss Teasely's brother left chits amounting to upward of ten thousand Mex. Miss Teasely felt it her honorable duty to pay off these chits. So she started her ice cream pidgin. She is an honorable and respected woman. I take pleasure in saying this for my race. We wish the Far East were full of Miss Teaselys."

Miss Teasely was blushing, and Miss O'Gilvie was gazing at her with glowing violet eyes—eyes radiant with romance. Well, Miss Teasely was romantic. She had executed a noble and romantic duty.

"You are not from Hong Kong, Mr. Tsing?"

"I am from Saigon," the Oriental said. "I run an ivory and jade shop on the Marche de Cho-dui. A well frog knows nothing of the sea, perhaps, yet rumors have a way of making channels— even into wells. Let us hear from this charming young person with the lovely eyes."

MISS O'GILVIE laughed softly. "I am simply nobody. I am a school teacher bound for Indo-China, but not Saigon. Hanoi."

"To teach school in Hanoi?" Miss Teasely asked sharply.

"Yes, Miss Teasely—Hanoi."

Miss Teasely of Hong Kong looked puzzled. "I cannot imag-

ine any one as young and lovely as you, Miss O'Gilvie, going to
a place like Hanoi—even to bring enlightenment to the little
heathen—if Mr. Tsing will pardon me. Hanoi! Hmph!"

Her air was close to suspicious. It created uneasiness. Mr.
Tsing broke it by bending forward and saying to Peter Moore:

"And you, Mr. Moore?"

"I have no claims at all to distinction," Peter replied.
"Compared to Miss Teasely's ice cream parlor and Miss O'Gilvie's school teaching and Mr. Tsing's jade and ivory shop, my
work is drier than dust."

He saw that, of the four at the table, three were watching and
listening with the keenest interest Captain Runk's piercing blue
eyes were fairly boring holes in Peter. Mr. Tsing, for the moment,
had put aside his smiles, and Miss O'Gilvie was staring at him
with a peculiar fascination. Only Miss Teasely seemed casual.

"I work in the research department of the radio division of the
General Electric Company, in Schenectady," Peter said. "What
could be drier than that?"

"I think it's fascinating," Miss O'Gilvie said, and her deep-violet eyes glowed. It was evident that, just as Confucius found
hopelessness in all humanity, Miss O'Gilvie found naught but
romance. "Why are you going to China?"

"I'm on my way to Hong Kong," Peter said, "to look up a
young Chinese genius named Fong Toy. Fong Toy has perfected,
in his private laboratory, a device which, it is said, will eliminate static. As you perhaps know, static is the one evil of radio
telephony and wireless telegraphy which we have so far been
unable to clean up.

"Fong Toy, like most geniuses, is a stubborn young man. He
refuses to come to the General Electric, so General Electric
must go to him."

"How perfectly fascinating!" Miss O'Gilvie breathed. "You're
going all the way to Hong Kong to look at some little gadget
that will make the air safe for the Wash 'Em Soap hour!"

Mr. Tsing found his smile. He said: "It is a curious coincidence. For several years a young man named Moore, a wireless operator on ships on this run, got himself into one kind of trouble after another in China. Once he almost precipitated a war. He was a reckless adventurer and a most dangerous young man. He took all laws unto himself. He was so bold, so audacious, that the Chinese coined a name for him—Ren-Beh-Tung, which means, The Brass Man. Among American and British residents he was known, whimsically, as Peter the Brazen. I believe his given name was Peter. That was it. Peter Moore!"

"That," said Peter dryly, "is curious. Very curious. My given name happens to be Peter, too."

The violet eyes of Miss O'Gilvie had grown very round.

"You aren't—" she impulsively began, and checked herself.

"I have heard of that young man," Miss Teasely put in. "Wasn't he ordered, by certain people, to leave China and never return?"

"He was," Captain Runk said emphatically. "He was told that if he ever returned, on any excuse whatever, his life would not be worth—that!" And very expressively indeed Captain Runk snapped his fingers.

"You must let people know that you are not Peter the Brazen," Miss Teasely said.

"Yes," Mr. Tsing agreed, "it would be an excellent plan to let it be known, Mr. Moore, that your intentions are peaceful and harmless."

"**OF COURSE,**" Peter said. He was conscious that the atmosphere at the table had subtly changed. It had become pervaded by a certain ominousness, as if a veiled threat hung in the very air.

Captain Runk had withdrawn into himself. Miss Teasely was no longer smiling. And Mr. Tsing had become suddenly affable; quickly he had changed the subject. He was now describing typhoons he had been in.

Only Miss O'Gilvie took no pains to hide her sudden interest in this golden-haired, blue-eyed, good-looking young man who bore the name of a notorious adventurer. She was gazing with glowing romantic eyes at Peter.

An interruption was provided by the first officer. In his dripping oilskins and sou'wester he came lurching across the rocking deck, to announce harshly:

"Cap'n, the chief wireless operator, O'Brien, must be lost overboard. I've searched the ship from stem to stern. He came down about an hour ago, so the second says, to deliver a message, and he never came back. The second is rattled and hysterical. O'Brien isn't in his stateroom, or the engine room, or the officers' mess. He isn't aboard."

Peter was watching Captain Rank. The skipper had not changed his expression. Only his eyes had slightly narrowed. And Peter was certain that Captain Runk had been previously aware that the wireless man was gone. He was doubly certain of it when the captain began to protest.

"You mustn't jump to conclusions like this, Mr. MacKenzie. Maybe he is somewhere, seasick; in some empty stateroom."

"No, sir; he never got seasick in his life. He was due to relieve Williams, the second operator, in five minutes. He went to deliver that message—and he never came back."

"You'll find he's on this ship somewhere, Mr. MacKenzie."

It was a dismissal and a reprimand, but the captain's attitude was not, to Peter, convincing. He felt sure Runk knew that the first operator had gone overboard; and Peter was equally sure that the man he had seen thrown overboard by the Chinese had been that wireless operator.

He looked quickly from the captain to Mr. Tsing. But the Oriental's emotions, whatever they may have been, were concealed behind an imperturbable mask.

First Officer MacKenzie lingered. And Captain Runk inquired sharply: "If you think a man has been lost overboard, do you want to put this ship about and look for him on a night like this?"

"I suppose it wouldn't be any use, sir. All I say is, it's mighty mysterious. Who was that message for?"

"He will show up with the rest of the convalescents as soon

as this sea goes down," Captain Runk said. But his voice and his expression lacked conviction.

THE FIRST officer withdrew. The threat in the air that Peter had sensed had become so pronounced that he was on the alert for the first word. He wanted to hear from Mr. Tsing. But Mr. Tsing said nothing. It was Miss O'Gilvie who broke the silence.

"How dreadful!" she exclaimed.

She was as white as when Peter had encountered her on the deck outside Mr. Tsing's suite. And her eyes were dark with terror.

Captain Runk was endeavoring to reassure her. It was nothing to be alarmed about. He'd had such experiences before. The wireless man had not been lost overboard. He must have given in to seasickness and crawled into the first empty stateroom he saw. He'd show up in the morning, never fear!

The dinner, which had started off so gayly, was finished in a queerly grim silence. Peter was the first to finish. As he rose from his chair and picked the napkin from his lap, a small white oblong fell to the floor.

Peter picked it up. It was a folded sheet of ship's stationery. Upon it was scrawled in sapphire-blue crayon:

A word to the wise: Don't interfere!

And under the scrawl, executed hastily in the sapphire-blue crayon, was a smile!

CHAPTER III

THE SULTAN OF SAKALA

PETER SECURED HIS trench coat from a hook in the little hall outside the dining saloon, and, tossing it over his shoulder, proceeded down the corridor toward the smoking room. Who, he wanted to know, had placed that warning in his lap? Miss

Teasely had sat next to him. Hers had been the easiest opportunity. But what did a cheerful little old lady who ran an ice cream parlor know of sapphire smiles and the intrigue which might lay behind them?

The note succeeded in making Peter Moore irritable. He had not the slightest desire to mount any more Chinese tigers; yet it seemed that, in spite of his anxiety to keep out of trouble, he was being drawn into it as inexorably as a chip is drawn toward the vortex of a whirlpool.

He wanted fresh air, and went on deck. Over the roaring of wind and waves he heard a sharp tapping of heels. Susan O'Gilvie, without hat or raincoat, fairly threw herself into his arms and clung to him. She backed him against the cabin wall. Her enormous dark eyes searched his. Over and over in a tense voice she said:

"Mr. Moore, you've got to help me! You've got to help me!"

To himself Peter said: "Don't weaken. Keep out of this." And aloud: "What's wrong, Miss O'Gilvie?"

She panted: "You know that that man we saw thrown overboard was the wireless operator! The captain knows he was thrown overboard. Did you watch his face?"

"Yes," Peter said.

"You've got to help me," she repeated. "You—you understand such things."

In more senses than one, Peter's back was to the wall.

"I don't understand what you're talking about."

Susan O'Gilvie had seized him by the upper arms.

"I'm frightened," said the girl with the violet eyes. "I've got myself into an awful predicament. And you're the only man who can help me. You *are* the Peter Moore they were talking about. You can help me. Will you?"

Peter freed one of his arms and fished the note he had found in his lap after dinner from his pocket. He held it, fluttering in the gale, before the girl's eyes. Susan O'Gilvie quickly read it, then glanced back to his eyes.

"But you're not afraid," she said. "You wouldn't let that note scare you. An ordinary man might; but you wouldn't."

"Miss O'Gilvie," Peter said sternly, "you heard the captain and Mr. Tsing and Miss Teasely at dinner. What they said was true. Five years ago I was requested by a powerful person in China not to return—for five years."

"Then the five years are up!"

"Not so fast," Peter said. "The five years are up, but there was another condition. If, at the expiration of five years, I returned, I was to notify this certain powerful person, and I was to promise to keep out of trouble. I am going to keep that promise."

"**BUT THIS** has nothing to do with China," Miss O'Gilvie wailed. "It's Indo-China. Really, I'm in dreadful trouble, and you must help me. Listen! That man you saw murder the wireless operator is one of two coolies who were delegated to guard me on this trip."

"To Hanoi?"

"Beyond Hanoi. They are Tonkinese."

"So is Mr. Tsing," Peter pointed out.

"I do not know Mr. Tsing. That is, I only met him tonight," she said.

"But the coolie who killed the wireless operator knows Mr. Tsing. After killing him, he vanished into Mr. Tsing's suite."

Susan O'Gilvie stared at him incredulously, and Peter was sure she was not acting. Undoubtedly she was a badly frightened girl, in need of help.

"I don't know what to make of it," she said. "Why should that coolie have killed the wireless man?"

"Perhaps," Peter suggested, "you'd better tell me all you can."

"Shall we go into the smoking room?"

She was so pale, and she was trembling so, that Peter was afraid she was about to faint. He took her arm and led her down the deck to the smoking room door. Except for the bar steward, the place was empty.

Susan O'Gilvie huddled down into a corner of a leather wall seat, and Peter sank down beside her. He wished she were not so disturbingly pretty. For reasons of his own he had put women behind him, and Susan O'Gilvie was altogether too appealing. And she was certainly a trouble maker. She was the romantic type that would look for trouble until she found it. This had been his very first impression of Susan O'Gilvie, and it was an impression that would be reënforced the longer he knew her.

She curled up in the leather corner, her legs tucked under her, with a naïve air that suggested a schoolgirl, safe is her bedroom, preparing to confide secrets to a bosom companion. She had slim, beautiful legs which Peter carefully ignored.

"About a month ago," Susan O'Gilvie began, "I met a perfectly fascinating Tonkinese, a native sultan, at a big dinner party in San Francisco. He absolutely fascinated me. He told me such weird stories about his sultanate, and he invited me to come and see it."

"The Sultan of Sakala?" Peter inquired.

"You know about him, Mr. Moore?"

"I only know that he was in the States about a month ago. And I know that when I was in the East before he had a very bad reputation."

"Well, he asked me to have tea with him in his suite at the St. Francis. It was terribly irregular, but—I went. He told me more about Sakala—and the awful ignorance of his subjects, and his efforts to make Sakala modern. It was simply fascinating. He is the last absolute monarch on earth. His grandfather made some kind of treaty with the French, whereby the Sultanate of Sakala is absolutely free of French control or supervision. His name is Chong Foo Shommon. Isn't that a fascinating name?"

Her eyes were glowing again and her smile was that of an excited small girl. And Peter's eyes were glowing responsively. Oh, he'd probably help her. He'd make a damned fool of himself again and get himself into more trouble than he ever had before. How could he avoid it?

"**HE WAS** terribly courteous and thoughtful and—everything," Susan O'Gilvie was saying. "And he asked me to tea the next afternoon. Of course, I went. Well, it seems that he had been thinking things over, and he asked me how I would like to go to Sakala and take charge of the school system—start overcoming the pathetic ignorance of those people."

"Are you," Peter interrupted, "an expert on education?"

"Well, not exactly," said the romantic girl, "but I have my B.A. degree from Berkeley, and the sultan was certain that I would do. But I told him I couldn't possibly go—because of my father."

Miss O'Gilvie paused and quickly nipped her lower lip with a row of beautiful white teeth.

"My father and I were terribly devoted," she explained. "Since my mother died we have been very close."

"Where was your father when you and Chong were becoming such good friends?"

"I was coming to that. He was at Catalina Island, fishing. A few days after the sultan sailed for the Far East, my father was—drowned." The mist in the lovely eyes had turned to tears. "He was out fishing—alone—he always fished alone—when a squall came up. His boat was capsized, and his body was later washed ashore below San Pedro. It—it almost killed me. And of all the people who were kind and thoughtful to me, the sultan was the kindest."

"I thought you said he had sailed for the Far East," Peter said.

"Oh, he had. But he heard of it by wireless, and he sent me the longest, sweetest messages! And his agents in San Francisco did everything they possibly could for me. They were wonderful! A few days later a young man—a Tonkinese who is now a student in Berkeley—came to me and said he had had several long messages from the sultan, telling him to look me up and suggesting that perhaps I might want to come to Sakala and pitch into the educational problem so as to—to forget."

"Did you suspect—" Peter began, and checked himself. "Go on, Miss O'Gilvie."

"It sounded so—so adventurous and romantic."

At all events, Peter reflected, Susan O'Gilvie ran true to form.

"Then, one day, this young Tonkinese student—Mr. Kang, his name was—came to me with a little white jade box with the most marvelous sapphires on it in the form of a smile—the one you saw. He said it was my passport to Sakala, that that sapphire smile would open the gates of forbidden cities to me and would guarantee my safe passage through Indo-China—and in any part of Indo-China. I was simply thrilled.

"He said if I would go, he would delegate two Tonkinese coolies to travel wherever I went, to see that I was protected. And it was one of those coolies who threw that wireless man into the sea! Why did he do that, Mr. Moore?"

"I don't know, Miss O'Gilvie."

"But why should he have thrown him into the sea? What could that possibly have to do with—with protecting me?"

PETER FROWNED. He lighted a cigarette and blew a puff thoughtfully at the ceiling.

"The first officer, when he came into the dining room tonight," Peter said, "mentioned that the wireless operator had gone below to deliver a message. Did you notice that the captain did not once ask whom that message was for?"

"I'm afraid of Captain Runk," said Miss O'Gilvie. "Since that man was thrown overboard, I—I'm afraid of everybody. Everybody but you. I'm—afraid to go on with this. I don't know what to do? What *shall* I do?"

"Tell me first what you were planning to do. First, of course, you were going to Hong Kong?"

"No," was the reply. "I wasn't going to Hong Kong." The girl lowered her voice to say. "I wasn't even going to Japan."

She paused. Peter was looking across the top of her shining dark head at a porthole. The porthole framed a pair of oblique shoe-button eyes. They were fixed upon Peter and Susan O'Gilvie in an inscrutable stare!

Peter got up quickly. It did not take him long to open the smoking room door and hasten on deck. There was no one in sight

He walked from the port to the starboard side. The deck was empty. The gale, it seemed to him, was moderating. The wind no longer screamed, and the pitching of the ship was less violent.

He returned to the smoking room and sat down.

Miss O'Gilvie considered him with glowing eyes. She sighed and smiled faintly. When she smiled she was, to use her favorite word—fascinating.

"I did not know," Peter said, "that this ship stopped anywhere between Honolulu and Yokohama."

"That is the point," the girl said mysteriously. "That is why I am in such trouble—so afraid to go on with this; that is why I need your advice and help. Am I making a fool of myself? Will you tell me frankly? The sultan, through Mr. Kang, said it would be much quicker, much safer, much wiser if I boarded a junk that would take me directly to Sakala—right up the Mokong River, without even stopping at Saigon."

It was the first point of her story that seemed really to capture the adventurer's entire interest.

"Where," he asked, "are you to board this junk?"

"At exactly latitude 30°, longitude 135°. Mr. Kang pledged me to secrecy, but I had to tell you—didn't I? You understand, don't you?"

"Yes," Peter said gently, "I understand."

"**THIS JUNK** is to be flying signals of distress. Captain Runk will stop to find out what the trouble is. A small fishing sampan will come around on the other side of this ship and take me and the two coolies off. It sounded so exciting and—and romantic when he told me. But I'm doubtful and I'm afraid. If I hadn't seen, with my own eyes, that coolie throwing that man overboard—"

She stopped impulsively, then went on: "I have a coolie

costume in my stateroom. It's all ready to put on. If I don't go aboard that sampan in the morning, I'm afraid they—they'll do something to me. I'm afraid of the captain. I'm afraid of Mr. Tsing. Mr. Moore, what do you think is behind it all? Is something menacing me—or is it my imagination?"

"Have you decided not to go aboard that junk?" Peter asked.

"Do you think I should?"

"I do not."

"Then," said Miss O'Gilvie with an air of vast relief, "I won't. What will I do?"

"You will go to Yokohama and take the first ship for California, won't you?"

She lowered her eyes. When she looked up, mischievous lights were sparkling in them. Peter would learn, in due course, that those lights invariably spelled trouble.

"I suppose so. I'll do whatever you say. If you only knew what a relief it was to be able to trust some one as I know I can trust you! I know I can depend on you to see me through this!"

"Thank you," Peter said dryly.

"What are we going to do first?" she questioned eagerly.

"You," Peter said, "are going to sit here while I go down to my cabin for a gun."

"Really?" she cried. "Oh, I think that's fascinating!"

"You'll promise not to move from here until I return?"

"I'll promise!"

"No matter who may bring you a message—or urge you to do this or that? I don't want you to leave this spot until I come back."

"I wouldn't dream of it!"

Peter left her with the awareness that, of the various charming, dangerous and beautiful women it had been his lot to know, Susan O'Gilvie had by long odds the most dangerous potentialities. He wondered if she were as innocent as she seemed.

Peter was wary. He had learned, in a hard school, that women are not always what they cleverly endeavor to seem. Could his old enemies in China have set her upon his trail—with this amazing story of a sultan and a junk?

CHAPTER IV

A SCREAM OF TERROR

PETER MOORE WENT swiftly through corridors, down a stairway to the deck below, and to his cabin. He pulled out the bag under his berth, unlocked it and removed from its oiled flannel wrapping a brand new Colt's automatic pistol.

He released the catch which permitted the clip of cartridges to fall into his hand. Examining them, he returned the clip to the butt, dropped the pistol into the right hand pocket of his trench coat and returned to the deck above.

He did not proceed at once to the smoking room. He let himself out on the starboard side and circled the deck until he reached the door opening upon the corridor into which the murderer of the wireless operator had run.

Pressing himself flat against the cabin wall, he inched his way along until, with one eye, he could look into Stateroom 117. The room was alight, but it was empty.

Peter ducked under it, passed the door and negotiated the next porthole, from which light was also streaming in a very thin beam.

Yellow silk curtains had been pulled across the porthole, but, fortunately, they had not been pulled all the way across. A crack perhaps three-eighths of an inch in width existed between the hems of the two curtains.

Glancing up and down the deck to make sure he was not observed, Peter peered into the cabin. What he saw interested him tremendously.

He saw Mr. Tsing Gow Lou seated in a wicker chair smoking

an opium pipe. Mr. Tsing was in the act of inhaling the sizzling lump of gum. He lowered the pipe, retained the smoke for a moment, then exhaled the smoke in a dense blue puff. A yellow hand reached up and accepted the pipe.

But this vision of Oriental self-indulgence was not what peculiarly interested Peter. To the right of Mr. Tsing was a teakwood table. Upon this table sat a very modern radio receiving set. Peter's experienced eye identified it instantly as an eight-tube set, so sensitive that, with its portable loop antennæ, it could readily pick up telegraphic signals from the most remote corners of the Pacific.

Seated before this set was the murderer of the wireless operator. Nickel headphones glittered at his ears.

Putting a very obvious two and two together, Peter realized that while Mr. Tsing indulged in his evening opium, an expert telegraph operator at his elbow conveyed to him all messages which were being sent from and received by the wireless apparatus of the *Queen of Asia!*

WHY, PETER wanted to know, did Mr. Tsing wish a record of all messages handled by the *Queen of Asia's* wireless? What particular message was he so anxious to intercept?

From these difficult queries, it was a simple matter for Peter to deduce that one such message had already been intercepted; that the wireless man who had been murdered had started off to deliver the message to some passenger; that Mr. Tsing had not wished the passenger to receive that message and had simply ordered the operator to be killed and tossed overboard! Simple and effective, indeed!

Peter shivered a little. His respect for Mr. Tsing was mounting. But just where did Miss O'Gilvie fit into this puzzle? He would, if possible, soon learn.

The opium pipe, with its new charge, reappeared. Mr. Tsing accepted it from the yellow claws of, Peter presumed, a servant who squatted on the floor and was toasting the pills as fast as Mr. Tsing consumed them.

Simultaneously, the man at the wireless receiver lifted his hand in a gesture to compel silence. He began to write rapidly on a block of yellow paper. He removed the receivers from his ears and turned excitedly to Mr. Tsing.

Mr. Tsing, in the act of lifting the pipe to his mouth, uttered a sharp sentence, presumably in Tonkinese. The Oriental wireless man reached to the table and picked up a brass-hafted curved dagger—an exceedingly wicked-looking dagger. He started for the door—and Peter started aft.

Unless he was mistaken, he had two people now to look after—Susan O'Gilvie and the wireless operator on watch. He hastened into the smoking room and found Miss O'Gilvie still sitting alone. He snapped:

"Come quick!"

Her beautiful eyes sparkling with the excitement of adventure, Susan O'Gilvie came running.

"This way," Peter said, and led her to the narrow iron ladder which ran up from the promenade to the boat deck. "Up there," he said, "and hang on. This wind is still strong enough to blow you overboard—and there's no rail around that deck."

Miss O'Gilvie fairly scampered up the ladder. Peter followed. In the stormy wet blackness of the boat deck, he encountered her hands. They fluttered to his and clung.

The deck began inclining to starboard. Smoke from the funnels shrouded a light far above them. Spray whipped into their faces. Peter clung to a funnel guy with his free hand and waited for the ship to right herself.

A hundred feet forward a light burned in a small square window. He knew it was the wireless shack. Dimly, in the light, he saw the white bellies of lifeboats; other guys and stays.

"Ready?" said Peter.

"Yes!"

The ship staggered and began to climb an invisible mountain. While it climbed, the man and the girl ran. Peter found the doorknob, twisted it, and threw open the door.

AT THE wireless instruments, beneath a powerful naked tungsten, sat a very pale young man. He removed the headphones from his ears and stared from Peter to Susan O'Gilvie. Even his eyes were pale, and his lips were gray.

"Is there," Peter said gruffly, "a key for this door?"

"Y-y-yes!" stammered the youthful operator. "Why?"

"Lock it!"

Confusedly, the young man pulled out a drawer under the instrument shelf, fished about among assorted odds and ends, found a key. He stumbled to the door and locked it.

"Now," Peter said, "climb over those condensers and pin some paper over that porthole."

"Say, who in the devil are you?"

"Do what I say—quick!"

While the operator obeyed him, Peter was pinning a folded Sunday supplement over the after window.

The operator climbed down. He looked dazed and scared—and sick.

"Did they find Williams?" the radio man asked.

"No. He went overboard."

The young man sank down in the chair and placed shaking hands to his temples.

"Will you tell me what's going on aboard this damned ship?" he said in a whimper. "First, they try to bribe us to let them read all the stuff we receive and send, next—"

"Who tried to bribe you?"

"Those Chinks!"

"Mr. Tsing?" Peter demanded.

"I don't know his name."

"A fat little fellow, always smiling?"

"That's the one! He offered us a thousand dollars each. Then he told us to name our own figures. Williams went to the skipper. And the skipper asked him why we were such suckers. Can you beat that? He would have stood for it! What kind of ship is this, anyhow, when your own skipper is a lousy crook? I don't believe Williams was washed overboard. I believe they killed him. What are they going to do to me? Am I—next?"

"No!" cried the romantic Miss O'Gilvie. "Mr. Moore will save you! Just do what he says."

"But who is he?"

"Haven't you ever heard of Peter the Brazen?"

"Good Lord—" Peter began. He didn't like dramatics.

The boy was staring at Peter.

"Are—you—Peter—Moore?"

"Yes!" said Miss O'Gilvie dramatically.

"Gee!" The boy continued to stare at him as though Peter were a ghost. And in the boy's mind he must have been some-thing of the kind—a heroic figure of legends told and retold in static rooms all over the Pacific.

"Well," he went on, "I—I wish you'd untangle this mystery, Mr. Moore. What's it all about, anyhow? I went down to help look for Williams, and while I was away from here, somebody came in and put my transmitting set on the bum. They changed every connection. I can't send, and they put the receiver on the fritz, too. I wish I'd never come on this damned run. They had me on the Honolulu run, and it was swell. Ever since I got into wireless, I've been hoping they'd put me on the China run. Now I wish I was home."

He was babbling. His voice had risen to a hysterical pitch. Obviously, this young man was cracking under the strain.

"**DID YOU** receive a message in the past few minutes?" Peter asked.

"No, Mr. Moore; how could I? They put my receiver on the bum! Now, why do you—"

A heavy banging on the door interrupted him. A muffled voice bellowed:

"Open that door!"

Peter said curtly to Miss O'Gilvie: "Stand over there." Then, more loudly: "Who's there?"

"The first mate!"

Peter unlocked the door. First Officer MacKenzie, dripping salt water from his sou'wester and oilskins, came stamping in. He looked with surprise at Peter, then at Susan O'Gilvie.

"What is this," he asked, "old home week?"

"We're trying," the operator said, "to figure out this mystery. This is Peter Moore, Mr. MacKenzie. Maybe you've heard of him."

"Yes," said Mr. MacKenzie bluntly, "I've heard of him. I might have known he was aboard this ship when all this trouble started. I won't make any bones about it, Mr. Moore. You sure did build up a great reputation for yourself a few years back as a trouble-maker, out this way."

"He is not at the bottom of this trouble," Miss O'Gilvie stated with dignity. "I am. He is merely helping me out."

"Well, I would be much obliged, miss, if you would bottle up this trouble and give us honest seamen some peace. Maybe you can tell me why we are ordered to check speed and to change our course so's we hit a particular latitude and longitude by exactly sun-up tomorrow mornin'?"

"I know nothing about it," Miss O'Gilvie said. "Rather, I have placed the entire matter in Mr. Moore's hands. He will speak for me."

"Oh, yes," said MacKenzie, "you will speak for her."

Peter grinned. "There's nothing to say—yet. But I'd appreciate it if you would send up your ablest and most trustworthy seaman to guard this wireless shack until we tie up in Yokohama."

"I'll send up the bosun's mate. He fought side by side with me through the war and I'd trust him through—"

THE SHRILL singing of the little wall telephone which communicated with the bridge interrupted him. He exclaimed: "There's the old man now, wantin' to know why I ain't on the bridge. I hope I roast in hell—if you'll pardon me, miss—if I ever sign articles on this old hooker again! Good night, everybody!"

He pulled open the door, sank his red neck, turtle-fashion, into the collar of his oilskins, and went out. The bell continued to ring. The wireless operator got up and answered it.

"Yes, sir," he said crisply. Then: "No, sir; I haven't got it fixed yet. It 'll take me another hour, anyhow. What's that, sir? All right, sir."

He replaced the receiver and turned to Peter. "It was the old man. He wants to see me in his cabin."

"Don't go," Peter warned.

"But I've got to go."

"I am advising you," Peter said, "not to leave this cabin until we are docked in Yokohama."

"I can't help that," said the young man. "When this skipper tells you to do a thing, you do it. If he gets any sorer at me than he is, he won't indorse my certificate at the end of the run. I'll be back as soon as I can."

Susan O'Gilvie slipped into the chair, crossed her beautiful knees and looked up at Peter.

"You see?" she said.

"I see," Peter growled. "We are going to run at reduced speed until we reach latitude 30°, longitude 135° exactly at sunrise. Then you're going aboard that sampan whether you want to or not."

"They can't force me to go!"

"You don't," Peter said wearily, "appreciate these people. Somehow, you will be aboard that sampan tomorrow morning unless—" he said thoughtfully and paused.

"Unless?" she prompted him.

"Unless I—" Peter began again, and stopped. He stared quickly at the girl, and the more or less innocent cause of all this trouble stared at him with suddenly round, terrified eyes.

The sound that had interrupted Peter came again—an unholy scream of agony or terror or both.

CHAPTER V

HONOLULU CALLING

PETER TOOK THE pistol out of his trench coat pocket, opened the door and listened. The scream was not repeated. It had seemed to come from a quarter just forward of the great funnels.

He snatched up a black tubular flash light from a bracket at the back of the instrument shelf and went on deck, flashing on the beam. Spray cut across it in long white diagonal streaks.

Holding the flash light in his left hand, his automatic in his right, Peter advanced through the spray until he saw two figures in the lee of a whale-boat, one lying crumpled on the deck; the other hovering over it—a black figure that reminded Peter of a great bat. As the pale beam of the flash light fell upon him, the standing figure straightened up.

Peter was not surprised. It was the man he had seen at the wireless receiving set in Mr. Tsing's cabin a few minutes ago— the man who had murdered the other operator!

There was a dagger in his right hand. The wicked, curved blade was dark and wet. He turned and started to run. Peter fired and saw the man stagger and half turn. Peter fired again. The Tonkinese clawed at the air with half-clenched hands, fell to the deck, and began to roll and slide. As the tilting of the deck increased, the man rolled and slid faster. A hoarse cry issued from his twisting lips.

As Peter had warned Miss O'Gilvie, there was no protective railing about the boat deck; there was not even a deck gutter.

Very much like a bundle of old clothing, the murderer rolled between the fore and after ends of two lifeboats, paused for a moment at the brink—and dropped from sight.

Some one caught Peter by the arm which held the pistol. He brought the flash light beam to bear upon the white face, the big excited eyes of Susan O'Gilvie.

She cried: "You shot him! You killed him! I saw him go!"

She was clinging to his arm, and trembling.

"Go back into that cabin," Peter ordered, "and lock the door. Stay there. If that phone rings, don't answer it. Don't open the door to anyone but me. I'll knock three times, then twice. Understand?"

"What are you going to do with this poor boy?"

"I'm going to take him to the captain."

"Oh, I think this is horrible!"

"Yes," Peter said. "Now, go back to that cabin."

She reluctantly returned to the wireless shack. Peter waited until the light from the open door was blanked out. Then he flashed the pale beam on the crumpled figure at his feet.

The wireless operator lay with his legs queerly twisted under him, with his mouth and eyes open. He was still breathing. Words came from his convulsing lips.

"You—you got him, didn't you, Mr. Moore? I'm glad of that."

"Where did he get you?"

"My back. I'm dying. I know I'm dying!"

Peter knew it, too. Somehow, the boy seemed to wilt. The eyes remained open, but the mouth sagged. Peter had seen this tragic phenomenon too often before; he knew the boy was dead.

He picked up the body and staggered forward. At the captain's door he stopped and kicked heavily at the lower panel.

THE DOOR was jerked open by Captain Runk, in undershirt and trousers. There was a glass half full of a brown liquid in his hand. He glared at Peter through the screen.

"What's going on out there?"

"This boy," Peter said, "was killed a moment ago by the same 'wave' that washed the other one overboard. Open this door!"

The captain opened the screen door. Peter carried his burden in and deposited on the couch. Beside the couch was a table. On the table, set in a square wooden holder so that it would not tip or spill, was a half-finished bottle of rye whisky.

The piercing blue eyes of Captain Runk were slightly blurred. The luxurious quarters reeked with whisky fumes.

"Who was shooting out there?"

"I was."

"Who were you shooting at?"

"I haven't the slightest idea," Peter said. "Perhaps it was a phantom." He was furious. "It was downright murder, captain, and you know it! Why did you send for that boy?"

"What business is it of yours? Look here," the big man bullied, "you keep out of it. Got a gun?"

"Yes."

"Give it to me."

"No, captain."

Captain Runk sank back against the door and glared at him. "Do you think you are running this ship?"

"No, but if I were, you're the first man I'd put in irons, captain. Two murders have been committed on this ship tonight. You've been aware of both. You knew both had been planned. You were an accessory, at least, to the last one."

"I don't know what you're talking about, Moore. What were you doing on this deck? Don't you know it's forbidden?"

"I'm making my own laws this evening, captain. I may not be the only man left aboard this ship who can operate that wireless plant, but at least I am the only man aboard who is going to."

"We'll see about that," said Captain Runk. "So you are up to your old stunts, are you, Moore? Well, you won't get far with them on this ship, let me tell you. You are not going to touch that wireless plant"

"Why not?"

"Because you are not a properly qualified wireless operator!"

"But I am, captain. I have never let my license expire."

Captain Runk took another tack. "Moore, we are wasting time. We are a pair of clever men. You are a dangerous man and I am a dangerous man. I am not in the least afraid of what you can do or what you will say. When this ship docks in Yokohama, you will not report what has happened during this voyage. You will not say a word to any one. Why not? Because you will not dare. To the proper authorities I will say that the senior wireless operator was washed overboard and that the junior operator regrettably met his death—a swinging block struck him in the head and crushed his skull. He will be buried before morning. So—you will say nothing to any one."

"Am I to assume," Peter said crisply, "that the gentleman in the jade mask is behind all of this?"

"You can assume anything you damn please. You gave a promise, did you not, to interfere in no way in any Chinese affairs?"

Peter nodded. "Yes, I did."

"Then don't interfere!"

THE CAPTAIN glared at Peter under half-lowered lids. He lifted the glass to his mouth and tossed the drink down.

"I don't trust you," he said. "I've decided that you are to be my guest until we tie up in Yokohama."

"You mean, your prisoner?" asked Peter softly.

"Call it anything you want. You are going to stay in this cabin until we dock in Yokohama."

"Captain," Peter said, "keep your hand away from that bell button." He withdrew the pistol from his pocket and leveled it at Runk's capacious chest. "You just told me I was a dangerous man. I'm going to show you a trick."

"Put that gun down!"

Peter grinned. He backed to the door and closed it. He turned the key in the lock, removed the key and dropped it into his pocket.

"What are you going to do?"

"I'm going to shoot you if you touch that button."

Captain Runk was glaring at him. His eyes had suddenly lost their blurriness. He looked a little more than half mad now. The muscles in his neck were bulging. His face, above the short black beard, was almost blood-red. The whites of his eyes seemed to increase in area.

"Now, back slowly to that door and open it."

"What door?" the captain asked.

"Your bedroom door."

Captain Runk hesitated. Then he backed to the bedroom door and opened it. The master's suite, as Peter had guessed, ran from starboard to port. Runk's office, where they were standing, occupied one-half of the space and his bedroom, bath and closets the other half. A door in the bedroom opened upon the port side of the boat deck.

"Do you know," Captain Runk snarled, "what will happen to you for this?"

Peter was examining the portholes in the bedroom. They were perhaps ten inches in diameter, the same size as the ones in the office. Captain Runk could not possibly squeeze through any of them.

"Now sit down on that bunk!"

The captain seated himself on the edge of the bunk. He grasped his knees so tightly that his knuckles went blue. He began to curse.

Peter, with the gun leveled at him, backed to the door, took the key out of the lock, opened the door and inserted the key in the lock from the outside.

He said crisply: "Good night, captain!" He slammed the door, turned the key and tossed it into the sea.

Then he ran aft. He had wanted only time enough to reach

the wireless cabin in safety. He knocked three times on the door, then twice.

Susan O'Gilvie let him in. Peter locked the door and looked at her. Her deep violet eyes were glowing more romantically than they ever had before.

"I'm sorry," Peter said, "but it is going to be necessary to place you in a compromising position. It will be necessary for us to stay in this locked cabin the rest of the night."

"As if I minded!"

"Well, you ought to mind."

"I think it's perfectly fascinating!"

Peter groaned. He said: "Captain Runk or Mr. Tsing or both—and God knows how many others—are going to try to get into this place."

"You mean, they're going to try to make me go aboard that sampan in the morning?"

"Yes."

She sat down suddenly on the couch.

"And you're saying that you cannot stop them! Will you get me a drink of water? I feel faint."

PETER WENT into the tiny bathroom which adjoined the wireless house and returned with a glass of water. Susan O'Gilvie sipped it. She returned the glass to him, smiled wanly and said in a sweet, husky voice:

"I think you're marvelous. I ought to be ashamed of myself for starting all of this trouble, but I'm not. It was worth it to meet a man like you. I wanted romance and adventure, but I didn't dream I'd meet the most famous adventurer in China!"

"Don't be silly," Peter muttered.

"I'm not being silly. I think you're fascinating."

She looked as if she might be preparing to throw her arms around his neck and kiss him. Her eyes, glowed with adoration. Peter backed away.

"You disapprove of me terribly, don't you—Peter?"

"No," Peter said with a tired smile. "I think you're—fascinating. Now, kindly keep still while I fix this wireless."

"Yes, Peter," she said meekly.

He was bending over the receiving apparatus, frowning. He opened the drawer, took out a screw driver and a pair of pincers. In thirty seconds he had forgotten Susan O'Gilvie's existence.

The girl sat primly, with hands in lap, on the edge of the couch. Her deep-violet eyes upon him were adoring. Once she protruded the tip of her pink tongue and ran it around the inner edges of her lips. She sighed audibly.

"May I smoke, Peter?"

"What?" He looked around, with deep creases between his blue eyes.

"I said, may I smoke?"

"Certainly."

She lighted a cigarette and blew smoke at his slender back.

"The gale seems to be abating."

Peter said nothing.

"I said, the gale seems to be abating."

Absently: "Yes?"

"Yes. The wind's gone down and we aren't plunging around nearly as much."

Silence from the wireless wizard.

"Peter, have you ever been in love?"

"What?"

"I said, have you ever been in love?"

Peter, turned around with screw driver in one hand, pincers in the other. His face was brick-red.

"Yes!" he snapped. "Dozens and dozens of times! Hundreds of times! How can I fix this thing, how can I concentrate, with you interrupting me?"

She smiled mistily at him. "I'm sorry. I think you're simply fascinating!"

Peter returned to his electrical crossword puzzle. In half an hour he had it solved. He sat down at the instrument board and turned switches.

An expression of satisfaction relieved the grimness of his face. He glanced at the printed list of call letters tacked on the wall, adjusted the head phones to his ears and listened to the shrill yapping of near-by Japanese stations. He tuned them out and picked up Honolulu. Honolulu was calling him. Over and over, the call came.

CHAPTER VI

THE ATTACK

PETER THREW THE switches to the transmitting position. His nimble fingers danced upon the hard rubber knob of the key. He was surprised that his fingers had lost none of their familiarity with the Continental Code. In brisk dots and dashes he spelled out to the listening Honolulu operator:

"Kindly repeat all messages you have transmitted to the *Queen of Asia* since five this evening."

And the answer came back: "Where have you been for the past five hours? I sent you a message at six three. Do you want that repeated?"

"Yes."

The message came trickling in. Origin, San Francisco. It ran:

MISS SUSAN O'GILVIE, aboard S.S. *Queen of Asia*, at sea.

A man named Kang Wan Chou was arrested this morning and charged with the murder of your father. Chief of my detective bureau reports you were on friendly terms with Kang before you sailed and he was somehow instrumental in persuading you to go to Far East. Do not know your plans, but would advise extreme caution. Would greatly appreciate your returning to San Francisco to testify against Kang. Advise.

Julius Donovan,
Chief of Police.

Peter's pencil flew over the message blank. The Honolulu operator said:

"Here's another from San Francisco:"

SUSAN O'GILVIE, aboard S.S. *Queen of Asia*, at sea.

Please let me know by return radio why you left without letting me know where you were going and why. It has placed me in a very embarrassing position. I thought we were engaged. Learned in newspapers this afternoon that your father was not drowned, as believed, but was murdered by an Indo-Chinese student at Berkeley named Kang Wan Chou. Police are holding Kang. I think you have given me a very raw deal, but will meet you in Shanghai or Hong Kong for immediate marriage if you say the word. Dearest love.

BEN.

The Honolulu operator wired: "That's all. Do you want weather report?"

"No," Peter flashed back. "I'll get it from Yokohama."

The Yokohama station promptly cut in. "Hurricane has moved on southward and will reach Formosa tomorrow noon. Forecast for northwestern Pacific and Japanese waters: fair with abating strong winds becoming gentle westerly. Do you want—"

The signals ended. As they ended, Peter heard a rattling and rasping on the roof overhead, and knew that the antennæ was down.

The telephone began sharply to ring. Peter tore off the two messages from the pad and handed them to Susan O'Gilvie as he went to the phone.

He picked up the receiver and said "Hello!" crisply. And the booming voice of Captain Runk came into his ear.

"Is that you, Moore?"

"Yes, captain."

"I'm going to give you five minutes to get out of that wireless house. If you're not out then, I'm going to shoot you out!"

"And Miss O'Gilvie?" Peter asked.

He placed his hand over the mouthpiece and turned to Miss O'Gilvie. She had finished reading the two messages and was staring at him, white-faced. He snapped:

"Turn out that light—quick!"

She got up with a dazed air and switched off the light. Peter listened to Captain Runk. He was cursing, and enumerating the dreadful things, he was going to do to Peter. When a pause came, Peter said:

"Captain, you should be thankful that I was so presumptuous. If it had not been for me, you might have lost this ship."

"Why?"

"I have just received a typhoon warning from the Yokohama station—it came in just before you had the aërial cut—and also a message from your own owners instructing you to lay a course to the westward to avoid that low-pressure area."

"You're lying!"

"Captain, I am nobly performing my duties as the wireless operator of this ship. On your present course you will run head-on into that low-pressure area. By encircling it, you will probably save your ship."

The line went dead. Captain Runk had hung up!

IN THE blackness beside him, the frightened voice of Susan O'Gilvie said: "Was that true—about the typhoon?"

"No," said Peter. "But what can he do? How can he find out through any other source that the weather ahead is fair and calm? If he believes me, he will change the course immediately. He doesn't want to believe me."

"Peter, how can we tell whether or not he changes the course?"

Peter answered by feeling about for the instrument shelf. Finding it, he climbed upon it and lifted the newspaper that the junior wireless operator had pinned over the window.

"Look," Peter said.

The girl climbed up beside him. He could feel the trembling of her body.

"That light you see 'way up there," Peter explained, "is on the top of the foremast. You can see the smoke cutting this way at an angle from the forward funnel."

"I understand. If he changes the course, the angle of the column of smoke will change."

"It will swing over to starboard," Peter said.

They watched. She said presently: "It isn't changing. He doesn't believe you. He's going straight ahead to that spot where the sampan and the junk will be waiting. Peter, what are we going to do? We're trapped!"

"Did you suspect before you read those messages that the Sultan of Sakala had had your father murdered—so there would be no obstacle in the way of your coming?"

"Of course not! I never dreamed of it! Does that explain why those two poor boys were murdered—so I would not receive these messages?"

"It does," Peter said briefly.

Susan O'Gilvie was beginning to whimper softly.

"I think it's horrible. My father and two other men have been murdered so that there wouldn't be the slightest slip-up in the sultan's plans to bring me to Sakala. What can we do?"

"Wait," Peter said.

"But while we're waiting, aren't they making plans to attack this cabin?"

"There isn't much doubt of it."

"But isn't there anything you can do?"

"Only wait," Peter reiterated.

Muffled faint sounds informed him that Miss O'Gilvie was beginning to cry. He said sharply: "Look up there!"

The faint muffled sounds stopped. The girl gasped: "It's changing! It's swinging around! He's changed the course!"

"Yes," said Peter.

"Then I'm safe!" she cried.

"You'll be safe," Peter said grimly, "when I have seen you aboard a steamer sailing for San Francisco."

A period to that dubious reassurance was uttered in the form of a splintering crash. The window in the after wall of the cabin had been smashed in!

CHAPTER VII

NEMESIS

PETER THREW HIS arm around Miss O'Gilvie's slim shoulders, leaped to the floor, and pulled her swiftly after him. "Crouch!" he whispered.

Splinters still remaining in the window frame glinted in the pale beams from a remote light. With pistol in hand, Peter waited. A full minute passed. Then some one knocked sharply on the door.

Peter, with his arm still around the girl's shoulders, moved his hand until his fingers found her mouth. His intention was to impress upon her the importance of silence. Her soft lips returned that warning pressure with a frank kiss.

Then a voice boomed: "Moore, if you don't unlock this door, I'll have it chopped down."

Peter was watching the shattered window. The Sunday supplement, dangling by one pin, was flapping to and fro in the wind. He saw the vague outlines of a round head. It was, he presumed, the head of Mr. Tsing. Anyhow, it looked like the head of Mr. Tsing.

Peter aimed deliberately and fired. There was a faint scream from Miss O'Gilvie and a louder yelp of pain or fury from the vicinity of the window. The round head had vanished.

A low voice, hardly audible above the wind, said: "Start chopping that door down."

Peter waited. At the first thud of the falling ax he fired again. A volley of profanity greeted that. A roaring voice shouted:

"To hell with it! You may be skipper of this ship, but you ain't goin' to make no lead puddin' outa me!" And there was a thud as the ax dropped to the deck.

Then Captain Runk's angry voice: "I'll be damned if I will. Do it yourself. I'm through!" Heavy footsteps receded.

"Now what?" whispered the girl.

And Peter shrugged.

"Let's," she said, "sit down on that couch. Oh, Lord—I'm going to faint!"

Suddenly she went limp. Peter picked her up and carried her to the couch. He sat her down, pulled her head over to his shoulder and began rubbing her hands. In a moment she said:

"I—I passed out cold. I wouldn't have had that happen for anything in the world. But you don't think—I'm a little coward, do you?"

"No."

The telephone began to ring. Peter cautiously got up and made his way to it. He picked up the receiver, placed it to his ear, and said in a low voice:

"Yes?"

Just outside the window a streak of fire-red flashed from a glinting blue muzzle. Peter dropped hastily to his hands and knees. Particles of broken glass and splinters of wood came cascading down on the back of his head and neck.

Susan was on her knees beside him. Hysterically she whispered, "Are you hurt?"

"No," he said, and added: "That was clever of them."

"Tricking you to the phone, and having a man stationed outside to fire at you when you answered? I think it was positively vicious. If they'd killed you, I—I would have died."

They found their way back to the couch, sat down side by side, and waited. The wind had suddenly dropped. Above it,

Peter heard the slatting of lifeboat tarpaulins. But there were no other sounds.

He wondered if the enemy had given it up as a bad job. Susan O'Gilvie was snuggled against him. Her head was on his shoulder. From time to time she uttered a sigh. She had infolded one of his hands in both of hers.

"Peter, will you be going on to Hong Kong?"

"Yes. Why?"

"Won't it be dangerous—now?"

"Possibly."

"Peter, what's to become of me?"

"You," Peter said, "will leave Yokohama on the first ship bound for San Francisco or Vancouver and—marry Ben."

SUSAN MADE no comment. Later she said: "I suppose you're going on to Hong Kong, buy that static gadget from Fong Toy or whatever his name is, go back to Schenectady—and stay there forever."

"Probably," Peter replied.

"You're simply impossible! Here is the most exciting part of the world—just beyond that window. China! And I'd like to share that excitement with you. I've got millions, Peter. Think of the—"

A growling voice outside the window interrupted her.

"Hey, Moore, you still in there?"

Peter did not answer. His hand slid into the pocket where the automatic lay.

"It's MacKenzie. Everything's all right. You two can come out now. The old man's dead. He and that fat Chink had a big row in his office, and the Chink stabbed him in the throat. I'm skipper now. I guess you can trust me. Anyhow, I ain't up to my ears in any of these damned mysteries."

Peter said cautiously: "Who killed the captain—Mr. Tsing?"

"Yes. That one. The fat boy. I've got him ironed to a stanchion in the chain locker. His last offer to let him go was a hundred thousand Mex."

Peter turned on the light and opened the door. The first mate, pale and haggard, was standing on the deck.

Susan walked out of the door. She turned and flashed a strange look at Peter.

"Does that mean I'm safe now?"

He nodded.

"Good night, Susan."

CHAPTER VIII

THE LURE OF THE EAST

PETER AWOKE LATE in the morning to an ocean that was cheerfully living up to its name. A dazzling spring sun sparkled on lazy blue wave crests. A faint odor of land came in at the porthole—the delicately spiced odor always present In a wind blowing offshore from Japan. A cloud of white gulls, their wings gilded by the sun, were fluttering about the ship.

Peter shaved, dressed, and went on deck. All of the vestiges of the gale had been cleared away. The steamer chairs were back in place, and they were filled with chattering passengers.

Peter took a turn about the deck. He would have sworn he was not looking for Susan O'Gilvie, but in his heart he knew otherwise. When a second turn about the deck did not reveal her, he was conscious of a vague disappointment.

He was fully aware that Susan O'Gilvie was a young woman of extremely dangerous potentialities. In her quest for romance she had already turned his life topsy-turvy. His old enemies in China would certainly hear of last night's activities—if they had not indeed had a part in it. Peter shivered slightly in the warm ocean breeze.

He assured himself that his interest in Susan was merely that of a well-wisher. After the stress and strain of last night's adventure, he simply wanted to make sure that she was quite all right. An impulse purely friendly.

He saw Miss Teasely. The little old lady smiled and bowed to him over her knitting. Her smile was without significance. A loud-voiced woman in the steamer chair on her right was relating the tragedies of last night with gusto. Two wireless operators had been washed overboard. The captain had been killed in a quarrel with an opium-besotted Chinaman. The ship was buzzing with it.

The *Queen of Asia* paused at noon for the captain's burial. Acting Captain MacKenzie performed the burial services in a stumbling voice. And a very dramatic incident in Peter Moore's life was, he presumed—and hoped—closed.

The feathery shoreline of Japan came up over the horizon. Boso Peninsula. Clusters of fishing sampans were to be seen on all sides.

Not until the *Queen of Asia* was made fast to her dock did Susan appear. Peter was in the throng at the rail when a slim figure in white pressed into a space beside him; a warm hand snuggled into his. And he looked down into the radiant upturned face of the beautiful Susan. Her violet eyes were sparkling. She smiled.

PETER FELT a sudden warmth in the vicinity of his heart. And he felt the heat of rich color creep up his neck and into his face when she said, in her sweet, clear voice:

"Good afternoon, darling."

"Good afternoon, Susan."

"Am I presentable?"

He smiled. "Fascinating!"

"Did you miss me?"

"Horribly!"

"Did you pace the deck and search the ship—and worry?"

"Every moment!"

Her eyes sparkled with that light that he was destined to know always meant mischief.

"Am I going to be spanked and sent home, Peter?"

Peter lifted his right hand and pointed to a glossy white hull across the way.

"Do you see that ship, Susan? That ship is the Empress of Japan. She is sailing in two hours for Vancouver. And you are sailing on her!"

"Is that final?"

"I can't give you orders," Peter said.

"You could if you would only be nice about it."

"But," Peter said determinedly, "I can make suggestions. I am strongly suggesting that when the Empress of Japan sails you be aboard her."

Susan sighed. She examined the glossy white liner with obvious disapproval.

"Will you go over with me while I see about reservations?"

"Yes."

"Peter, you are the most difficult man I ever knew in my life. The romance and adventure of the entire East is calling to us. Can't you hear those temple bells? Can't you smell that incense smoke? Can't you hear the *clunk-clunk* of the caravans crossing the mountains and the deserts?"

"Don't!" Peter said.

"You're weakening!"

"No."

"You mean," Susan persisted, "you can hear nothing but the ticking of the gadget in Mr. Fong Toy's laboratory that will make the world safe for the Hundred Fathom Fish Hour?"

"Yes," Peter said.

"Very well," Susan retorted crisply. "Let's go ashore. They've got the gangplank down. All I can say is that when I started out from San Francisco I certainly believed I'd see more of the Orient than a concrete dock in Yokohama!"

THEY FOLLOWED the long queue of passengers down the gangplank and to the dock. The Empress of Japan's purser could, he said, let Miss O'Gilvie have one of the finest suites aboard. It had been canceled at the last moment. Gravely Susan paid for the suite with crisp hundred-dollar bills.

When the transaction was completed she took Peter's arm and led him out on deck.

"We'll say good-by here and now," she said. "I—I feel a little shaky still, after last night."

They stood at the rail. Her small white hand lingered on his arm. She patted it. Her eyes looking up at him were misty and mysterious. They had taken on that haunting look that moved him so.

"Well—good-by, Peter. Kiss me."

Peter bent down swiftly to kiss her. Her arms flew about his neck. She kissed his mouth, his cheeks, his eyes. She clung to him. Then she pushed him away and looked up at him with sparkling bright eyes.

"I hope," she said, "that you'll live to regret that you ever let me say good-by to you, Peter."

Peter turned and walked very unsteadily away. He left the ship, but he did not leave the dock. When the Empress of Japan sailed, he was in the crowd at the end of the pier. He had never felt so lonesome in his life. He hated Japan.

He did not expect to see her on deck, but, at the end, he caught sight of her—a slim figure in white. She did not wave. She stood with her hands on the rail and looked down at him.

When the ship swung about, Peter joined the crowd moving toward the inshore end of the pier. His eyes roved over the hills of this blatantly modern Yokohama. Rickshaw coolies yelped at him. He pressed on past them.

He hoped that Fong Toy's static eliminator was all that it was cracked up to be. If it wasn't, he would wring that youthful Chinaman's neck!

"I'm glad she's gone," Peter tried to console himself. "She's nothing but a romance chaser. Star-struck! If I'd let her stay—"

Gloomily he reached into his pocket for a cigarette. His fingers encountered, not a yielding paper packet, but a cold, hard surface. He pulled the object out of his pocket and shivered involuntarily. It was the white jade box!

In the dusk the sapphires sparkled like drops of a magical blue liquid. And it seemed to Peter that the sapphire smile was not quite a smile, but a somewhat disdainful sneer.

THE MAN IN THE JADE MASK

*No man knew better than the too-adventurous
Peter the Brazen how deadly Shanghai could
be—and no man tried more earnestly and more
unsuccessfully to keep out of its devious intrigues*

CHAPTER I

NIGHT LIFE IN SHANGHAI

LIKE AN ARMY of Manchu ghosts, the pale green fog of the Yangtze delta swept down the Whang-po valley and on over the Yellow Sea. Anchor chains rumbled as ships surrendered to the pallid invasion. Junks and sampans became yellow wraiths glimpsed for a moment and gone. Sounds became muffled. The most familiar objects were made mysterious and fantastic.

In Shanghai the fog plated the streets and house fronts with a layer of shining silver, turned street lights blind, and gave a more sinister purpose to those shapes of evil which stalk after dark.

In Native City a brazen uproar battled with the muffling fog. A Chinese opium king had died during the afternoon. Priests were clashing brass cymbals and setting off strings of firecrackers to frighten the devils away.

The streets of "the wickedest city in the world" were emptying. Sikh policemen in red turbans appeared in groups of two and three where only one had been seen before.

River rats, two- and four-legged, crawled out of their water front holes and prepared for their night's work. On such a night thieves and footpads reaped their largest harvests.

Women with sensuous eyes yawned through perfumed lips, awoke and began to make themselves fascinating for the men of a dozen nationalities.

These same men were industriously tossing down the last of their before-dinner cocktails.

The business day was over and relaxation and mirth invited.

"This way, Mr. Moore," warned the man with the gun.

Night-time Shanghai was waking up, preparing for the fever-ish tempo of jazz orchestras and the popping of convivial corks.

In the cheerful brightness of the American Club, the merry clatter of cocktail shakers and the roar of genial voices created such a din that a man had to shout to make himself heard. From end to end that famous bar—only very recently it lost to Austra-lia the proud distinction of being the longest bar on earth—was packed two and three deep.

Midway along it, a bronze-skinned, blue-eyed young man in a gray four-dent Stetson and a gray trench coat tossed down what remained of his dry Martini and said to the man on his right:

"I've got to be getting back to my hotel. I've decided that if Simpson doesn't show up on that noon train from Nanking, I'll take tomorrow's express to Hong Kong. Business there won't wait."

"But you'll join our party tonight," the man insisted. "Come on! Weaken! There'll be some of the prettiest girls in Shanghai. We'll have dinner at the Carlton and then go on to the Parisi-enne and make whoopee. I'll promise you a girl who'll knock your eye out!"

The young man in the gray trench coat laughed. "Thanks,"

he said; "but if you don't mind, I'll just duck. I have a report to write up. I'm tired and I want to turn in early and read a book."

"A book!" his companion roared. "Whoever heard of anybody comin' to this town to read a book? Shanghai isn't for readin' books, old top. This is China—the glitterin', fabulous, mysterious, exotic East! You haven't been out after dark since you've been here. Come on! Weaken! Let me show you China after dark!"

"Not tonight—thanks," the bronzed, blue-eyed young man said firmly. He ticked the brim of his hat with his finger tips in an amiable military salute. "Good night, Mr. Jessop! See you in the morning!"

He turned and made his way down the crowded room toward the door which opened upon the Bund or water front. His erstwhile companion, Jim Jessop, addressed the man on his left. Bill Withrow stood with one foot hoisted on the brass rail, his two elbows hooked comfortably over the edge of the bar.

"Bill," roared Jessop above the bedlam, "how do you figure a feller like that? He hasn't been in China a week, and what do you suppose he does nights? He reads a book!"

Bill Withrow, of the A.B.C., jerked his head around and gazed after the receding tall young man.

"Oh, yeah?" he drawled. "Do you happen to know who that bookworm is?"

Jessop snorted. "I ought to know! Haven't I spent the past week with him? He's doing some special research work for General Electric, and he must be a big shot because the letter he brought from Schenectady made me nothin' but his errand boy. But wouldn't they send me a feller who wants to read books at night! You'd think he'd want to get acquainted with Shanghai night life."

"Well," Withrow drawled, "I can tell you something about the book he's going to read. He reads it in his hotel bedroom with the door bolted and the lights out. The name of it is Colt Thirty-eight. It has six chapters, and there's a death in every chapter!"

"Roll over," Jessop chuckled, "and dream another one!"

But Bill Withrow was not smiling. "I can tell you something even funnier," he said. "It isn't his first trip out here—or his tenth. He used to be a wireless operator on the China run. Five or six years ago. That boy caused more trouble and raised more hell up and down the China coast than a dozen Boxer rebellions. He was ordered out of China, and he was told to stay out. How do I know? Because I was attached to the American embassy at Pekin when it was happening! His middle name is dynamite. The reason he won't put his head out of his hotel after dark is— he doesn't want it shot off! And you want to show *him* China!"

Jim Jessop was grinning. "If I were you, Bill, I'd change my brand of liquor. Or, perhaps," he added, "drink less."

But the other man was not drunk, not by any means. His eyes had a faraway look. As if to himself, he murmured:

"So Peter Moore is back in China! Now, I wonder what that youngster is up to?"

Bill Withrow was not the only person in China that night who wanted an answer to that question.

CHAPTER II

HOUSE OF A THOUSAND DOORS

THE YOUNG MAN in the gray trench coat had stopped near the street door and was now buttoning the flap of his coat collar under his chin. He lighted a cigarette, pulled down his hat and slightly clenched his fists, as if he were gathering himself together. He opened the door and went out.

A blank wall of fog met him. It seemed to swirl about him, to reach out long tenuous fingers at him. Nearby street lights burned mistily like the ghosts of lights. On the river, which swept past unseen just beyond the Bund, the whistle of a river steamer fumbling her way to a mooring was hoarse and muffled. A phantom ricksha flitted past with the ghost of a coolie between the shafts.

The man in the gray trench coat put two fingers into his mouth and produced a piercing whistle, but the ricksha did not pause. It would be hard getting a ricksha tonight.

A thin crouching shadow on his right mysteriously moved; was suddenly and startlingly a live thing that came hurtling through the fog—a phantom born of the fog. The long curving blade of a knife gleamed wetly. The man in the gray trench coat glimpsed distorted Asiatic features. He reached automatically to his right hip pocket, but the gesture was an empty one. His hand fell away.

Before he could move, the half-naked yellow man was upon him, one clawlike hand reaching for his throat, the other swinging the knife upward, over and down in a misty shining arc.

From perhaps twenty feet away two brief blue flames spat

out. They were accompanied by the double crashing discharge of a pistol or revolver.

The Asiatic went slithering to the wet sidewalk at Peter Moore's feet, one outstretched hand relaxing in death as it quivered at his left foot.

Very quickly the American glanced into the fog from whence those brief blue knifelike flames had leaped; but he saw nothing. The fog moved by like a curtain being drawn over that act of deliverance.

Peter Moore crouched down and pulled back the coolie's jacket from his right shoulder. And on the upper part of the right shoulder blade he found what he had hoped he would not find: a circle of grass-green tattoo about two inches in diameter; within the circle a grass-green isosceles triangle; within the triangle one round green dot!

He pulled the dead Oriental's jacket back into place as he heard feet thumping along the street toward him. They would be Sikh policemen, attracted by the sound of the shooting. And in a moment men would pour from the nearby club.

Peter Moore did not want to answer any one's questions. Nor did he wish to appear before the International Court in the morning to answer even more embarrassing questions.

He stepped over the dead body and slid along the face of the building; heard explosive Hindustani, and knew that his guess was right. He would have slipped off into the fog and essayed his return to the Astor afoot but for the fact that his departure was summarily arrested.

A suave voice, invisible in the fog, purred:

"A four-horse chariot cannot overtake the spoken word, Mr. Moore. But a bullet is faster than the wind. Two bullets may be faster even than life."

PETER MOORE stopped short. The gun that had so conveniently intercepted the intended assassin was prodding him ever so gently in the side. He did not look down. He did not have to look down. He knew that he would see a tall, handsome Chinese of forty, with shoe-button eyes, a sardonic smile, attired as fault-lessly as a Parisian *boulevardier*.

"Do I make myself clear? He who rides a tiger dares not dismount!"

"I understand," Peter said wearily. "That one had orders to get me, and you couldn't head him off with anything but a bullet. But why the delay?"

The man with the gun chuckled. "Good words are like a string of pearls. To see one's self is to be clearsighted. It is a pleasure to meet you again. Will you come?"

The gun's pressure against Peter's side became perceptibly greater.

"Where?" he asked in the same weary tone.

"To meet an old friend in a distant country," said the Chinese gunman, "is like the delight of rain after a long drought. This way."

"You might hold that gun an inch farther away," Peter suggested dryly. "I think we are of the same mind."

"Ah?" his companion chuckled. "If two men are of the same mind, their sharpness can divide metal. *Desu-ka?*"

A black limousine was at the curb.

"If you will get in, Mr. Moore. And if you will oblige me by not slipping out the other door!"

Peter said angrily: "You've got me covered, haven't you?"

"Covered, yes—but not delivered. You have such a surprising nature, Mr. Moore! No, I have not forgotten. Past events are as clear as a mirror; future events, as dark as lacquer."

The American sank into the deep upholstery. The Chinese gunman followed. The door shut with a velvety, luxurious click. The car started with a whispering of costly gears; slid off into the fog, a black and shining argosy of mystery.

"Where to?" Peter asked.

"Not to know," the gunman answered, "is to be a Buddha."

"Is this the new Chinese version," Peter asked, "of being taken for a ride?"

The gunman laughed. "You may console yourself, Mr. Moore. As far as I am concerned, your destination is not death. That is, not at my hands."

"Where? The House of a Thousand Doors?"

"Where else, indeed?"

"An invitation from K'ang?"

"Who else, Mr. Moore?"

"But what have I done to K'ang this time?"

"We Chinese are so distrustful, Mr. Moore. You Americans have coined an expression: 'Clever people, these Chinese.' By nature man is evil; if he is good, that is an artificial result. K'ang prefers to take no chances."

Peter Moore lighted a cigarette with steady hands, "You and I," he said coldly, "have met too often. The last time it was Hong Kong."

"**I AM** flattered," responded the humorous gunman. "I will refresh your memory further. In a port in Java, you once tossed me over the rail from a steamer. My name is Wah. Yes, the last time was Hong Kong. There was a very beautiful Persian girl— and an emerald as large as a dove's egg."

"I thought you were dead."

"Ah! I am like a cat, Mr. Moore. You shot me neatly through the left shoulder. I prize the scar, but I have no wish to collect other souvenirs of your ability. Do not forget that I have you covered, Mr. Moore. Do you know what happened to that Persian girl?"

"No."

"Ah! Would you like to know?"

"I would not."

As if his feelings had been hurt, Mr. Wah settled back in his corner of the seat. The black limousine swam through the fog, swinging right from the Bund into the Rue du Consulat, left into the Rue Montauban, then a left jog into the Avenue de Deux Republiques.

The Avenue of the Two Republics—the deadline of Shanghai! Where the French section of China's greatest city came to an abrupt end and China began. One stepped or rode through a gate, crossed an imaginary line—and turned his watch back four thousand years!

The laws of the white man terminated at that imaginary line. Once across the boundary, any white man surrendered his claim to European protection and American protection. He crossed at his own risk. Chinese City was dangerous by day. At night, a white man took his life in his hands when he entered it. Cautious white men did not enter Chinese City after dark.

The limousine sped through the North Gate. In a twinkling, Peter Moore had left Western civilization behind him; was plunged into the heart of the dragon that never progresses, never changes. Asphalt streets suddenly gave way to lanes and alleys of mud. Modern structures of stone and brick gave way to ramshackle buildings of unpainted teak and pine.

The limousine proceeded slowly now, its fenders all but scraping doors and posts on either side. Colored banners hung down from ropes and wires suspended from rooftops. They mingled the advertisements of fish and vegetables with lurid appeals to barbaric gods.

The din that the American had heard on leaving the club became louder. In a side street the priests were gathered, clashing brass cymbals. From the roof peak of the house of the dead opium king great strings of firecrackers hung down. At intervals one of these strings was set off. The street flickered and crackled with the explosions.

These sounds were left behind as the black limousine proceeded. Sloe eyes in yellow faces stared into the car; dirty faces, cruel faces, vicious faces.

The American nervously smoked cigarettes and looked

forward with uneasiness to the impending interview with K'ang in the House of a Thousand Doors.

THE LIMOUSINE presently drew up before this fabulous and sinister house. It probably did not have even a small fraction of its reputed thousand doors, but it had more entrances and, exits than any other structure Peter Moore had ever entered. Some of them you would not suspect were doors. And he knew that there were passages under the house. He had seen a horde of five hundred men vanish from that house in less than thirty seconds—and no passer-by in any of the surrounding streets would have been aware of their going!

The House of a Thousand Doors was, he reflected as Mr. Wah nudged him in the ribs with a gun, admirably suited to the purposes of K'ang. And the thought of entering it made his heart race.

"You will get out, please," said Mr. Wah, "and go to the green door. Do not attempt to run."

Peter had no intention of running. He alighted and walked straight to the green door. He heard Mr. Wah wading through the mud behind him, and he heard massive bolts shoot back.

The door, of solid teak five inches in thickness, armored with mighty straps of bronze, swung open without sound.

"Enter," said Mr. Wah.

Peter entered a square hall from which three flights of stairs ascended to upper regions and from which, by count, he knew that fourteen doors opened.

A grinning yellow giant peered into Peter's face and stood aside. He was naked to the waist. Light from dongs suspended by fine brass chains from the teak ceiling struck gleams from the coolie's oily skin. There was a bone-handled dagger thrust into a cord about his waist. In the air was the pungent odor of sandalwood incense and the more acrid flavor of opium.

The door closed behind Mr. Wah with a soft thud.

"This way, Mr. Moore."

He led the way down the hall, with Peter following, and the half-naked coolie bringing up the rear.

Mr. Wah held open a door. It gave upon a flight of descending steps. Mr, Wah went down—and down. Peter had never been down these steps. They spiralled within a round well carved from the mud and crudely plastered. The plaster was green with mold. Farther down it was white with fungus. But the air rising up this well was warm and still scented with incense and opium.

At the bottom of the winding stairs was another square room. More doors—at least a dozen.

"This way, Mr. Moore."

The suspicion was stealing over the American that he was not going to leave this house alive.

Mr. Wah was holding open another door. His expression was grim, and his little black shoe-button eyes were glinting. His revolver was no longer in evidence. He looked very serious, and Peter immediately found out the reason.

A diffusion of cold green light—as cold and as green as the light that is given back from a gray day by an iceberg—flooded Peter's face. He had heard of K'ang's Green Room, sometimes known as the Room of Questions and sometimes as the Room of Easy Death, but he had not been privileged to enter it on his previous visit to the House of a Thousand Doors.

PETER FELT his pulses ticking sharply and rapidly in his ears, took a long breath—and entered the famous room. It was absolutely barren of furniture or furnishings of any kind.

Floor, walls and ceiling were a glaze of the cold green lacquer, which held and at the same time reflected the outpouring of green light. Not unlike the light of the mercury vapor arc, it gave the human flesh a ghastly greenish-yellow hue like the flesh of a corpse that has met death by strangling. The source of the deathly light was mystifying. It seemed to come from everywhere, as if it emanated from ceiling, walls, and floor. Cold and green and terrifying, it cast no shadow.

Peter knew that the purpose of this room was to terrify the

man who entered it. It was barbarically imaginative and as sinister as the leer of a Chinese executionier.

Knowing what he knew about the room, Peter could well understand its perverse and powerful influence. He could readily picture a scared man gibbering in terror in this awful light. The room of a thousand questions! Well, let K'ang question him. He had certainly not crossed K'ang's path, or trifled with any of K'ang's sinister affairs—at least, not for several years!

He had nothing to fear from K'ang; yet the green diffusion drenching him made him decidedly uneasy. Peter looked behind. Without a sound the door had closed. He had heard that sections of the green walls were transparent; and he had heard reputedly true stories—or empty fables—to the effect that when K'ang received a man in this room, his council of ten stood behind the transparent sections, watched the behavior of the man under examination, heard his words—and coldly voted upon his disposal.

Looking along the glazed green walls, Peter saw, or imagined he saw, shadows and the pale ovals of faces. But he was more interested in the heavy green brocaded curtains which hung from the ceiling at the far end of the vast room.

The curtains parted. A man in green robes, their color perfectly matching the walls, floor and ceiling, stepped out. He was alone. He was K'ang! His voice, thin and metallic and with a curious whispery quality, came down the green immensity.

"You will approach me—slowly—Mr. Moore." More the voice of a mechanical creature than a man of flesh and blood.

Peter began walking down the middle of the room. He tried to walk steadily; tried not to reveal his uneasiness. He was thinking of that coolie whom K'ang had sent to stab him to death as he emerged from the American Club, wondering why those orders had been countermanded.

He was prepared for anything. He was prepared for the grass-green circle embroidered on the front of K'ang's green robe; within the circle a triangle, and within the triangle a round dot.

But he was not prepared for K'ang's countenance. It was not a face. It was a caricature in kingfisher jade, a mask with slits for eyes and a carved green grin for a mouth.

That jade countenance somehow added to the greenly glowing room a proper Oriental climax. Hiding even the expression in his eyes, it gave K'ang an advantage over any visitor.

When Peter was ten feet away from him, the thin, whispery voice again issued from the carved lips.

"Stop where you are, Mr. Moore!" ordered the man in the jade mask.

CHAPTER III

THE STOLEN SCEPTER

PETER MOORE, AMERICAN citizen, obeyed the voice. He stopped and plunged his hands into his pants pockets. Hands are revealing. And Peter knew he was playing poker with death. The expression on his face was as unrevealing as the jade mask.

Boldly he asked: "K'ang, why have you brought me here? What have I done?"

The man in the jade mask had folded his arms upon his breast. Through the jade lips came his answer: "Mr. Moore, five years ago you were definitely instructed never to return to China. Why have you violated that order?"

Peter replied: "K'ang, it was stipulated that if I ever returned to China I would first communicate with your San Francisco agents and notify them of my intentions. Before sailing from San Francisco, about a month ago, I communicated with your agents."

"Yes. You said you were coming to China to carry out certain scientific investigations, in connection with wireless telephony, for the General Electric Company. That was your avowed purpose."

"It is my actual purpose, K'ang."

"Yet," said the man in the jade mask, "I am informed that you were the center of a serious disturbance aboard the ship on which you crossed the Pacific. Two Chinese and a white man were killed."

"I was not," Peter answered firmly, "the center of that trouble. I participated to save from mischief—"

K'ang checked him with a curt wave of one ghastly green-ish-yellow hand. "I know, I know. A beautiful young Ameri-can. You are always saving from mischief some beautiful young American—as an excuse to cover your actual purposes!"

Peter leaped on this as a golden opportunity. It was evident to him that K'ang was not thoroughly acquainted with the facts. Through this loophole he might escape!

"If your investigators had given you a full report," he retorted, "you would have learned that the beautiful young American returned to America from Yokohama."

The man in the jade mask said coldly: "We will dismiss that for the moment. You arrived in Shanghai eight days ago. Your mission was to proceed to Hong Kong to investigate some invention of a man named Fong Toy. Why are you staying here?"

"To see a man named Simpson, who is on his way from Nanking. He, also, is an inventor." Peter took a deep breath and plunged. "K'ang, it is a distinction to meet you again, but I swear I have done nothing that could possibly displease any member of your order. I am through with adventure. I am a research engineer. What more can I say to assure you of my honest intentions?"

The man in the jade mask took so long to reply that Peter grew nervous again. He realized now that all this talk had been but a preliminary to whatever topic it was that K'ang had brought him here to discuss. Beads of cold sweat gathered on Peter's forehead.

THE WHISPERY voice continued: "Since you have been in Shanghai I have had you carefully watched."

Peter nodded. "I've been aware of the man with the scar."

"Where," inquired the man in the jade mask, "were you between the hours of nine and one last night?"

Peter was surprised. He wished he could see through that gleaming green mask.

"Last night, between those hours," he replied, "I was in my room at the Hotel Astor."

"We have reasons to believe," K'ang said harshly, "that you were elsewhere!"

The American was bewildered. He had not left his hotel bedroom all night.

"Where," asked K'ang, "is the Ming scepter?"

Peter stared at the jade mask. He knew his eyes were round with amazement. "The emerald scepter?"

"Yes!"

The American shook his head.

"K'ang, I know nothing about this. I was not out of my room last night. The man with the scar should be able to tell you that!"

"Six years ago, Mr. Moore, you boasted that you would some day enter this house and steal that scepter. It was a very rash boast. Last night some daring thief entered this house and took the scepter. We know you made the boast; we know you were in Shanghai last night."

Peter realized that the Ming scepter was to members of the Green Circle what the lock of Buddha's hair was to devout pilgrims who visited the Schwe Dagon pagoda in Rangoon, what the Silver Chalice of Antioch was to pious Christians—a mystic symbol with a sentimental and historic value beyond all cost.

"K'ang," he said, "you are a just man. You know that I do not lie. Six years ago, when I was a wireless operator on American ships running to the Orient, I took part, I admit, in a variety of intrigues. I caused you no end of trouble. We were enemies. We parted, if not friends, at least with a certain mutual respect—and a perfect understanding.

"I got tired of adventuring—very tired. I have become a peaceful business man. I don't go looking for trouble any more. My errand in China is strictly a business matter. I want no adventures, no trouble, no excitement. I know nothing of the theft of the Ming scepter. I have never seen it. What else can I say?"

The man in the jade mask slowly nodded.

"You have said enough. I believe you, but I will exact a promise from you to keep to your business interests. Great troubles are brewing in China. If you interfere in any way, I warn you that you will be harshly punished. If we find that you have been lying, that you are implicated in the theft of the Ming scepter, your fate will be—the *ling chi!*"

Peter hastily gave his promise. He had seen men put to death by the horrible *ling chi*—the death of a thousand cuts. The victim was strapped to a post and slashed with a razor sharp knife—not deep, not fatal slashes, but slight ones, in his hands, his arms, his abdomen and legs, until he went mad with pain and died. The headsman's ax would have been more merciful.

"You may go," announced the man in the jade mask.

PETER TURNED and walked to the door through which he had entered, and his legs were unsteady.

Mr. Wah opened the door. His expression was inscrutable. Peter wondered if he had overheard that remarkable conversation.

They ascended the winding staircase to the floor above. At the outer door, in the muddy lane, the black limousine was waiting.

With something of a flourish Mr. Wah said:

"Bear in mind, my friend, the superior man does not pull up his shoes in a melon field, nor under a plum tree pause to straighten his hat."

Peter gave him a cold smile.

"Damned clever, you Chinese!"

And as the limousine started he carried away with him a

memory of little black shoe-button eyes filled with implacable hatred.

He was worried no longer. He was, as a matter of fact, so amused by his recent adventure that he chuckled at intervals during the tortuous ride back to his hotel through the fog.

The Green Circle was, perhaps, the oldest and most powerful secret organization in the world. It had been in existence for centuries when the first of the Mings ascended the Chinese throne. It was this emperor who had presented to the Green Circle that priceless emerald scepter which was now missing. Some bold robber had stolen it under the very nose of K'ang; and the more Peter thought about it, the more mirthful he became.

He hated the Green Circle. Often, in the past, he had encountered its sinister, far-reaching power. He wished now that he had given no promise to K'ang. He would like to find that famous scepter!

But he was through with adventure. He was trying to establish a name for himself in the realms of science, of American business. The amber-lighted lobby of his hotel was, as the limousine purred over the Garden Bridge, a reminder of this. It stood for civilization, peace, business. Adventure was behind him—forever!

Leaving the limousine, he crossed the lobby and entered the bar. Jim Jessop had shifted his scene of operations from the American Club; was now the center of a hilarious crowd. Seeing Peter, he yelled:

"Hey, there, bookworm! I thought you were goin' to bed!"

"I am," Peter laughed.

"You look pale."

"I need a drink."

"Sure you won't change your mind about lettin' me show you China as it really is—the bafflin', mysterious, exotic, fabulous East?"

Peter's polite refusal was interrupted by one of the hotel boys, a worried-looking Chinese youth who announced:

"Mist' Moo', that big-eye lady wanchee you chop-chop!"

Peter's smile went away. He said sharply: "What name that big-eye lady hab got?"

"No talkee name," the boy panted. "My no savee name. She wanchee you chop-chop! She talkee my bling you chop-chop!"

Peter frowned. He knew no "big-eye lady" in Shanghai—certainly, no "big-eye lady" he wanted to see.

He said: "Young lady or old lady?"

"Young lady! Plitty lady?" the China boy panted. "You come along my? You takee look-see?"

"Yes," Peter answered nervously, "I'll take a look-see."

He followed the boy into the lobby. He was given a confused impression very suddenly of swirling silver fox fur, of a white face with a scarlet mouth, of a girl's laughter, as she jumped up from a deep chair beside a pillar and threw slender, fierce arms about his neck, crying, "Peter—darling!" and kissed him!

CHAPTER IV

PLAYING WITH FIRE

THE BIG-EYE LADY grasped Peter's coat lapels and looked up at him with an expression which mingled hope with eagerness—eagerness at seeing him and hope that he would not be angry.

She was a little thing, not much more than five feet tall, and her eyes were large, as the bell hop had said. Susan O'Gilvie had not blue but deep violet eyes. Her voice resembled the sound of pure metal struck upon sharply; clear and rather sweet and, like the rest of her, curiously suggestive of romance.

Breathless with excitement, Susan O'Gilvie was saying: "Oh,

I think it's wonderful to find you here! I was so afraid you had gone on to Hong Kong. Now, don't be angry."

Peter was surprised that he wasn't angrier. As a matter of fact he wasn't angry at all. Warmth was coursing through him. He was blushing. He was telling himself that he hadn't realized how pretty Susan O'Gilvie was, or how much he had really been missing her.

But he was amazed to see her here. Less than two weeks ago he had personally placed Susan aboard the Empress of China in Yokohama; had seen the liner pull out, America-bound, with Susan staring at him reproachfully from the rail, an appealing and heart-saddening vision of loveliness and despair.

It had been more of a wrench than he had been willing to admit, seeing her go away. As far as Peter was concerned, it had been farewell forever.

His blood was racing now. He had convinced himself that he was not in love with Susan; could never fall for a girl like Susan. She was too romantic, too excitable, too adventurous. What he was determined to put forever behind him was the one thing in life she wanted—high adventure.

He had met Susan on the trip across, been captivated by her sheer loveliness, and had saved her from being victimized at the hands of an unscrupulous Cambodian sultan. In Yokohama, as soon as the ship landed, he felt that he was being not a little noble in packing her off on the first homeward bound ship. So many men would have taken advantage of a girl as rich and beautiful and innocent as Susan!

With great enthusiasm and lively gestures, she was explaining why and how and when she had disobeyed his stern orders.

"I was dying of loneliness. I had to see you again. I bribed the pilot to take me ashore when we were clear of Yokohama harbor."

She was gazing up at him with big starry eyes, hopefully.

"You know, Peter, I'd never been in the Far East before. And I was simply fascinated!"

Said Peter: "The Far East is dangerous for an inexperienced girl traveling alone."

"Yes," she agreed. "I know. But I'm not alone now. You're going to protect me." Before he could interrupt, she hastened to say: "Japan was simply wonderful, Peter. I adored it. I climbed Fujiyama—and I had tea with the Empress. She's a darling!"

That, Peter dryly reflected, was what money could buy—tea with empresses and the privilege of doing just what you damned well pleased, regardless of friendly advice or brotherly bossing.

He wondered idly, as he looked down into that small lovely upturned face, just how many millions Susan was worth. As if she knew—or cared! Her ideas about money were as reckless as were her ideas on everything else. Money was for spending, for providing bigger and better thrills, wilder escapades.

AFTER HAVING had tea with the "darling Empress," Susan had decided to follow Peter. At first, she hadn't dared.

"But the more I thought of you, the surer I was that I had to see you—and have another talk."

Peter vividly recalled their other "talks." They were mostly monologues delivered by Susan on what a poor stick he was not to abandon all his business schemes and enter upon a career of reckless adventuring with Susan.

There was the treasure of Kubla Khan, buried somewhere in the wilds of Afghanistan. They would organize a band and, suitably armed, travel into the heart of Afghanistan and seize the fabulous treasure. What they would do with it when they got it was unimportant. The fun would be in the getting it. Susan had plenty of other ideas, too, all just as thrilling.

"I couldn't get you out of my mind, Peter. You positively slayed me! And I thought of you being all alone in China, surrounded by your old enemies, trying so hard to be good, and—I couldn't stand it. You needed me, and so I came! Now, tell me you're a little glad and not a bit peeved!"

Peter smiled. He was so glad to see her that he could have folded her in his arms and kissed her until she was breathless.

But she spelled trouble. And Peter was trying so hard to keep out of trouble!

"You ought to be paddled," he said affectionately.

Her large violet eyes sparkled up at him. Her smile was winning. Feminine instinct told her that this tall, stern young man with the curly blond hair and adventurous blue eyes was weakening; she had only to play her cards cleverly!

"Let's sit down and have a chin-chin, darling," she cooed demurely.

Peter led her to a lounge and seated himself beside her, realizing that, in his present state of lonesomeness, it was going to be hard to treat Susan O'Gilvie like a young sister.

She snuggled her hand in his.

"When," Peter asked, "did you hit town?"

"This morning. And right off the bat, I met the most fascinating Chinaman—Mr. Chung. Do you happen to know Mr. Chung?"

Peter, reflecting that it would be like her to meet a fascinating Chinaman before she had been in Shanghai an hour, replied:

"The name Chung in China is like the name Smith in America."

"Well, this one," Susan eagerly confided, "is very tall and good-looking. He speaks English perfectly—without a trace of accent. And he seemed to know all about me. He said he knew I'd come to China looking for thrills and adventure—What did you say?"

"I just growled," Peter replied.

"Why?"

"What's Mr. Chung trying to sell you?"

"How did you know he's trying to sell me anything? Do I look so gullible? Well, Peter, he really gave me a thrill. He told me some things in strictest confidence, and—"

"Do you think you ought to break that confidence?" Peter interrupted dryly.

"Aren't you my protector?" the girl laughed. "And isn't it my duty to tell my protector everything? Did you ever hear of a mysterious, powerful, sinister Chinese organization known as the Green Circle?"

PETER STIFFENED. His eyes, which had grown warm and even affectionate, came to a sharp focus on her lovely piquant profile, and narrowed.

"What about it?" he asked.

Susan did not seem to notice the hardness in his voice.

She said, gayly: "It seems that the Green Circle is so old, so powerful, and so dangerous that no one dares plot or plan against it. You must have heard of the Green Circle, Peter!"

"Susan," Peter replied in a low voice, "do you see that short, broad-shouldered man with the scar on his cheek standing by that little table? He is a member of the Green Circle. For days, he has been just about that far away from me, whether I'm asleep or awake. If we must discuss the Green Circle, let's not give him any tales to carry."

Susan had seized his thumb. She was squeezing it. Her shoulder was pressing against his. She said, in a breathless whisper:

"Oh, I think that's perfectly wonderful! Why is the Green Circle so interested in you—were they your enemies before?"

"Yes!"

"Well, then," Susan announced loyally, "they're my enemies now. Have you ever heard of the House of a Thousand Doors?"

"I just came from there," Peter said.

"Darling!" she exclaimed. "How perfectly adorable! Then you've decided to fight them again!"

"On the contrary," Peter corrected her, "I was called there tonight to give a promise to behave. I promised."

"Oh, how could you?"

"There is a room in that house," Peter replied, "called the Room of Questions, or the Room of Easy Death. The ruler, or head, of the Green Circle is a man named K'ang. How he gets the job, I don't know. Since the Green Circle was first organized, thousands of years ago, the head of it has been called K'ang. Now, this man K'ang wears on his face a mask of kingfisher jade. The room he received me in was green—as big as all outdoors and just as green as his mask. A terrifying room."

Susan was gazing at him with tense violet eyes. Her lovely lips were parted. Her cheeks were pink with excitement.

"He asked me questions. He told me if I interfered in any way with the Green Circle's plans, I would be put to death by the *ling chi*—the death of a thousand cuts."

"How perfectly fascinating!" Susan breathed. "But we aren't afraid, Peter! We can lick the Green Circle!"

"Can we?" Peter asked briefly.

"I'll tell you what my plan is. Do you know what *joss* means to a Chinaman? I don't mean the incense they call joss-sticks. Of course, you know. It means luck, fate, destiny—all sorts of queer things. Well, the *joss* of the Green Circle has depended for years on a marvelous green scepter. Centuries ago, it was given to them by an emperor of the Ming dynasty. It's known as the Ming scepter. That scepter is the Green Circle's big *joss*. Without it, according to these funny Chinese notions, the Green Circle is helpless."

"Did Mr. Chung," Peter interrupted, "tell you all this?"

"He did! And more! And what do you think my scheme is?"

"I am beginning to have dark and terrible suspicions!"

"Peter," Susan said reproachfully, "stop laughing at me. I'm terribly serious. I mean what I'm saying. Mr. Chung has the emerald scepter in his possession! And I'm going to buy it."

CHAPTER V

THE FIVE-TOED DRAGON

PETER MOORE'S IMMEDIATE sensations were those of a man half awake into whose face had been thrown a bucket of ice water. He was startled and shocked to the awareness that Susan O'Gilvie was much more dangerous to herself and to any one with whom she came in contact than he had ever imagined.

"Let me get this straight," he whispered, glancing at the back of the scar-faced man near the little table. "Mr. Chung has the emerald scepter. He is bringing it to you and you expect to buy it."

"Not exactly," Susan explained gayly. "He has it, but he isn't bringing it to me. I am going to get it. At exactly ten o'clock, I leave here in a ricksha which he will send for me. The ricksha will take me to where Mr. Chung is, with the scepter. I will give him a check made out to 'Bearer'—and I get the scepter!"

"How much?" Peter asked.

Susan nipped her lip between two lines of perfect white teeth. "You'll be furious, darling," she said. "You'll say I'm a fool. Two hundred and fifty thousand dollars!"

"Gold or Mex?"

"Gold. Are you furious?"

"Not at all," Peter answered coldly.

"But you are mad!"

"No," said Peter, still more coldly. "Now, if you'll pay close attention, I'll be just as brief as possible. Would you deliberately put the muzzle of a shotgun in your mouth and push your toe against the trigger?"

"Don't be silly!"

"It would be just as safe as having anything to do with that Ming scepter, Susan."

"But the Green Circle wouldn't know I had it, Peter! My whole idea is to destroy the Green Circle's ugly, sinister power. You see? I am trying to do some good in the world. The Green Circle *is* a horrible, unscrupulous body of men. By taking the Ming scepter from them, I destroy their power!"

"And your own life!"

"Peter, my mind is made up."

"The Green Circle," Peter explained quietly, "knew that, six years ago, I had recklessly said I would some day make off with that scepter. Maybe I meant it, maybe I didn't. No matter. I said it. That was enough. Last night, that scepter was stolen somehow from the House of a Thousand Doors. I was in Shanghai, being closely watched. Even so, K'ang was overlooking no possibilities. That was why I was taken to him and questioned."

Susan sighed. "I think you're wonderful, darling! And you will go with me and protect me while I buy it from Mr. Chung, won't you?"

"No."

"Then I'm going alone!"

"In spite of my warning?"

SUSAN GLANCED at her wrist watch, a trifle of platinum and diamonds that had probably cost five thousand dollars.

"In fifteen minutes that ricksha will come. When it comes— I'm going, Peter. You're a terrible disappointment. I thought you were joking. I thought you were as anxious for excitement and adventure as I am."

She had risen. She stood looking down on Peter, with disapproval in every line of her taut little body, in the set of her mouth—a haughty American princess. Accustomed to being adored and unquestionably obeyed by all the men she knew, she was furious at this man who would not side with her on this "wonderful plan."

Peter watched her with a slow smile.

"After all," he said, "what do you know about human nature?

What do you know about Chinese nature? It's a little different from the American nature, Susan. How do you know that this Mr. Chung isn't a scheming, lying crook?"

"My judgment of human nature," Susan said frostily, "is quite sound, thank you!"

Peter's smile widened. She was so cute'n when she was mad!

"Give me an example of it!" he challenged.

"When I was in real trouble, I picked out you to protect me, didn't I?"

He laughed. "You evidently weren't such a good picker, at that, Susan. Listen! Let me make a suggestion. Forget about the Ming scepter. Forget about warring on this dangerous old Chinese secret society—and let's go to the Parisienne and dance."

Susan stamped her diminutive foot. "You make me furious! Treating me like a child! Are you going with me to meet Mr. Chung—or aren't you?"

"I am not," said Peter.

"I thought so!" she taunted. "Scared!"

Peter got up. He was no longer smiling.

"I'm asking you to drop this whole thing. I wouldn't trust your Mr. Chung any farther than I could throw him by his ears. Promise me you'll drop it."

She looked up at him with blazing eyes.

"I don't care if I never see you again as long as I live!"

"That would be okay with me," said Peter.

With a final blasting glare, she spun about and walked away.

Peter waited until she had gone from sight down a corridor, then started back toward the bar. He had decided that he would, after all, join Jim Jessop's party and "do" Shanghai until daylight. Halfway to the bar, he changed his mind again. He turned into an elevator; went up to his floor and to his room.

Peter sat down on the edge of his bed to think things over. He told himself that he owed absolutely no responsibility to

Susan O'Gilvie. She was of age. Theoretically, she had a brain and knew how to use it.

He had warned her of the urgent danger of having any kind of traffic with a mysterious Mr. Chung, or in any way involving herself in trouble with the Green Circle. She ought to have learned by now that he knew his China. If she wanted to dismiss his friendly advice and plunge, eyes open, into the greatest danger—that was her lookout.

Yet Peter could not rid himself of the feeling that somehow he owed it to that spoiled young brat to protect her from trouble. If anything should happen to her; if the mysterious Mr. Chung should get her in his clutches—Who in the devil was Mr. Chung?

PETER CONSULTED his watch. Five minutes of ten. In five minutes a mysterious ricksha would pull up under the Astor's *porte-cochère*. Susan O'Gilvie, thrilling to the romance of the unknown, would climb into it and be driven—where?

Peter got up and hastened to the bureau. He opened a drawer and removed from it a Colt's .38 caliber Police Positive revolver. It was shiny and blue and new. He released the catch and flipped out the cylinder. There was a shell in each chamber.

But long experience with wily Asiatics had taught him to distrust a firearm which had been out of his sight for very long. He ejected the shells and made sure that the action was in proper working order. He unlocked his wardrobe trunk and opened a fresh box of shells. He reloaded the arm, dropped a half dozen extra shells into a pocket, and disposed the revolver on his hip. Then he bolted out of the room.

When Peter reached the lobby, Susan was nowhere in sight. A ricksha with a curiously high fan-shaped back was wheeling out of the *porte-cochère* and starting toward the bridge over Soochow Creek when Peter went out. Even as he looked at that distinguishing fan-shaped back, it was swallowed by the fog which poured through Shanghai now like a great turgid river.

Of the gigantic red-turbaned Sikh doorman Peter sharply inquired: "Do you savvy Miss O'Gilvie?"

"Yes, *sahib*."

"Seen her in the past five minutes?"

"Yes, *sahib*. Miss O'Gilvie just came out, all excited. Asked if a ricksha had come, and just then one arrived with a note for her. *Sahib*, I know nothing of Miss O'Gilvie except what the Numbah One dining room boy told me—that she is a *pukka* rich American girl. But I do not savvy this ricksha pidgin. There was a look in her eyes. And when a beautiful woman gets that look in her eyes, *sahib*—"

"How long ago did she leave?" Peter curtly stopped him.

"A moment before you came out, *sahib*."

"That black ricksha with the fan-shaped back?"

"Aie, sahib!"

"Get me a ricksha!" Peter snapped.

The big, slow-thinking doorman spread out his large hands in a gesture of helplessness.

"Alas, *sahib*, there are none in the ricksha compound."

Peter rushed out of the *porte-cochère*. He hastened along Whang-po to Seward Road. He dashed across the bridge and all but collided with a ricksha coolie who, between the shafts of his vehicle, was just swinging from Soochow Road into the Bund.

The American stopped him, climbed into the seat and barked: "Down the Bund! Chop-chop—*cumshaw!* No chop-chop, no *cumshaw!*"

Which meant, hurry and you get a tip; don't hurry and you won't!

The ricksha coolie gasped, "My savvy, masta," and hurried.

He was the kind of coolie, so small, so thin, so generally undernourished and pathetic-looking, that makes riding in a Shanghai ricksha seem an act of human cruelty. But his looks were deceiving. His large bare feet plop-plopped down the wet pavement, his pipe-stem legs twinkled.

Peter, crouching forward, staring into the fog, hoped that he could head off that reckless brat. He would use force! He would compel her to return to the Astor with him!

FOG SWIRLED past him. Under a light as he sped past Jin Kee Road, Peter caught a glimpse of the black ricksha with the fan-shaped back, and yelled at his coolie to go faster. But the coolie could not go faster. And under another street light, a few blocks farther along, Peter saw that the black ricksha was easily maintaining the distance between them. A long-legged Mongolian was between the shafts; his calves were like hams, and he ran like the wind.

"You catchee him," Peter shouted, "you catchee five dollar!"

But his coolie could run no faster. Once, the tall, lean Mongolian glanced back—and went still faster.

It became a race down the Bund—to where? The lights of the customs house, blurred and eerie in the fog, flashed past, then the pink glow of the Café Parisienne.

Another ricksha was following. Peter heard the coolie gasping behind his own vehicle, sometimes a hundred feet away, sometimes closer, his feet plop-plopping on the wet pavement. Peter had forgotten about the man with the scar; had forgotten that K'ang and the Green Circle were interested in his every movement.

The three racing rickshas beat down the Bund until it became the French Bund. The black ricksha darted into Canton Road, and twisted south again into Kiang Se Road.

Peter anxiously wondered if that meant North Gate. It evidently did. The black ricksha raced on into the French section, swung west into the Avenue of the Two Republics— and plunged through North Gate into the ill-smelling misty darkness, the greaselike mud, of Chinese City.

Ahead of him, the tall Mongolian coolie was shouting to clear the way.

An old man with two varnished ducks slung from his shoulder by a rope interfered with his progress. The Mongolian, not pausing in his stride, put out a stiffened arm, very much as a running football player shoots out a stiff arm into the face of a tackle, and caught the fellow sharply on the chin.

The old Chinese sprawled backward into the mud. He picked himself up, yelling. And suddenly every one in the street was yelling. None of them knew what the trouble was, but trouble in any Chinese city these days can be ignited as easily as an explosion can be started by dropping a match into a powder magazine.

The old man recovered his ducks from a mud puddle. He picked up also a block of wood. The black ricksha was well beyond range by this time, but Peter wasn't. The old man hurled the block of wood, not at him, but at his coolie. It struck him in the forehead, and the coolie went down to hands and knees in the mud, shaking his head after the dazed manner of a prize fighter who has caught an unexpected punch on the jaw.

The sudden stopping of his ricksha threw Peter out, but he landed on his feet. He pulled out a roll of bills, stuffed a five-dollar note of the Bank of Hong Kong into the dazed coolie's hand, and fought his way down the lane, through yelling Chinese, after the black ricksha.

PETER KNEW that the man with the scar was close behind, and wondered if he would shoot him in the back.

But there was no shot. Yellow clawlike hands clutched at Peter; he pushed them aside. A tall coolie with the "chop" of a Jap steamship line sewn on the front of his faded blue blouse got in Peter's way. Peter hesitated to strike him. Chinese mobs were dangerous. But he was driven to it by the thought of the vanishing black ricksha ahead and by the thought of a shot in the back from the man with the scar.

No, it didn't take long to fan the hatred of these people into murderous fire. The steamship coolie had a knife in his hand. Peter struck him full in the jaw, leaped over him and ran through the mud.

Occupants of the stores and houses along the muddy lane were pouring out, some with clubs, others with knives. Their yells drowned out the popping of firecrackers and clashing of cymbals where the priests were still endeavoring to drive devils away from the corpse of the opium king.

The lane became a gantlet that Peter had to run, and it might well become a gantlet of death. A hated white man was running—running at top speed—and the sight affected the Chinese very much as the sight of a running fox affects a pack of hounds.

But he fought his way on, dodged clubs and knives, met opposition with his fists only when it was necessary—and saw the black ricksha swing into a lane at the left.

This lane was, when the American gained it, more like a river of mud than a thoroughfare for pedestrians or vehicles.

Perhaps a hundred yards along it the black ricksha stopped.

A man with a flaming oil torch planted himself squarely in Peter's path. Peter snatched the torch from the man's hand and began brandishing it. That solved his problems. Gray shapes stepped aside for him.

Over tossing heads and shoulders Peter saw Susan O'Gilvie alight from the black ricksha and run into a building which blazed with yellow light.

In front of this building hung a varnished and lacquered silhouette in teakwood of a five-toed dragon. In China's less troublous days the five-toed dragon stood for the majesty of the imperial government; the three-toed dragon was a symbol merely of mystic, musty legends.

The revered five-toed dragon had fallen to this: the name and address of Shanghai's most notorious joy joint; a hang-out for the toughest and hardest of China's upcoming generation; a rendezvous for outcast Americans, for beach combers with prices on their heads, for pariahs of every nationality; a dispensary of wicked native booze, an opium joint, an Oriental interpretation of the jazz idea where singsong girls displayed their dubious charms, where young China met and raised an Oriental variety of hell.

The Five-toed Dragon!

And into this wanton hole had skipped Susan O'Gilvie, an innocent, beautiful and wealthy American orphan!

Susan had gone to the right place for thrills!

CHAPTER VI

THE MYSTERIOUS MR. CHUNG

NOW PETER KNEW the Five-toed Dragon from experience aforetime; knew the character of its proprietor and the nature of its clientele, an equally lawless crew. It had been necessary one time for him to acquaint himself thoroughly with the layout of the Five-toed Dragon, with its rambling halls, its stairways and devious underground passages. He knew the tunnel that led down, like a drift in an abandoned coal mine, to the edge of the Whang-po; another tunnel that led to an exit in a vegetable shop not fifty feet from the North Gate. But it had been more than five years since he had opened the swinging front door of the Five-toed Dragon.

Peter tossed the flaming torch into the mud and entered. Time had effected at least one change. Opposite the entry was a square hole through the wall. On the other side of the hole stood a fat, smirking Chinese girl powdered and lip-sticked until she looked like a caricature. Her face might have been dipped in flour, and she was the hat-check girl.

That was a new institution. Peter flung off his trench coat and Stetson, and received in return a square brass check with the number 24 in Chinese engraved upon it. Well, twenty-four was his lucky number, and he had every reason to believe that he was going to need an abundance of luck to pull through this night without drastic consequences.

He pushed on into a smoke-filled; noisy room, an Oriental imitation of the blowsiest kind of American night club. Chinese men and girls sat about at small square tables on teak benches, sipping *saki* and *samshu* and trade gin while a Chinese orchestra rendered its version of American jazz, and in a two-by-four space in the center of the room couples swayed and rocked and tried to dance.

Smoke from hundreds of cigarettes rose to join the dense blue fog at the ceiling. This fog was in swimming layers, each layer a little less dense than the one above; and mingled with it was the distinctive soporific aroma of opium.

A slim Eurasian girl with hair as black as midnight, eyes puffed and glittering, swayed up and caught at Peter's hand. Her breath, sour with absinthe, rushed into his face. She brokenly entreated:

"Sweet w'ite man buy his 'Stelle a lil drink—heh?"

Peter pushed her fumbling hands away and crossed the room, with 'Stelle screeching curses after him. An insolent young Jap looked up at Peter and made an insulting remark in Japanese that Peter understood perfectly but did nothing about. It was a tough crew, and a well-dressed American wasn't popular here. He belonged on the other side of the deadline.

He found that everything in the Five-toed Dragon was about the same as it had been five years before. Same smells, same blare of noise, same types of people.

Peter looked in vain for Susan O'Gilvie. The thrill-seeker was not in this room. He had not, as a matter of fact, expected to see her here. Before he took steps toward finding her, he wanted to refamiliarize himself with the lay of things.

He realized that if he were to rescue the restless, reckless girl from this place and take her to the comparative safety of the northern side of Shanghai's deadline, he must find her quickly and act with decision.

The moment it was known that Peter Moore was in the Five-toed Dragon, trouble would start. Plenty of trouble. Trouble in generous amounts had always started when he had been here before—and tonight might well see him establish a record!

Susan, of course, was the dangerous factor. He knew that Susan was the kind of girl who could not resist trying anything exciting. She would not hesitate to sample opium. They would not even have to offer it to her. Knowing that the Five-toed Dragon was, among other things, a hop joint, she would promptly ask for opium. Peter imagined he could hear her sweet, clear, lilting voice as she watched the pill being toasted: "Oh, I think this is perfectly fascinating!"

Yes, whatever the mysterious Mr. Chung's scheme was, it was hard to visualize an easier, more eager victim than Susan. The very roots of her character were sunk in volcanic soil. She would go more than halfway to meet any kind of excitement. She was anybody's victim!

PETER'S PLAN was simple. Knowing the place as he did, and taking advantage of opportunities, he would somehow, if he possibly could, contrive to rescue her, take her back to the Astor, give her a brief lecture on the follies of playing with Oriental dynamite—and let it go at that.

He would settle that debt with his conscience, but thereafter Susan O'Gilvie could pursue her own sweet way to the devil. He reiterated to himself that he was not in love with Susan, that he would have gone to such pains with any girl.

Quietly, Peter made a tour of the large room. Off the large room were smaller rooms, or stalls, each containing a table, two chairs and a couch, so-called private dining rooms, where a man could take a girl, or where a man could go alone and be waited upon by a wise little Chinese miss who knew how to roll a proper pill.

But Peter was sure that Susan had been taken elsewhere. He was convinced that the mysterious Mr. Chung was no other than Mr. Lee Hung Gow, the middle-aged proprietor of the Five-toed Dragon.

Mr. Lee Hung Gow matched the description Susan had given of "Mr. Chung." He was tall, suave, and he spoke perfect

English. He was the kind of modern Chinese who would have hit upon such a clever scheme for getting Susan into his toils.

Mr. Lee Hung Gow, as Peter knew from experience, had palatial quarters on the floor above—the sort of exotic headquarters that befitted the Oriental gangster and racketeer that he was. A ruthless man and a sworn enemy of Peter was Lee Hung Gow.

As quickly as he could do so, Peter would ascend to the floor above and continue his investigations.

Just now he was somewhat concerned over the presence, near a post beside the orchestra, of the man with the scar. This one might readily complicate matters.

A Chinese Rudy Vallee was crooning through a megaphone. There was no applause when he and the orchestra stopped. The roar of voices took the place of the music.

Peter sidled toward a doorway. Glances being sent in his direction convinced him that he had no time to waste.

Two tall and pugilistic waiters, or bouncers in the garb of waiters, were eying him nastily. Girls were smirking at him. Numbers of the younger China element were gazing at him with the ugly looks which were, throughout China, being addressed more and more frankly at prosperous Americans and Europeans.

Peter felt sure that the moment he was recognized, trouble would start. He gained the doorway which he knew opened upon stairs leading up to Mr. Lee Hung Gow's apartment. He placed his back against it for a final survey of a situation which was rapidly growing tense.

Suddenly he saw a man jump up from a table—a white man with carrot-colored hair—speak excitedly to one of the big Chinese waiters, then gesticulate in the direction of the American. The fellow started toward Peter. Paralleling him, a few tables away, came the other big waiter. And bringing up the rear, as if he had reached a sudden decision, was the man with the scar!

Peter hesitated no longer. He threw open the door, let himself into the small hall, and pulled the door shut after him.

Voices came down the stairs: the argumentative voices of

men, the thin, high protesting voice of a girl. This voice—Peter could not yet be sure that it was Susan's—rose to a scream as he started up the stairs.

Peter removed the revolver from his hip and started up the stairs, two at a bound.

CHAPTER VII

THROUGH THE SECRET DOOR

THERE WAS TIME and opportunity to act only upon that split-second decision. Retreat was cut off. Ahead lay the most serious possibilities.

If he had made a mistake in his reasoning—if the girl who had screamed should prove not to be Susan O'Gilvie, which might well be the case, he had lost his chance. In either event, the chances of his getting out of the Five-toed Dragon alive were exceedingly slim.

Pale, grim and desperately ready for eventualities, Peter raced up the stairs with the gun ready.

He was promptly given an opportunity to demonstrate the ruthlessness with which he was prepared to meet Mr. Lee Hung Gow's resistance.

A Chinese guard, stationed at the head of the stairs to anticipate just such interruptions, leaped out from a curtained recess with a steel bar in his upraised hand. His lips were drawn back in a grin of murderous fury. It was, perhaps, the chance he had been hoping for all his life—to bring death to just one hated white invader!

The steel bar, a most dangerous kind of club, gleamed above Peter's head, and for a sickening moment the American visualized that shining weapon crashing into his own skull.

Unhesitatingly he fired. Then he stepped back as the Oriental plunged forward with a shriek of agony.

Peter ran to the end of the short hall. He parted thick black curtains and stepped into the room from which had come the voices of men and the woman's scream.

An interrupted tableau almost froze him for the moment. With sharp relief he saw Susan struggling, as he had expected, in the arms of the tall, handsome Lee Hung Gow. The girl's violet eyes were dilated with terror, but she was no longer screaming. A large yellow hand with elegantly pointed fingernails had been clapped over her mouth.

On a low teak taboret in the very center of the room, sparkling and glittering like the eyes of a nest of snakes, lay the famous Ming scepter! Above it burned an oil dong—only light in the room.

That was the first surprise, the first upset of Peter Moore's shrewd calculations.

But the surprise for which the American was not in the least prepared—which so astounded him that it almost cost his life—was the presence of a second man, a figure Peter gazed at with utter incredulity.

The suave, the unctuous gunman who had escorted him from the American Club to the House of a Thousand Doors in the purring black limousine! Mr. Wah!

Susan had suddenly stopped struggling. She was staring, over that hand clapped upon her mouth, at Peter.

IN A sudden breathless hush, three men acted. Mr. Lee pushed Susan away with such violence that she stumbled and fell at Peter's feet. He reached swiftly for his hip. Mr. Wah did likewise, his hand darting down with the swiftness and accuracy of a striking snake.

Peter, it so chanced, was a split second ahead of either of them. He fired at Wah, flicked his revolver muzzle to the left and fired at Lee.

Lee fell in a sudden writhing heap across Susan's legs.

But Mr. Wah only staggered, and began fumbling wildly for

his weapon. Peter steadied his gun, deliberately aimed at Mr. Wah's heart—and again pressed the trigger.

Mr. Wah ceased fumbling wildly. An expression of amazement flitted over his handsome face. And then a gasp, the last breath he would ever exhale.

Voices clamored on the stairway. In seconds, Peter would be outnumbered, surrounded.

He saw the curtains part; the face of one of the big waiters, scarred with smallpox, was poised there momentarily as if it hung down from the ceiling by a wire.

Peter fired twice—once at the pockmarked face, once at the light over the taboret. The face vanished—and the light went out!

In the instant flood of blackness, Susan's hysterical voice pierced the shouts in the little corridor.

"Peter—where are you?"

"Keep still," he whispered. "Give me your hand."

"I can't walk!" she wailed. "I'm scared stiff! I'm going to faint! How can we get out of here?"

Peter picked her up in his arms and, with racing pulses, ran down the room to the southern wall. He fumbled at a well-remembered panel and hoped to heaven that it had not been altered.

Under the velvet overhang he found the circular lump with groping fingers; pressed it mightily, and had the satisfaction of knowing that they were, at least for the moment, out of danger.

The panel swung outward. Peter stepped into blackness; kicked the secret door shut after him.

He whispered: "Are you all right?"

"Yes! Oh, I think this is perfectly horrible! Where are we?"

"There's a steep flight of stairs running down to a network of passages underground—with an old iron ship's ladder at the bottom. Take my hand and I'll lead the way. Can you walk?"

"I'll t-t-try!" she chattered.

Peter led the way. He had forgotten the number of steps. He knew only that they went down and down—and he dared not strike matches—yet.

Presently he whispered: "Easy, Susan! Here's the ladder!"

"Peter, I'm so s-s-sorry!"

"Never mind," he grunted. "We've got to work fast. Come on!"

He grasped a slim silk-clad ankle and placed her foot on the first rung. A damp, sour, cold wind blew up past them.

Down and down they went. Once Peter touched the wall. It was cold and slimy.

Not until he felt moist brickwork under his feet did he strike a match. For a moment it illuminated a square room, with walls of yellow brick, measuring about twenty feet on a side. The flickering flame disclosed coils of rope, water-logged boxes, several kegs.

In the center of either side was a door. One led to the river, one to a vegetable stand near the North Gate. Where the other two led, Peter did not know, and probably never would know.

A BABBLE of excited voices above caused Peter to squeeze out the flame between his fingers.

He said: "They're after us! Come on, Susan!"

"Where do those d-doors go?" she stuttered, clinging to him.

He told her. "We're taking the one to the river."

"Why?"

"Because they'll expect us to go to the North Gate."

"Darling," she whispered, "you—you're wonderful! Can you ever forgive me?"

"We've got to run," he told her. "Take my hand and duck your head. Parts of this passage are under five feet high. Steady, Susan!"—for she was beginning to tremble.

"I'm scared."

"We'll be out of it in two minutes."

"Then what?"

"A sampan—hotel—civilization!"

"Peter, I was a fool. Will you ever forgive me?"

"Don't worry about it."

"But I was so gullible. I—"

"Oh, we all make mistakes!"

"But people with sense learn. I don't. I'm positively disgusted with myself. I'll do just what you tell me. I'll never be such an idiot again."

"We'd better go faster," said Peter.

"Yes," she panted. "I thought it would be thrilling. They—they showed me that scepter, then they told me to write out the check for two hundred and fifty thousand dollars, gold, on my New York bank. And the minute I wrote it out, that horrible beast grabbed me. What would he have done?" She shuddered.

"Held you for ransom, perhaps," Peter answered calmly. "Sold you to some up-country Chinese millionaire, maybe. Who knows?"

"You killed them both!"

"Let's hurry!"

A damp, chill breath from the river was flowing in their faces. Suddenly they were stumbling over steps. The steps led up and into a small brick structure, like a sentry box, on a jetty.

The shouts behind them were louder now. Susan drew a deep grateful breath of the foggy air, and suddenly threw her arms around Peter's neck. She was crying.

Peter pushed her away.

"But, darling, aren't we safe?"

"Not until we're out of this Chinese settlement and back in Shanghai."

He pushed her ahead of him out of the low doorway and onto the wet planks of the jetty. Perhaps a dozen feet away from the side of the jetty on which they had emerged, a dong burned dimly in the low thatched cabin of a sampan.

Peter later recalled that he opened his mouth to awaken the *fokie* on that sampan; that, from everywhere, soft feet were rushing toward him, making no sound but a whisper on the wet planking.

None of this he saw, for there was no light but that dim effulgence in the sampan's low cabin.

His next actual impression was that, from the heart of the river, a living red flame had shot up and engulfed the universe. He carried the amazement of this into prompt unconsciousness. Susan later declared that, at this precise moment, she had screamed. But Peter had no recollection of such a sound.

CHAPTER VIII

THE DOUBLE CROSSER

A GENTLE, RHYTHMIC swaying brought Peter back to consciousness. Then he heard the steady plop-plop of naked feet in mud. A fiery pain burned and throbbed from temple to temple. He tried to think, tried to orient himself.

The rhythmic swaying persisted. He reached out weakly with his hands, and drew in his breath as sharply as a man might who finds he has been sealed alive in a tomb. Then he realized, as his fingers scraped along the velvet lining of the swaying tomb, that he was in a sedan chair—being transported where?

He tried to call, but when his muffled voice banged dully in his ears he realized that a hood had been strapped over his head. It was not strapped; it was wired. Dozens of turns of stout wire were wrapped about the base of the hood around his neck.

Peter realized that he had, at the very moment of escape, fallen into the hands of the enemy. But which enemy?

He fumbled at his coat pocket. The revolver was gone!

The swaying motion stopped. A hand fumbled at his knee, a cold, wet hand with long finger nails. In Chinese a harsh voice bade him to arise.

Still weak and sick, reeling from the blow that had knocked

him unconscious, Peter obeyed his captor, and stepped out of the chair into ankle-deep mud.

Hands seized his elbows. He heard the bolt of a door shoot back; he heard other feet making sucking sounds in the thick mud. Then the door closed behind him.

Where was he? Where was Susan?

Hands plucked at his sleeves, at his elbows, at his hands. He was urged along some sort of hall. Another door opened and closed. Still another. Because of the thick hood over his head, he could smell nothing; and all sounds were muffled. He had no means of knowing where he was.

Peter was taken down a flight of steps. He counted them. Twenty. Up another flight of steps. Again he counted. Ten. Down another flight. Thirty. Another door opened and closed.

Silence.

It was as though all the hands which had been plucking at him, pawing him, were retreating. He could almost see them becoming smaller and smaller, more and more vague.

Then a pressure at his neck informed him that the binding wire was being unwound. He tried to control his shaking. The suspense of not knowing where he was, where Susan was, and what their fate might be, was more than his nervous system could stand.

Peter was prepared for almost anything. But he was utterly unprepared for that which he beheld when, suddenly, the hood was snatched from his head.

A cold green radiance flooded his eyes. Originating at no given point, it was taken in and thrown back by glassy green walls, ceiling, floor. Just ahead of him, stretching from green ceiling to green floor, hung a pair of green brocade curtains.

A FLUTTERING voice cried:

"Peter—darling!"

He looked quickly, to see Susan standing perhaps a dozen feet behind him—a limp, bedraggled Susan, her little shoes and slim ankles coated with mud; her face as white as death, her large violet eyes swimming.

He hastened to her side. Limply she sank against him. Her voice, no louder than a breath, floated up from gray lips.

"Where are we? What's going to happen?"

Peter said quietly:

"We're in the green room—in the House of a Thousand Doors. If I knew what was going to happen I would be a Buddha!"

"They'll kill us, Peter!"

The curtains parted.

Susan's voice died to a little gurgle in her throat.

K'ang—the man in the jade mask—stepped before them.

The cold, thin, whispery voice issued from the jade slit, and Peter felt Susan's hand, clutching his arm, fiercely tighten.

"Mr. Moore, I suppose you realize perfectly what this means. You have broken your oath to me. Where is the emerald scepter?"

Peter looked steadily at the gleaming slits behind which this man, whose face he had never seen, must be peering out at him.

"The last I saw of the Ming scepter, K'ang," Peter quietly answered, "was in Lee Hung Gow's private room in the Five-toed Dragon. It was on a taboret under a single light. When that light went out I escaped with Miss O'Gilvie."

For a long time the man in the jade mask made no comment. Peter saw him take a short backward step. In an ordinary man he would have taken that as an indication of astonishment. But the American was convinced—had for years been convinced—that K'ang was no ordinary man. So complete was the legend which attributed to K'ang the coldness and wisdom of the serpent that Peter had accepted it at its face value.

He was amazed when, instead of the thin, whispery voice, a full-bodied voice quivering with emotion issued from the jade lips.

"You saw the Ming scepter in the Five-toed Dragon?"

"I did, K'ang."

"I—" K'ang began, and stopped. Then, in a low roar: "Who took the scepter?"

"K'ang," Peter quietly replied, "I saw no one take the scepter. I was surrounded by enemies. I had gone to the Five-toed Dragon because Miss O'Gilvie, against her better judgment, had accepted an invitation from Lee Hung Gow—to go there and buy the scepter."

The gleaming jade face turned toward Susan.

"Who offered to sell you the scepter?"

"Lee Hung Gow," she answered in a husky little voice.

"What was the price?"

"A quarter of a million dollars—gold."

"Did you pay this price?"

"I did—with a check."

"Made payable to whom?"

"Lee Hung Gow."

"You signed it and gave it to him?"

"I did."

"And they showed you the Ming scepter?"

"They did."

THE MAN in the jade mask was folding and unfolding his hands. In his previous encounters with this mysterious Oriental power, Peter had not once seen him betray the slightest symptom of an emotion: nothing but coldness—a machine-like coldness.

And it suddenly flashed upon Peter that the power of K'ang was slipping—or past. He scented intrigues within walls which had, for centuries, hatched the most ingenious and elaborate of intrigues. Wheels within wheels, spinning at counter purposes.

It startled him to realize that in spite of the elaborate care taken to capture him and Susan, K'ang was in utter ignorance of what had happened in that room in the Five-toed Dragon.

He said quickly: "K'ang, what are you going to do with us?"

And K'ang said harshly. "You—the *ling chi,* as I promised. The girl—I do not know."

Peter felt Susan's hand contracting about his arm, heard the breath leave her lips as a gasp.

Then, suddenly, she sagged. He reached down and turned only in time to catch her as she fell.

He gathered her in his arms, one arm under her neck, the other under her knees.

Holding her close, he turned back to K'ang.

He felt the cold moisture that had formed on his forehead. His heart was beating slowly and dully, like the clapper of a lifeless bell thumping. For him—the *ling chi,* the death of a thousand cuts. For Susan—

Peter took a gambler's chance. It was the only chance. It was based solely on his guess that K'ang, the mysterious power who ruled the Green Circle, was no longer a power.

"K'ang," he said in a steady voice, "I can prove to you that I am not a traitor to my promise, but that I have befriended you, and in so doing am entitled to my freedom, and Miss O'Gilvie to hers. I have ridded you of the man who has been, like a cancer, eating at the heart of the Green Circle."

And Peter realized that, on his next words, he would live or die.

"Did you know, K'ang, that I had shot Mr. Wah—in the Five-toed Dragon?"

If the man in the jade mask had taken it calmly, coldly, Peter would have known that his shaft had missed its mark.

But if K'ang betrayed any emotion, there was a chance.

For at least ten seconds K'ang did nothing, said nothing. Then he took another of those unaccustomed backward steps, as a man might retire in the face of a crushing, humiliating fact.

K'ang burst into Chinese. He spoke so rapidly that Peter, well-versed as he was in the tongue, caught only occasional words. Glancing behind him, Peter saw that the man with the scar was standing there.

He was nodding. His eyes were terrified. He was simply verifying what Peter had said. In English, he finally stated:

"It is true, K'ang. Wah is dead."

"Where is the scepter?"

"K'ang, I do not know. A hundred of my men are searching for it!"

The man in the jade mask spoke again.

"You may go, Mr. Moore. But wait! You are clever! All the time you remain in China, I will have you watched. If you interfere in any way with my plans, I will carry out my threat—the *ling chi!*"

CHAPTER IX

WHAT PETER MISSED

THE BLACK LIMOUSINE carried Peter and the half-conscious girl back across the deadline and into the civilized community of Shanghai. It purred down the Bund.

The fog was lifting. It was possible, now, to see the riding lights of ships at anchor. The thinning mist was palely glowing. Dawn was at hand.

Susan, huddled against him, then slowly lifted her head. She shook it dazedly.

"Peter—where are we?"

"On the way back to the Aston"

"But—what happened?"

Briefly and modestly, Peter told her.

Susan snuggled against him and breathed: "Oh, I think it's been perfectly fascinating!"

"I'm glad you enjoyed it," Peter said dryly.

"Oh, but I did, darling—now that the danger's all over! Do

you know what I think? I think I was born under a lucky star. I wouldn't have missed tonight for worlds!"

Peter said nothing. Susan O'Gilvie had tasted of that heady, bitter-sweet wine—dangerous adventure. She had had two sips so far. And with that wine in her blood, she would want to go on. She wouldn't be satisfied until she got herself killed.

The adventurer was neither disappointed nor angry. He knew just how she felt. He had sipped plenty of that wine himself.

The girl yawned—and snuggled her hand into his.

"I'm dead tired," she said. "I'm going to bed and leave a call for five this afternoon. We'll have tea and talk plans. I knew, if I once got you started, you wouldn't stop. Peter, what fun we're going to have!"

In the lobby of the Astor she put up her face and sleepily kissed him. Peter did not release her as soon as he might have. Whether he loved her or not was no longer a consideration.

He had put adventure behind him. He was a research engineer in the employ of a great American organization. And he was going to stick to his vocation. Susan O'Gilvie was not for him.

"Good-by," he said.

"Until this afternoon at five, darling!"

Peter did not answer, but watched the girl until she entered an elevator and the door clanged behind her. Then he went up to his room and packed. There was, he knew, a tub of a steamer, a Chinese coastwise ship, leaving for Hong Kong in a very few hours. It would put in at Amoy and Soochow and other dreary places. He was going to take that steamer.

Peter shaved, bathed and changed to fresh clothes. When he was dressed and had finished his packing, he sat down and wrote a brief note.

DEAR SUSAN:

I suppose I'm a coward for doing this, but I'm afraid that if I stay behind I might fall. You should have learned that adventure

in China isn't for a nice kid like you. I'm not packing you off for
home this time, but I'm heartily recommending it.

I'm inclosing a souvenir of our night's excitement. Do what
you wish with it. I'm off for Hong Kong.

Good-by and good luck!

PETER.

For several minutes Peter examined the famous Ming scepter which he had carried, for the latter half of the night, tucked
down inside his shirt under his belt. If it had been necessary to
surrender it to K'ang, he would have surrendered it. But it hadn't
been necessary.

And Susan would appreciate it. The crude emeralds flashed
and sparkled in the wrought gold handle. The *joss* of the Green
Circle! Well, perhaps the loss of it would put the Green Circle
to an end. Perhaps!

HE WRAPPED it up carefully in the note; found wrapping
paper and cord and made a neat package. He descended to the
lobby and left the package at the desk, with instructions that it
be delivered to Miss Susan O'Gilvie at five o'clock.

Then Peter went into the dining room and ordered break-
fast. He was enjoying ham and eggs, coffee and toast, when Jim
Jessop, his Tuxedo rumpled, his shirt front no longer white and
glossy, and his tie entirely missing, came weaving in, bellowing
for strong black coffee. Then he espied Peter, and he ambled over.

"Well, well, well! 'At's a boy! Up bright and early—you little
worm catcher! Boy, if you only knew what you missed last night!
I took my gang into Chinese City—and we crashed the toughest
joint in all of China! The Five-toed Dragon! There'd been a riot
there just before we went in. A lot of Chinks shot? Boy—the
fun you missed! If you'd only gone along, you'd have seen China
from the inside—the fabulous, exotic, mysterious East!"

THAT CARGO OF OPIUM

*Peter the Brazen was running away—
from a thrill-seeking, adventure-crazy girl;
but wherever he went in the China Seas,
trouble clung to him like iron to a magnet*

CHAPTER I

TRAMP OF THE CHINA SEAS

THE FIRST RAYS of the rising sun struck down through the fog like javelins of gold. It was beginning to thin. The rolling billows of mist, as if mysteriously illuminated from the inside, glowed saffron to yellow; yellow to gold.

The modern city of Shanghai emerged dripping from the mist. The Whangpo-kiang, rolling down to the Yellow Sea in a gurgling brown tide, once more became visible. Ships at moorings and at anchor, brown junks with bare masts, stood out against the pearly background, where Pootung Point lay, like ships of black jade carved upon a field of alabaster.

The City of Swatow, a frowzy, rusty-sided tramp—mute testimony to the deplorable lack of efficiency or good management betrayed by all native-owned ships—rode at her forward and after anchors. She might have been hauled only recently from the ooze of the sea bottom.

Seaweed hung down in long green beards from the hawseholes out of which stood her anchor chains. Her bright work had become gray. Her white superstructure was slate. Rivet heads drooled rust down her shabby, battered sides.

A stem of smoke seemed to struggle with difficulty out of her skinny funnel, which was askew.

The term, "scum of the seas," took on realistic meaning when one glanced at the City of Swatow.

Seated in the bow of a sampan that was fishtailing out from the mouth of Soochow Creek, a young man gazed at her with

She blew a kiss toward receding Shanghai.

eyes trained to estimate the worth of any ship at a glance. On his crisp lips was a faintly derisive smile mingled with a twirk of sadness. With such an expression, any man of the sea might have looked at the City of Swatow; for any man who loves the sea hates to see a ship sink so low.

His shrewd blue eyes pierced through her pitted iron hide, into the heart of her engine room—and saw there disorder and shameful neglect: steam leaking from rags wrapped around steam-line joints; caked grease and mud where mirror-like metal should have been, temporary patches of strap-iron that had become permanent.

Years ago no doubt a crack ship in the transatlantic service, the City of Swatow had been doomed to end her days, neglected and unloved, a frowzy old vagabond of the sea, creaking up and down the China coast.

The young man in the sampan, sitting astride his steamer trunk, glanced at the brown-red pile of masonry, across Soochow Creek beyond the northern end of the Bund, Shanghai's famous water front.

His faint smile went away, and only the twirk of sadness remained. For fully a minute he gazed back at the Astor Hotel with eyes glazed by dreams and speculation. Then he definitely shook his head, as if to shake the visions out, and squared his shoulders.

Unless he broke cleanly with Susan O'Gilvie—put her geographically well beyond reach—he was lost. She was too appealing, too provocative, and entirely too dangerous. And the City of Swatow, in her own good time, would carry him well beyond Susan's reach.

HE SAW, with faint displeasure, the blackened strands of a wireless machine's antenna hanging slack between the masts. He would rather have been cut off from the world entirely. It would hurt, leaving Susan forever; but he wanted to make the break a clean one. He could hear Susan's voice, sweet and clear, like good metal struck upon sharply: "Peter, I think you're perfectly *cruel!*"

Peter Moore, veteran of more hair-raising adventures in China than he cared to think about, wanted his hair raised no more.

Grinning, he dropped a kiss onto the tips of his fingers and flicked it at the pile of brown-red masonry. Then he turned back again to face the future—and the City of Swatow.

She would touch at Soochow, Amoy, Swatow and Hong Kong, picking up a load here, dropping a load there. It would be a slow trip, but it would give him time to rest up from the recent adventures into which Susan O'Gilvie—whose thirst for danger and adventure nothing could quench—had plunged him.

The sampan swung in beside the rickety ship's ladder which ran up the City of Swatow's blistered side. Peter gave the deserted-looking tramp a hail.

"Hi—yah!" he yelled.

A China boy in a shabby, soiled white coat and faded blue pants eased out of a doorway. His eyes looked down at Peter blankly. Without a word, he vanished, to reappear presently with another man in tow. This one was presumably white. He wore the unpressed blue uniform with the tarnished brass buttons of a ship's officer.

He, too, scrutinized Peter Moore without enthusiasm. He placed his hands on the rail and called down, hoarsely, in coast pidgin:

"What thing wanchee, mister?"

"A passage to Hong Kong."

The purser and supercargo, as Peter later learned he was, looked still more dubious.

"It's a long slow trip, mister."

"The slower the better," Peter answered, cheerfully.

"Well, I don't know, mister. We don't carry many passengers."

Another man appeared. That is to say, a door forward on the top deck opened and a man came out of it. He was tall, solidly built, and Chinese. In a deep-throated voice he bellowed:

"What's all the *bhobbery?*"

And the purser yelled: "Here's a guy who wants a passage to Hong Kong, captain."

The captain now came to the rail of the boat deck and looked down suspiciously at Peter, who grinned back at him from the sampan.

"We're booked up," stated the captain.

"All right," Peter said. "I'll go as a deck passenger. Come down here, you, and hustle this trunk." This was addressed to the deck boy or steward, who had first appeared.

The China boy hesitated. He and the purser went into a huddle. Peter grew impatient. In river Chinese, he told his boat-man, the *fokie,* to take an end of the trunk. Peter tossed the suitcase over the rail and onto the deck; picked up one end of the trunk. He and the *fokie* carried it up the ladder to the deck.

The big Chinese captain had, in the meantime, joined the purser and the deck boy. With suspicious, hostile eyes the trio stared at Peter. The audacious American grinned at the captain, flipped an airy salute at him, and said:

"When do we pull out?"

"As soon as the mate comes aboard with clearance papers.

That's his sampan now." The captain's small black eyes were glinting with hostility. "What is your name?"

"Peter Moore—Schenectady, New York," Peter cheerfully answered. "Radio research division of the General Electric Company."

THE CAPTAIN grunted. "I thought so. They used to call you *Ren-Beh-Tung*—Peter the Brazen—on this coast, a matter of five or six years ago. You are a trouble-maker. I do not care to take you to Hong Kong on my ship."

"Captain," Peter said gravely, "for certain reasons, I must travel to Hong Kong on this vessel."

The skipper solidly stood his ground. "One of the Dollar Line ships is leaving for Hong Kong this afternoon. She is faster, much more comfortable."

Peter's smile had hardened. There was trouble brewing on the City of Swatow. With senses delicately adjusted to trouble, he was made aware of it. It wouldn't have surprised him to learn that the big Chinese captain was planning to sink this old hulk for the insurance. Perhaps that was not what he detected in the air; but trouble of some kind was brewing. And he would rather chance trouble on the City of Swatow than the kind of trouble he was more than likely to encounter on the Dollar liner. It was not improbable that Susan O'Gilvie would be a passenger on the Dollar liner.

"I like slow ships," he said.

And the Chinese captain harshly answered: "I will not take you to Hong Kong on this ship."

Peter planted his fists on his hips. He had been through this sort of thing before, in the old days.

Quietly he announced: "Captain, you and I know maritime law. If you put me off this ship, I'll libel you before you can get your anchors out of the mud. I'll tie you up in Shanghai law courts indefinitely. Where's my stateroom?"

The captain shrugged. Almost in so many words his attitude said: "Very well, I've warned you; you can take the consequences." Aloud, to the purser he ordered: "Give Mr. Moore a cabin."

So, a few minutes later, Peter Moore was being installed in one of the City of Swatow's cabins. Dust lay thickly upon its furniture. The linen on the bunk was damp and moldy. It smelled of Chinese rivers. But the cabin was commodious. Its big portholes would give Peter plenty of ventilation, and there was a door which opened conveniently on the small promenade deck. The food would be awful, but he was inured to awful food.

Realizing the voyage would be a long one, the young man unpacked his trunk and disposed its contents in the spacious wardrobe. Then he adjusted the porthole lights, drew curtains over them, turned down the bed, undressed, and put on his pyjamas.

He was tired. Because Susan O'Gilvie had involved herself with a crowd of cutthroat Chinese the night before, Peter had gone without sleep.

He got into bed now and, for a little while, lay in that pleasant hazy borderland between sleeping and waking. Dimly he heard the mooing of the City of Swatow's whistle, the deep rumbling of anchor chains. A little later, in his dreams, he heard the vibration of the ship and the rhythmic creaking of woodwork as the loose old engines took up their work.

ANOTHER SOUND penetrated to Peter's dreams—a voice, sweet and clear, like good metal struck upon sharply, was calling:

"Ship ahoy! Ahoy!"

The adventurer who had put all adventure forever behind him smiled in his slumber. He knew he was dreaming. And even in his dreams he had the canniness to reflect that it was far better, far safer, to deal with Susan in his dreams than with Susan in reality.

"Ahoy, there! I want to come aboard!"

The young man came swimming up from the depths of sleep with the horrifying premonition that it wasn't a dream, after all. He saw sunlight falling, through the crack in the curtains over one of the big portholes and lying in a golden puddle on the dusty green carpet.

He heard the creaking of the old woodwork, the faint persistent shudder which he knew was the voice of the old hull responding to the laboring of the antique engines.

Again the familiar clear golden voice:

"Lend me a hand with this luggage, will you? *Chop-chop!*"

Another voice, the deck boy's: "No can catchum, missee."

The golden voice rose sharp and indignant: "You'd better catchum—or when I catchum you, there'll be war!"

Peter groaned. He sat up, reached for a dressing gown and slippers; got into them and opened the door. The fog was gone. The sun had transformed the Whangpo into a swirling river of gold. A sweet breath of spring was in the air. The sky was a brilliant miraculous blue. It was the kind of morning that ordinarily would cause any man to rejoice.

Peter failed to rejoice. Silhouetted against the blue and gold of it, out on the river beyond the rail, was a battered old sampan, in the bows of which stood a slender girl. She was not more than five feet tall. Her eyes were not blue but deep violet. Her face was pale.

A close-fitting blue *béret* sat jauntily on the side of her small head. The folds of a gray squirrel coat were wrapped snugly about her. She might have been the season's loveliest, most popular debutante. Behind her, on the deck, was a small mountain of trunks.

There was a small wad of handkerchief in one gloved hand. The newcomer raised this to her eyes, dabbed at them. As Peter watched, she turned slowly to face the receding city of Shanghai. She was looking back at the Astor Hotel. She lifted her finger tips to her mouth, dropped a kiss upon them and blew the kiss in the direction of the red-brown pile.

Astonished, Peter watched this. He saw her shoulders rise and fall in a sigh. The girl turned about to face the ship again, and he noticed that her large, lovely eyes were misted with tears.

Suddenly it all became clear to Peter. Susan was giving him up. That is, she thought she was giving him up. She was making a beautiful gesture of renunciation. Susan probably believed he was back there, asleep, in his room in that red-brown pile of masonry. She was saying farewell to him forever!

CHAPTER II

CONTRABAND OPIUM

PETER WITHDREW INTO his stateroom and softly closed the door. The humor of the situation made him want to laugh, but he didn't even smile.

He refrained from smiling because the results were apt to be serious. He had been on the verge of falling for Susan ever since he had met her, a few weeks ago, on the crossing from San Francisco to Yokohama. Susan appealed to him more than any girl he had known; but he didn't choose to fall in love with Susan. Her craving for thrills had twice plunged him into serious trouble—and he wanted no more.

He heard her luggage coming aboard—trunk after trunk being dragged along the deck. He heard her imperious voice, demanding the best accommodations on board; the voice of the purser, protesting. She was evidently as unwelcome a passenger as was Peter—and she was quite as determined to make the trip.

"This means," Peter reflected, "that I will be asking her to marry me before we reach Foochow. I could slip ashore at Woosung. But I won't. Maybe Fate has a hand in this."

He would not have been so amused if he could have foreseen what Fate had up her sleeve. He heard the tone of the purser's voice change from one of protest to one of conciliation. Evidently Susan had mentioned who she was. That name, with the millions behind it, would command respect and deference in any part of the world. Then Peter heard the name "Fung Low"—

Mr. Fung Low, and some reference to the small Whango port of Woosung.

But Peter was too sleepy to put two and two together. He climbed back into his bunk, and was very promptly asleep, dreaming a very wild dream of himself and Susan conducting a camel caravan over the Goblyn Gobi in search of Kublai Khan's fabulous hidden treasure. This treasure was in a cave, guarded by bloodthirsty Tartars. It was necessary to mow down these Tartars with a sub-machine gun.

Peter heard the *tat-tat-tat-tat* of the machine gun, awoke momentarily to realize that what he had heard was the rapid-fire exhaust of some fast motor boat; and dozed off again.

Late in the afternoon he came fully awake. He lay in his bunk listening to the creaking of the woodwork and the persistent shudder of the City of Swatow's ancient hull.

As he was dressing, he heard the sharp tapping of high heels on the deck. He looked out the porthole and saw Susan walk past, smiling up at a tall, dark-skinned Chinese.

Peter said "H'm," very thoughtfully to himself and finished dressing. Now and then he smiled. Unless Susan had heard of his presence aboard, which was unlikely, he could imagine her surprise and delight at seeing him.

When Peter went out on deck, the sun was setting—an inflamed, evil-looking sun, like a grape squatting on the western skyline. The Yellow Sea, through which the City of Swatow slowly plowed, was as calm as an inland lake. Fishing junks and sampans were like painted ships on a painted sea.

Peter walked forward with his pulses racing. Susan O'Gilvie was leaning on the rail at the forward turn of the deck, looking down at the deck well. The hatch covers had been removed and Susan was gazing into the cargo hold.

THE TALL Chinese with whom Peter had seen her was standing beside Susan—very close beside Susan—talking to her in a low voice. His clothes had obviously been made in London.

He even wore a bowler, set on his head at the proper Piccadilly angle. His manner was assured, even proprietary.

It was also confidential. He was gesturing with free, graceful motions at the cargo hold and murmuring into Susan's ear. It seemed to be a receptive ear. The little enthusiast nodded her head eagerly and looked up with an eager smile into the tall man's face.

Peter distinctly heard the man say, "Fifty thousand—gold, Miss O'Gilvie?"

And Susan's answer, laughingly: "It still seems like a lot of money, Mr. Fung."

Then Peter was beside her; looking over the top of her head into the shiny black eyes of Mr. Fung. All pretense of humor and politeness went out of Mr. Fung's eyes, and Peter quickly estimated the man: Southern Chinese; perhaps Cantonese or even Annamite; a smooth, polished rogue. He had met Mr. Fung's type before—not always to his advantage.

With a faint smile, Peter waited for Susan to acknowledge his presence. He was prepared for her squeal of delight.

For several seconds Susan took no heed of him. Then she became aware that Mr. Fung was staring with cold dislike at some one beside her, and she turned to find out who it might be.

Susan slowly turned. The eager smile inspired by Mr. Fung slowly left her lips as she stared up at Peter. Then the color slowly receded from her face. Her eyes widened. One hand flew up to her shoulder. She stared at Peter with the round mouth of astonishment.

"Peter!" she whispered. Then: "It can't be!" She quickly reached out and touched his cheek with her finger tips.

"Why!" she said, with amazement. "It's you! It really *is* you!"

"In the flesh," Peter nodded.

"But—but—why did you follow me?"

There was no sweetness in her voice or delight in her eyes. The scene was not progressing exactly as Peter had visualized it.

"I didn't follow you."

"Where," she demanded, "did you come aboard?"

"Shanghai."

"Then you did follow me! You followed my sampan!" Susan suddenly drew back from him. "Peter Moore, you make me furious!" she cried. "I'm perfectly capable of taking care of myself. I didn't ask you for your help. I think it's mighty presumptuous of you to force it on me—now!"

"I'm not forcing it on you," Peter said calmly. "I'm not even offering it."

"If you'll pardon me—" said the suave Mr. Fung.

Susan turned excitedly. "Yes. I'll join you in the smoke-room in a moment, Mr. Fung."

She turned back to Peter. Her eyes were narrow now. And they glittered with an emotion that could not be called, by any stretch of the imagination, delight.

In syllables as rapid as a machine gun burst she shot at him:

"Why did you follow me out to this ship?"

PETER LEISURELY lighted a cigarette. He flipped the match over the rail into the Yellow Sea, puffed several times and expelled deep lungfuls of smoke in the general direction of a fishing junk a mile away.

"I came aboard this venerable relic," he said, "a half hour before the anchors were weighed."

"You knew I was coming!"

"How," he calmly asked, "could I guess? I thought you were asleep in your little bed. I wrote you a farewell note. Did you get it?"

"I did," she snapped. "And that emerald scepter. You nearly frightened me out of my wits!"

She was referring to a priceless golden scepter, inset with emeralds, which Peter had secured during a fight in the native section of Shanghai the night before.

"I'm sorry," he said. "I thought you'd like it as a souvenir. If you don't want it, you can return it to Mr. K'ang—of the Green Circle."

"I did."

She was looking up at him, out of a very pale face with indignant eyes.

"I see," she said. "You were running away. Isn't that a scream? You were running away from me!"

But her voice and her expression did not indicate she found it very funny.

"I believe you," Susan went on, in the same coldly furious little voice. "You didn't follow me. You were running away from me. I'm glad. I'm terribly glad—because I'm running away from you, too! I'm still running."

She was on the verge of tears. Susan was, Peter reflected, far prettier when she was mad than when she wasn't.

"I suppose," she said, "you're booked for Hong Kong."

"Yes, Susan."

"Well, so am I—and it's a long trip. And the thought of you and me being shut up on this little tub for two weeks is more than I can bear!"

"It needn't be," Peter said.

"I'm not going to speak to you during the entire trip!"

"I was about to suggest something of the kind," Peter agreed. "Ignore me."

"I hate you!"

"That's my misfortune."

"I came on this old tub," said Susan angrily, "to have some excitement—some fun. I'm going to have it. And I positively won't let you interfere with it!"

"I haven't the slightest intention of interfering. Have as much excitement as you like. Consider me erased. But if you should decide to sink the ship, will you drop me a note?"

The heiress to no-one-knew-how-many American millions looked up at him with undiminished fury.

"You know, I don't care what you think of me. Once I did. But not now. I'm absolutely washed up with you. I was going to slip away from Shanghai and—and forget you. Well, I have! I'm going adventuring on my own hook!"

"Is there really any adventure on this old hulk?"

"There is for me—and you're not to meddle with it!"

"I've given my promise, Susan. I won't meddle or annoy you. I will stay out of your way. Your majesty, I am eliminated!"

PETER MADE an exaggerated bow and added gravely: "I wonder if it concerns those crates down there."

Susan glanced from Peter Moore to the cargo hold. Then she looked sharply back at him.

"Those crates," she said steadily, "contain earthen jugs of ginger in syrup."

Peter lifted his eyebrows and slowly nodded as if with comprehension.

"Interesting stuff—ginger in syrup. It comes from Canton. Figure that out."

"What do you mean?"

"It doesn't seem to make sense," Peter answered. "Ginger comes from Canton. This ship is going to Hong Kong, which is a stone's throw from Canton. If those crates of ginger came from Canton, as they must have, why are they going back to Canton? Maybe you can explain that."

"I can," said Susan. "They were consigned to an exporter in Shanghai. For some reason, he refused to accept them. They're going back to the consignor."

"That holds water," Peter admitted. "Now tell me why, if those crates contain ginger in syrup, it is necessary to open that hatch to ventilate them? Why do waterproof jugs, well-corked and sealed, require ventilation?"

"I don't know what you're talking about," Susan protested.

"Let's go down there, and I'll explain," said Peter.

She started to refuse, then changed her mind. With a danger-

ous light in her eyes, Susan followed Peter, down the iron stairway and into the deck well; through a manhole, down a steel
ladder into the hold.

Beside one of the long, coffin-shaped crates Peter stopped.
He was looking at the black lettering.

"Ginger in syrup," he commented. "It's the first time I knew
that ginger came from Benares, India, to China. Queer, isn't it?
Rather like shipping coals to Newcastle."

Susan said nothing. She was looking at him with narrow eyes.
Her face was white. Even her lips were gray.

"Look!" said Peter.

With a quick gesture he seized one of the boards on the lid
of the box. He gave a yank. The loose board came free with a
shrieking of nails.

Within the box were what appeared at first glance to be care-
lessly made cannon balls. Rough round balls about six inches in
diameter were packed in the crate in neat rows.

Peter lifted out one of the balls and gently shook it.

"This kind of ginger in syrup doesn't gurgle," he said. "Funny
stuff, Susan, this Benares 'ginger.' There's enough in this one ball
to last the most ginger-loving Chinaman about a year. Let's see.
The outer layer is an inch thick. The ginger center weighs about
four pounds. Refined, there will be about two pounds left.

"Interesting old stuff, this ginger, Susan. It comes out of
poppy petals, and this is particularly fine ginger. The poppy is
pricked, its juice is extracted, and when enough of it has been
collected it is shipped in a wad to the factory at Ghazeepore.
The workmen in the factory work the wad into these round balls.
There's an inch layer of *lewah,* a kind of paste, used to make the
poppy petals stick to the ball. Unless I'm mistaken, there are
forty balls of Benares 'ginger' in this case. At least, it always used
to be shipped that way."

THERE WAS a dangerous light in Susan's eyes.

"I don't think you're at all funny," she said. "What if it is opium? It's Benares opium—the best in the world. There's fifty cases of it in this cargo hold. I'm buying them!"

Her air was one of hostile defiance.

But Peter's air was one of amiable indifference. "Am I supposed to get excited because you've bought—or are buying—fifty cases of Benares opium?"

"I don't care what you think!"

"Susan," said Peter, "what I'm thinking isn't fit for utterance. I didn't know you were so fond of opium. At the rate of twenty pipes a day, you've got enough 'black smoke' here to last you—let's see—just about two thousand years. A long life and a merry one!"

"I don't think you're amusing," Susan stated. "I'm buying this opium because—because I understand!"

"Stop me if I seem inquisitive. But just what is it that you understand?"

"The villainous attempts of America and other countries to prevent the Chinese from having their opium! It's nothing but jealousy of England!"

"I see," said Peter.

"Opium," Susan went on angrily, "is not the dreadful poison that it is supposed to be. It is wonderful in helping to cure malaria and tuberculosis and—and other sicknesses! And in China it is often used just as cocktails are used in America—or tea. There's nothing so terribly wrong about opium. Used in moderation, it is no worse than alcohol."

"Mr. Fung," Peter retorted coldly, "must be the world's most expert salesman."

"He is telling the truth! Like all Americans, you're simply prejudiced."

"You might amend that," Peter said, "to 'like all decent people.' Any one who tells you that opium is no more harmful than tea or cocktails is a damned liar. You ought to be spanked and sent to bed for talking such rot. What are you going to do with your cargo of opium—smuggle it into Macao?"

"I told you I would not let you interfere!"

"I won't interfere. Go as far as you like. But since you've taken up opium smuggling on an ethical basis, I'll give you some arguments on the other side."

"You're wasting your time."

"Did Mr. Fung happen to mention," Peter asked, "that the opium addicts of China spend upward of a third of their wages for the stuff?"

"I don't believe it. Statistics don't mean anything!"

"To a woman," Peter agreed. "Did Mr. Fung happen to mention what the final stage of opium addiction is like? The first two stages aren't so bad. But in the third stage an opium addict smokes to stop the pain he suffers if he doesn't smoke. Get that? The vicious circle. I'll quote the description that a Hong Kong doctor once gave me of the last sufferings of an opium smoker. I can still remember it word for word:

" 'The cry of conscience is drowned by a louder call—a call so loud and urgent that if it be not heard, and the stimulant supplied, reason will forsake her seat, and the cast-off slave of pleasure will find his sure and speedy end in the grave of his own vice!' "

Susan uttered a short, hard little laugh.

"Go on!" she cried. "You ought to be a missionary! Tell me more about opium!"

"I'LL GIVE you a motion picture," Peter obliged. "In a Peking museum there are a series of drawings by a Chinese artist showing the various stages through which an opium victim passes. Want to hear about them?"

"Go on," she begged him angrily. "I adore talkies."

"We'll skip to the last stages," Peter said cheerfully, "when the opium smoker has a sallow complexion, sunken eyes with a dark ring around the lids, and bloodless lips. As he smokes more and more, his skin becomes waxlike, his eyes sink deeper and lose their luster, the eyelids and mouth become depressed and look as if some dark matter were deposited beneath the skin. Want to hear more?"

"Yes!" Susan snapped. "I think it is positively fascinating!"

"The lips of the smoker protrude and become more and more swollen from the frequent use of the large mouthpiece of the pipe. Ever see an opium pipe, Susan?"

"No, but I intend to."

"You probably intend to acquire the habit."

"Perhaps you'd stop me if you could!"

"No. I'm not interfering."

"Then what happens?"

"The opium smoker goes through terrific agony. He loses his appetite. He has awful mental depression. He loses all sense of right and wrong. All he thinks of is opium. All he can do is smoke. He must indulge almost constantly or he will go mad. Pretty picture, isn't it?"

"Perfectly marvelous! Do tell me more!"

"I'll quote Dr. Kolster again. He was quite lurid about it. He said: 'When the weary wretch retires to rest, the demon of his own creating pursues him still, and frightful dreams disturb his broken slumbers.' Want more, Susan? Shall I describe his death agonies?"

Susan was looking steadily into Peter's eyes. "No. You've told me enough. Your arguments aren't true. They're nothing but malicious propaganda. Opium when taken to excess is bad, perhaps. But it is seldom taken to excess. Smoking opium to excess is no worse than drinking to excess. Opium is, in China, just like cocktails in America or tea in England, or coffee in the Scandinavian countries. People—nice people—in China meet and smoke a few pipes just as you meet your friends in America and have a few cocktails. It is stimulating to the mind—it simply peps you up."

"Don't forget the celestial dreams," Peter said dryly.

"I won't," Susan snapped.

And Peter knew he was wasting his time. Susan O'Gilvie was looking for trouble. She wanted excitement, adventure, thrills. She'd find a few in opium. Peter tossed the ball of crude opium into the chest. A voice behind him demanded sharply:

"What are you doing here?"

The American looked slowly around. The fashionable Mr. Fung was standing near a stanchion with a short black pistol in one hand. The light of the waning afternoon struck ugly glints from it.

"Looking," Peter said calmly, "at your cargo of—ginger."

With the pistol bearing squarely on Peter's stomach, the tall, elegant Chinese circled about a pile of the chests and stood beside Susan and asked:

"Is this man annoying you?"

"No," the girl replied quickly.

"Get out of here," said Mr. Fung. "I don't know what you are doing aboard this ship, but I am advising you to start no trouble."

Peter smiled. He looked at Susan. She was pale, and she was staring at him defiantly.

She said in a husky voice:

"Let's have this perfectly understood. I don't want to have anything more to do with you—ever."

"That arrangement," Peter answered, "suits me perfectly."

CHAPTER III

A RENDEZVOUS WITH PIRATES

PETER RETURNED, VERY thoughtfully, to the little promenade deck. He suspected that Susan's hostile attitude was the result largely of pique. It was quite all right for her to run away from him, because the girl thought she was falling in love and dreaded the consequences, but for Peter to pursue such a course was cruel, unjust—cowardly!

He was standing against the rail, outside his stateroom, smoking, when Susan and her fascinating Chinaman came up from the cargo hold. Susan had taken Mr. Fung's arm. Her small, lovely face was tilted up to his; her cheeks were pink. Mr. Fung's attitude, it seemed to Peter, was too proprietary. Damn Mr. Fung!

They were excitedly discussing something in tones too low for Peter to hear. They passed. The murmur of their voices ceased.

The American snapped his cigarette angrily overboard. He didn't care where they went, what they did. He wished he had never met Susan O'Gilvie. She was nothing but a spoiled brat. Thank God, he was washed up with her!

Felt sandals whispered on the planking behind Peter. He whirled about. Lee, the deck steward, was standing there, arms folded on chest, his expression as inscrutable as that of a bronze Buddha.

And Peter barked: "What thing wanchee?"

Said Lee: "That sparky pidgin man talkee my him wanchee Masta Moo' topside that sparky pidgin house. Can do?" Which meant, translated: "The wireless operator wants to know if you will come to the wireless house. Will you go?"

Peter thanked him curtly, angrily wondered what the City of Swatow's wireless man could want of him, and went aft to the tiny iron ladder that ran up the cabin wall to the boat deck.

He climbed this ladder and found that the wireless cabin was situated, as it generally was on China coasters, just abaft the wheelhouse and master's quarters.

A red-haired man whose face was startlingly familiar was standing in the doorway with headphones clamped over his ears. His snub-nose was freckled; his chin was pugnacious.

"Randy Nichols!" Peter said, almost explosively, and wished that he could have recalled the words. He knew what Randy Nichols was doing on this old tramp. How long ago had Randy

Nichols been an idol of the American public, one of the greatest pitchers in one of the greatest leagues? Was it three, four—five? Peter didn't exactly recall. But he did recall the circumstances under which Nichols had vanished abruptly from the American sporting scene.

Randy had accepted—how much was it?—five thousand—ten thousand?—to "lay down" and lose the pennant for his team. Peter wasn't much interested in baseball. He did not even recall what team Randy had played on. He had never seen him pitch, but he would have recognized him anywhere in the world from published photographs.

The China coast swallowed up a great many men like Randy Nichols. Disgraced and humiliated, they slunk off to this remote coast where recognition by their fellows was most unlikely.

THE FAMOUS baseball pitcher was staring hard at Peter, but his grin was shy and friendly. He did not look like the kind of man who would have sold out.

As Peter crossed the deck, the wireless operator plucked the phones from his head and laid them on a table inside the door.

Peter was embarrassed. He had been cornered by men like Nichols before, and the experience had always been painful. They wanted to talk by the hour about the land from which they were exiled; they wanted to discuss "that mistake." It was always a mistake, whether it had been a bank robbery, murder or bigamy. They generally got tight and sobbed.

Peter inquired: "You asked to see me?"

The ex-pitcher nodded. "You spotted me right off, didn't you?"

"Yes."

"Surprised to find me here, ain't you?"

"Nothing in China," said Peter, "surprises me."

The red-head lighted a cigarette and ejected twin quills of blue smoke from hairy nostrils.

"I ain't kickin'. This is a rotten old tub, but I'm satisfied. You're the first guy I've run into in two years who recognized me, and you wouldn't have seen me if I hadn't sent for you. You used to be a wireless operator, didn't you?"

"Yes."

"Yeah. I've heard all about you. You punched brass in these waters five, six years ago, and you got into all kinds of hot water. Boy, you sure left a fancy reputation behind you on this lousy old coast! I hear that you quit the racket to go into the radio research department of the General Electric."

"I'm on my way to Hong Kong," Peter satisfied his curiosity, "to look up a Chinese student by the name of Fong Toy who, I understand, has perfected a static eliminator that really works."

The green-blue eyes of the ex-pitcher seemed to gleam. He looked behind him and all around the deck, as if to satisfy himself that their conversation was not being overheard. In a cautious voice, he said:

"Whaddaya say we slip inside and shut this door? I want to have a talk with you, Mr. Moore."

Peter supposed that he would now hear the tragic story of Randy Nichols's famous double cross. But he was mistaken.

He went in, glanced at the antiquated wireless equipment, and seated himself in one of the two chairs which the small room contained. The red-head shut the door and disposed himself in the other chair. There was a feeling of tension in the room which Peter quickly sensed.

Randy Nichols, with the cigarette drooping from one corner of his generous mouth, began:

"Seems kinda funny that you should be travelin' to Hong Kong on this lousy old tub when one of the classy Dollar Line boats was leavin' Shanghai for Hong Kong this afternoon—and is due in Hong Kong better than a week ahead of us."

"I wasn't in a hurry," Peter said, and wondered what was coming next.

"I wonder," the famous pitcher went on, "if you think I invited you up here to listen to my tale of woe—about the dirty deal I got when they kicked me out of the league, and what a tough break it is for a guy hammerin' brass on an old derelict like this. Well, I'm not."

PETER FELT a little uncomfortable.

"I invited you up here," went on the blue-eyed red-head, "because—" Nichols hesitated. He seemed embarrassed. He looked uneasily about the cubicle, cleared his throat nervously and, with his tongue, deftly shifted the cigarette to the other corner of his mouth.

"—because," he finished hoarsely, "I thought you might be gonna start somethin'. I mean," he explained hastily, "I know your reputation. I know how you used to rise hell with these Chink crooks and all. What I mean, Mr. Moore, is that if you're here to start trouble—just count me in, will you?"

Peter grinned. "Did you ever hear the old saying about a dog with a bad name?" he said. "Well, I'm that dog. Thanks for the compliment, but I'm not hell-raising any more. I am a peaceable business man."

"Yeah?" The red-head was skeptical.

"Yeah," said Peter firmly.

"You mean," Nichols inquired with disappointment, "this opium cargo we've got don't suggest any ideas to you?"

Peter's grin widened. "I'm not saying it doesn't suggest ideas. I'm saying I'm not going to put any of them to work."

Nichols shook his head sadly. "Well, that sure is tough. I was hopin', when I heard you was aboard, that you was gonna start somethin'. You better change your mind. Say! Come clean, will you? What are you doin' on this old tramp?"

"Traveling to Hong Kong!"

Nichols discarded his cigarette and lighted another.

"How about this million-dollar baby?"

"You mean Miss O'Gilvie?"

"Sure. Her."

"What about her?"

"Well, I've been hearin' funny things about that dame. I got it pretty straight that she came over to the coast here to spend a few of her millions lookin' for thrills. I heard she teamed up with you on the way over, and you pulled her out of a couple of mean scrapes by the hair of her neck. I heard that; maybe it ain't so. But here's somethin' I do know. She's on board this old can to buy up that cargo of opium from Mr. Fung. I've got reasons to believe she's already paid for it. You're on here, ain't you, as a matter of fact, to steer her out of more trouble?"

Peter waited.

"Because if you are," Nichols concluded, "you have certainly sawed yourself off the toughest job of your career, Mr. Moore— and there ain't any 'ifs' sprinkled along through that, either! That cargo of opium is jinxed, hoodooed—it's got the Indian sign on it!"

"But I'm not," Peter said, "on board to help her."

The red-head looked at him owlishly. "Yeah? Now it's my turn to tell one. Maybe you don't know all the ins and outs about this load of hop. How are they gonna land it? Tell me that, will you? You're a smart feller. How're they gonna get that stuff ashore?"

Peter's answer was another grin.

"LOOK HERE," said the red-head. "Maybe you understand all this, maybe you don't. Fung owns the opium. He owns this ship. But do you know how long that cargo of hop has been on board here?"

"No."

"Goin' on three months! Get that? Three months! I wouldn't take that bunch of hop for a gift. What would I do with it? What's the million-dollar baby gonna do with it? What would you do with it? Listen!

"Just about three months ago, one dark and lousy night, we hove to about twenty miles off Hong Kong. Out of the dark came another old tub. I'd seen her in Hong Kong often. She was in the India run, see? All right. We hove to, and this old can, she comes alongside and transfers into our forward hold those fifty crates of crude opium. Three months ago! Keep that in mind, Mr. Moore."

"You couldn't land with it," Peter guessed.

"Mr. Moore, sayin' we couldn't land it is like sayin' that a kick in the shin by a mule tickles! It's got to be the joke of the China coast, this load of Numbah One Pukka Benares opium! Finer than Malwa! Finer than Patna!

"Listen! We barged on into Hong Kong harbor. Fung was aboard. He was gonna slip on up to Lintin, where the old opium smugglers landed the stuff, and put it ashore there. All arrangements were made. Don't I know? Didn't I make the arrangements myself over this bunch of haywire?" He tapped the radio set.

"And what happens when we start sneakin' into Hong Kong? Searchlights from the fort play on us, searchlights from a dozen gunboats turn night into day. I tell you, it was a riot! No sooner do we drop the hook than out from shore comes a boatload so full of officers it was a wonder it didn't sink! And do they stay aboard of us day and night until we leave? You bet your life they do!

"So down the coast we go boomin', stoppin' at Soochow and Foochow and Swatow and Amoy; and are we welcomed everywhere we stop like visitin' royalty? We are! Everything but guns goin' off—and if we had made one funny move, they would of gone off!

"And what happens when we hit the end of the run—Shanghai? Nothin' but spies afloat and ashore, watching to see that we don't smuggle a ball of the stuff ashore. More spies than there was in the whole German army durin' the war! We got a destroyer escort down the river and out to sea, and we got a destroyer escort at every port we touched ever since."

Peter was beginning to laugh. And Randy Nichols, chuckling, proceeded with his story.

"Fung got nervouser and nervouser. Here he had gone and sunk maybe forty thousand gold in them fifty cases of hop—

and how was he gonna get his money out? If he had declared it in the first place, okay. But he didn't declare it—and you know the British.

"Now, along comes another complication. You know and I know that opium is perishable stuff—the crude gum. Sea air and the river air don't do raw opium a bit of good. It gets moldy. It ought to get to the refinery as fast as it can. Now, moldy opium brings a low price. And this opium is gettin' moldier and moldier. Every day, its value drops. So what is poor Mr. Fung gonna do?"

"SUPPOSING," PETER suggested dryly, "we break down and cry about poor Mr. Fung!"

The red-head grinned. "And here's another, funnier complication, Mr. Moore. You know and I know that Chinese pirates aren't any more stamped out, just because there's a law against them, than thirst is in the United States of America, just because there's a prohibition law. Fifty cases of opium—Number One Benares opium—would make a nice haul for any Chino pirate, So any day, any night, we are apt to have a visit by pirates."

Peter had stopped smiling. "You mean a prearranged visit?"

Nichols nodded his red head vigorously. "Boy," he said, "you know your China coast, all right. Sure! And if you got aboard this boat to stay out of trouble, you sure did take the wrong boat!"

"What's the plan?" Peter asked sharply.

"Some of it I can tell you, and some of it I can only guess. But, first of all, here is what I know. The million-dollar baby is buyin' the lot of hop from Fung. Maybe you know why. I don't. If you aren't helpin' her, what's she gonna do with it?"

Peter shrugged. "I've been wondering."

"Now, look. Is she a nice kid or is she a sap?"

"She's a nice kid," Peter said, "who needs a good old-fashioned licking."

"Well, she's gonna get it! And here's the dope. Some time tonight, unless I read the signs wrong, we're gonna run close by a coupla big junks. Just when we get abreast of 'em, that old tin teapot of an engine of ours is gonna sprain an ankle. While we're lyin' to, gettin' it fixed, the junks come up under the bow; the pirates come aboard—and *sayonara* goes the cargo of hop! Simple, sweet and pretty—huh?"

"Friends of Fung?"

"Friends, my eye! He fixed it up in Amoy with them throat-slitters. When I hear that engine lay down, I'm gonna buckle on my trusty gat and shoot the first yellow face that heaves my way. I take no chances. And now listen, Mr. Moore. Can you see all this go on and stand by, doin' nothin'?"

"I'm not interested," Peter replied firmly. "in that cargo of opium."

"But how about the girl friend—the million-dollar baby? She's plunked out fifty grand, hasn't she, for opium that Fung has already sold to somebody else—these 'pirates'? You can't let a poor innocent kid like that be skunked, can you?"

"That poor innocent kid," said Peter dryly, "wants to have a thrill. She would willingly pay fifty thousand to see Chinese pirates attack a merchant ship. She wants thrills. She wants danger, adventure, excitement. I'm not standing in her way."

"It ain't the money," the red-head argued; "it's the principle. A coupla good guys like us can't stand by and let a lousy Chino put something over on her. And I'm tellin' you that guy is bad— he's bad with women."

"Supposing," Peter said, "you go down and tell her that."

"She wouldn't listen to me."

"And she won't listen to me. A few minutes ago, she told me very emphatically to mind my own business. She said she was going into this opium deal with her eyes wide open, and that I was not to interfere."

RANDY NICHOLS nodded gloomily. "Yeah, I put her down for one of those haughty dames. Well, Mr. Moore, all I gotta say is this: If you should happen to change your mind and decide to mix into this—just let me know. If there's one thing I like, it's a fight. I like to throw things. I used to be pretty good at throwin'—things. I've heard a whole lot about the way you handle yourself in a fight, and I sure would like the experience of fightin' shoulder to shoulder with you once."

He looked at Peter with that strange, owlish expression. And Peter said:

"How does the crew stand on this opium shipment?"

"I was gonna mention that, Mr. Moore. That visit by the pirates ain't the only bit of excitement that's apt to happen on board this old hooker tonight. The crew is pretty restless."

Peter lighted a fresh cigarette.

"Where does the skipper stand?"

"I wish I knew. He's a bad boy. He's been in trouble with the authorities on and off ever since he got his ticket. He used to be in the slave trade—and they caught him at that. He used to do some pearl poaching—and the Japs got him red-handed at that. He may have some scheme up his sleeve."

"How about the rest of the crew?"

"Well, for one thing, they don't trust these pirates. They know the pirates are comin' aboard to take the opium off. From what I've heard, the pirates have agreed not to come aft of that forward deck well. But supposin' they don't keep their word? Supposin' they decide to make a clean sweep of the ship? Supposin' Fung has got it rigged up for the pirates to polish us all off—and sink the old can? Why not? He's been wantin' to sink her for the insurance for a long time.

"And a lot of plots are bein' hatched among the crew to get the opium for themselves. The most dangerous of the lot is the first mate, a big, mean Chino by the name of Wang. Wang has been cookin' up a scheme of his own to grab off that bunch of hop. I know he's been arguin' about it with the deck hands and some of the black gang and the engine-room crew. Why ain't it a good idea? They grab the stuff themselves, throw Fung and maybe the skipper overboard, run this old can up on some beach and take the stuff ashore, divide it up and scatter. Why not? I tell you, Mr. Moore, there's trouble on board this ship—and it's gonna pop soon!"

Peter stood up. The wireless room was almost dark.

"Supposing you meet me in the smoke-room after dinner," he suggested. "I'm going to look things over."

The ex-pitcher said in a low, sibilant whisper: *"Psst!* Wang is lookin' in here through that after porthole! He'd stick a knife into you, that guy, as quick as he'd look at you."

Peter, with his hand on the doorknob, turned and looked at the porthole. The face that was framed by the large disc of dirty glass was startling. Long and emaciated, it was more like a skull than a human face.

The yellow, pock-marked skin was stretched so tightly upon it that it glistened. There were dark rings on the eyelids. The eyes were sunken, as were the cheeks. Upper and lower lips were swollen and protruding.

Peter had seen enough opium victims to realize promptly that Wang, the first mate, was a very dangerous specimen.

In Wang's eyes there was no light. Like the eyes of a dead man, they were without lustre. And in the expression of his pock-marked face was the latent madness of his kind.

Peter did not require Randy Nichols's warning to realize that Wang was peculiarly interested in that cargo of opium.

CHAPTER IV

A NEW THRILL FOR SUSAN

NIGHT HAD FALLEN over the Yellow Sea. Deck lights were burning greasily when Peter descended the iron ladder at the after end of the boat deck and made his way forward. A long, oily swell was rolling up from the southeast, and, in the after-glow, blue-black clouds massed on the southeastern horizon indicated that a gale might be on its way.

The hush that had fallen over the sea made Peter uneasy. And the state of affairs on board the City of Swatow worried him. Opium had always been associated with violence, bloodshed. Fifty cases of Number One Benares! To any Chinese in the crew, one of those cases represented a fortune—more money than he could earn in seven years! A dangerous cargo, that opium!

Peter circled the deck. On his second lap, as he passed an open porthole, he detected the acrid, pungent odor of opium. He thought at first that it was in his imagination, but a second sniff assured him that it was in the air.

He returned to the porthole and glanced in. And the tableau that greeted him caused Peter to gasp.

Mr. Fung was squatted cross-legged on the floor of a stateroom with an opium pipe in one hand. On the floor beside him were one of the familiar flat tins of refined opium, a spirit lamp and a brass tray.

In Mr. Fung's right hand was a length of wire. This he dipped into the tin. Extracting a small amount of opium from the brownish mass he quickly held it over the blue flame of the spirit lamp, slowly turning it and pressing it from time to time against the flat bowl of the pipe. He turned the little brown lump over and over, carefully working it on the end of the wire until it was reduced to a plastic state. The lump, as Mr. Fung continued to heat and work it, swelled up and began to sizzle.

Suddenly Mr. Fung inserted the little sizzling wad into the pipe. He pressed down, twirling the wire, until the opium adhered to the walls of the pipe. In a nervous voice he said clearly:

"Now, Miss O'Gilvie—quickly!"

He handed up the pipe. Peter came nearer the porthole and stared. It was his first intimation that Mr. Fung was not alone. Now he saw Susan. Bright of eyes and pink of cheek, she sat on a low stool to the left of the Chinese.

She reached down quickly, seized the pipe, placed the large bit of it between her lips, held the bowl into the spirit flame which Mr. Fung raised conveniently for her—and inhaled.

Three puffs. Peter counted them. Always three. The pale, thick, blue-gray smoke spouted from Susan's lips. She began to cough. In a husky little voice she said: "It tickles."

Mr. Fung ran insolent eyes up to her face and answered: "One more."

"But aren't two enough?"

"One more," Mr. Fung repeated.

"But won't it make me sick?"

"It will make of earth heaven."

Peter swallowed with difficulty. He had promised not to interfere; to mind his own business and let Susan go her merry way after thrills and new adventures. He forgot his promise.

HE YANKED at the handle of the stateroom door. It was locked. Backing across the deck, Peter paused and charged the door with his shoulder down and struck it with a splintering crash. Rotten old lock and hinges gave way, all but the top hinge. The door hung askew, dangling from that hinge. Peter went well into the room by the momentum of his charge.

Mr. Fung sprang up with the pipe in his hand. He lifted it with the apparent intention of using it as a weapon. Peter struck him across the face with the back of his fist. The Chinese went sprawling into a corner. There, reclining on shoulders, elbows and one hip, he glared up at the intruder.

Peter picked up the pipe, the spirit lamp and the tin of opium and hurled them, one at a time, out the window.

Susan had sprung up. With her feverishly bright eyes and her flushed cheeks, she looked wild.

"I told you," she said thickly, "to let me alone."

And Peter, with fists at sides, chest heaving, answered: "Yes, Susan. I know. But a man has to draw the line somewhere. Get out of here."

"I won't!"

He seized her by the shoulders, spun her about and pushed her out the door. Then he linked her arm forcibly with his and propelled her along the deck.

Susan didn't want to go for a walk. Susan was so mad she cried. And the fumes of opium on her breath were so strong that Peter felt a little sick.

He was furious. So was Susan. She tried to yank her arm away, but Peter held on. So, arm in arm, they encircled the deck.

"Take deep breaths," said Peter.

"You make me furious," Susan stormed. "You're acting as if I'm tight. I'm not tight. I feel wonderful."

"I hate the smell of that stuff. It may be cocktails to you, but it's poison to me."

"Lend me your handkerchief."

Peter gave her a handkerchief. She wept into it. She hated him. All he did was spoil her fun. Sobbing, she permitted him to walk her around the deck a second time.

"You're absolutely wrong," she said presently. She stumbled over her feet and would have fallen if Peter had not quickly jerked her up.

"Everything looks so smooth and shiny," Susan said. "You're absolutely wrong," she repeated. "It's wonderful. It isn't at all like cocktails. It's perfectly fascinating. I feel as if I were floating. My head's so clear. And I think so quickly. I never thought so clearly or quickly before. Peter, haven't you ever tried it?"

"Oh, my God!" Peter said.

"Oh, don't be such a damned missionary! Why! I can understand things I never dreamed I'd understand, I know what life's about."

"What's it about?"

"It's wonderful. One thing I can see more clearly than anything else. That's you."

"Oh, yes?"

"Yes. You're a terrible person. You're an awful person. You're a dragon dressed up as a man."

"Breathing fire and everything," Peter supplemented.

"But you've been awfully sweet to me, Peter. Too sweet."

"Yes," Peter agreed.

"THAT'S THE trouble. You're too attractive. You're just too damned attractive. That's the trouble. If you weren't so attractive, I wouldn't be crazy about you. But I am. That's what's the matter. I'm crazy about you."

"Susan, please shut up!"

"I won't shut up. If you knew how clearly I could see everything!" Susan began to sob again; "That's the trouble. But I can see a way around everything. I can do anything. So I'm going to hate you. I do. I think you're poisonous. There! That's settled."

"Would you mind," Peter groaned, "taking deep breaths of this nice fresh air?"

"Of course I wouldn't mind, darling. I am absolutely putty in your hands. That's the trouble with us women. We're putty in the hands of the men we fall for. But I haven't fallen for you. I loathe you."

"Yes," said Peter.

"When we get to Hong Kong, we are going to flip a coin to see which goes north and which goes south. We will part—and never see each other again." Her sobs broke out afresh.

"You're breaking my heart," she said. "You're the only man I ever met I've been crazy about—and you don't see me for dust. Peter! Isn't it a glorious night? Look at those stars!"

"There aren't any stars," Peter contradicted. "The sky is overcast. It's getting ready to blow."

The girl vigorously disagreed. There were stars, she insisted. She flung out her arms and lifted her face to the clouds.

"Life is glorious!"

They had reached the forward turn of the deck again, and in the darkness of the well Peter heard the wheezing and clanking of a leaky old donkey engine. Then a lantern appeared. A dim and shadowy figure was unlashing one of the cargo booms.

As Susan leaned against him and wept at the sheer beauty of existence, Peter glowered down into the deck well. Another lantern appeared and flitted about like a firefly. There were men in the cargo-hold. Deck hands.

What were they up to? Was one of the schemes Randy Nichols had mentioned already afoot?

Then Peter saw, for a fleeting moment, the long, aristocratic face of Mr. Fung. What was going on down there?

The donkey engine wheezed and clanked. Peter saw a steel cable, coiling and writhing, drop like the head of a snake into the hold. A moment later, one of the long cases of Benares opium came floating up through the hatch to be deposited on the forepeak.

To the clanking and wheezing of the old deck engine, other cases magically floated up to join the first one.

And Susan suddenly took cognizance of it. She seized Peter's arm and gasped: "Peter! Peter! What are they doing with my opium?"

"Is it your opium?"

"It is!"

"Stop payment on the check you gave Fung, if he double-crosses you. That's easy."

"But I paid him in gold! I gave him a check this morning in Shanghai. He cashed it while we were going down the river. Then he followed us in a fast motor boat and came aboard at Woosung!"

"How much?"

"Fifty thousand. Do something about it! What is he doing with my opium?"

Peter shrugged. He wondered what Susan had been like as a little girl. What she had asked for, she had got.

HUSKILY, SUSAN cried out: "Mr. Fung, what are you doing with my opium?"

The wheezing and rattling of the old donkey engine answered her.

Peter inquired: "Susan, what were you going to do with it?"

"I am going to smuggle it ashore at Canton! Mr. Fung said he'd help me!"

"I'm afraid," said Peter, "that you'd better charge that fifty thousand off to experience."

"But I won't be swindled!" Her hand began to tremble. She whispered: "Peter, I feel funny. Everything's getting shinier and shinier. It's like glass. You face is like bronze. It's all shiny."

Peter groaned. Why did this otherwise perfect girl have this terrific craving for experiment?

"Peter! Hang onto me. Don't let me slide. I'm going down and down. Oh, gee, Peter; this is horrible! I didn't know it was like this. I'm passing out. Take care of me, Peter. Promise me you'll take care of me!"

"I'll take care of you," said Peter.

She sagged heavily and limply against him. In the glow of a deck light overhead, her face was gray, her lips parted and moist. Her eyes, half shut, seemed to swim.

Susan was all dead weight. Peter picked her up, with an arm under her knees, another arm under her neck. Her head rolled against his chest.

Peter strode aft. He didn't know where her stateroom was. Lee, the deck steward, supplied him with the information. Stateroom twenty-two. It was around on the port side.

Peter carried her into the room, arranged her on the bunk, pulled up a light blanket under her chin, opened the ports, turned out the light and went out. He shut the door and locked it, putting the key in his pocket.

A brazen uproar behind him as he started aft made Peter jump, but it was only a dining room boy beating the first strokes of warning for dinner on a brass cymbal.

Peter decided that he needed a drink. He'd have the drink, then go to his stateroom for his revolver. Unless he was mistaken, he would need a revolver tonight.

The smoke-room, when Peter entered it, was empty. The bar, a tiny square room beyond a half-door at the far side, was open. The bar steward was polishing glasses.

Peter lighted a cigarette and called to him: "Pay my one dry Martini. Can do?"

And the bar boy answered: "Can do, masta."

Peter smoked, occupied himself with his problems, and waited. He heard the bar boy cracking ice. Behind Peter was an open porthole. A draft of warm air floated about his shoulders.

The feeling grew upon Peter that some one out there on deck was looking in at him. A little icy something raced down his spine. He did not like the feel of things. It was like sitting on a load of dynamite that might decide at any moment to blow him to kingdom come.

CHAPTER V

THE POISONED COCKTAIL

A GLANCE ASSURED Peter Moore that the porthole behind him was empty. The next time he glanced up it was to glimpse, with a start, the shocking skull-like face of Wang, the first mate—Wang, with his opium-smoker's dead, staring eyes, his puffed lips, his eyelids with their hideous dark circles.

Wang vanished.

Peter inquired sharply of the attendant in the smoke-room: "Boy, what's the *bhobbery?* Pay my that cocktail *chop-chop.* My wanchee now—or *maskee cumshaw.*"

"Yes, masta." The threat of "no tip" seemed efficacious.

Again that icy trickling down the spine. Peter glanced sharply behind him. Some distance from the porthole was another face—the gloomy, saturnine face of Chou, captain of the City of Swatow.

His inscrutable black eyes stared at Peter, and it occurred to Peter that not only Wang, but Mr. Fung and Captain Chou and heaven only knew how many other men aboard looked upon him as the focal point of a deep and absorbing mystery. He held, in a way, a key position—his old reputation gave him an exaggerated importance in their minds.

What Wang wanted to know, what Captain Chou wanted to know was: what were the American's plans? Peter divined that the City of Swatow was fairly athrob with intrigues and counter-intrigues, all centering on that cargo of opium. What, then, was his disposition?

He stood up and looked out the porthole, hating, just now, to expose his back to any vacancy. This smoke-room, with its various entrances and exits, was a dangerous vacancy to which to expose one's back. There was, at least, Mr. Fung to consider.

At least two of the bubbling counter-intrigues came to a definite crisis as he gazed out that porthole. Captain Chou had swung about and was crossing the traverse to the port side. And at that moment, Wang came furtively into view.

Trying to piece some orderly scheme out of the fragments that he had picked up, Peter concluded at once that these two had been carefully avoiding each other. It was not only a crisis; it was a clash, and there would be some resulting rearranging of a critical balance.

He guessed this—and it was sufficiently upheld when Wang's right hand darted to his belt and came out with a knife. It was a wicked one, the kind that river Chinese are so fond of carrying—long and curved like a horn.

Captain Chou spat out some river idiom at his first officer, but Wang said nothing. He sprang. Captain Chou had likewise found keen and ready metal. The two knives met in midair in a *snick* that fairly produced sparks.

From his grand stand seat, Peter watched the duel and coldly

"Drink that cocktail!" the Chinese commanded.

weighed the results of the outcome. Captain Chou might be more sinister, but he was certainly less mad. It would be better for the rest of the world if the two of them carved their hearts out.

Peter would give Wang the benefit of the doubt for sixty seconds. The strength of madness would carry him no farther than that. Then he would wilt like a punctured toy balloon.

WANG, HOWEVER, was the cleverer knife man. The two knives were locked. Peter would never know quite what Wang did; but it was doubtless some good trick. The captain's knife left his hand and cut a slow shining parabola over the rail and into the sea.

And next moment, the first officer's knife was imbedded to its hilt in Captain Chou's throat.

Wang now drove the heel of his palm into the chin of his victim. The dying man's head snapped back, and the knife came out of the wound with an audible pop. Blood in a thick red cascade followed.

The first officer lifted the knife again, to plunge it with perfect accuracy between ribs and into Captain Chou's heart.

Wang now acted with trained decision. He held the captain erect and wiped the knife on the breast of the dying man's coat. Then he carried him to the rail, gave a push and sent him overboard.

The first mate—was he now elevated to the captaincy?—returned the knife to the sheath at his belt, planted his bloody hands on his hips and stared at Peter.

His eyes were still those of a dead man, but—for the first time—there was some ghost of an expression on his skull-like face.

It was pride, or vanity. He had definitely shown this white man who was master of the situation.

Something like a smile twitched Wang's puffed and protruding lips. Then he turned on his heel and went.

If Wang was, as it now appeared, in control of the situation, what would happen to Mr. Fung, to Peter, to Susan—and to that cargo of opium?

THE SMOKE-ROOM door opened and Mr. Fung came in. There was a slight cut on his right cheek which, Peter supposed, was the result of that hard slap with which he had sent the Chinese ship-owner tumbling into the corner of his stateroom.

Mr. Fung glanced at Peter, hesitated, then walked rapidly to the bar. Mechanically, the bar steward handed him a bottle and a small glass. Mr. Fung poured himself a stiff drink, tossed it down, and began talking in low tones to the bar boy.

Peter lighted a fresh cigarette, placed the package and matches on the table before him and waited.

The bar boy came out with Peter's dry Martini on a small red lacquer tray. Peter could see the colored sugar on the rim of the glass sparkling. Sugaring the rim of a cocktail glass was a habit of these Oriental bar boys; they dipped the rim in water, then into colored granulated sugar, unless you instructed them not to.

The sugar was of different colors—red, green, blue. Being wet, it sparkled like a crust of rubies and emeralds and sapphires.

The bar boy carefully placed the cocktail on the table beside the cigarettes and matches. Peter paid him and picked up the cocktail. The glass was within an inch of his lips when, lifting his eyes, he saw Mr. Fung, across the room, staring at him with an expression of such malignancy, such greedy absorption, that Peter involuntarily straightened up and stared back.

It was, perhaps, the narrowest escape from death he had ever experienced. A faint acrid perfume, as of almonds, rose into his nostrils—a vapor of sudden and violent death.

Peter carefully replaced the poisoned cocktail on the table. As he did so, Mr. Fung came across the room.

Mr. Fung seated himself on the leather wall seat before Peter. The ugly little automatic that he had once before displayed to Peter was in his hand.

Never, Peter was certain, had he seen such hatred in a man's eyes and face as he now beheld in the Chinese ship-owner's. His countenance was so pale that it actually looked green. His eyes were squeezed to such thin cracks that only a glimmering hairline was visible. And his mouth was engaged in making strange grimaces.

And Peter abruptly concluded that Wang was not the only madman aboard. Mr. Fung was in a murderous rage. Peter was prepared to hear his voice in the form of a shout. Such distorted features generally were accompanied by shouts—or uncontrollable shrieks. But Mr. Fung did not shout—or shriek. In the most controlled of voices, he said:

"Don't move, Mr. Moore."

A little pale, Peter watched him as a man might watch a cobra poising to strike. There was not the slightest doubt in Peter's mind that Mr. Fung was as dangerous as any cobra.

The ugly little automatic was pressing into Peter's side.

"Drink your cocktail!" Mr. Fung commanded.

Peter replied levelly: "I have never cultivated a fondness, Mr. Fung, for prussic acid."

The Chinese, opening his eyes a trifle, slowly nodded. As if in confirmation of a thought, he said: "Yes. Yes—you are a very clever man, Mr. Moore."

Peter watched him. Mr. Fung's eyes were alarming.

"But you are not clever enough," the Chinese added.

Peter did not answer. He did not intend to answer, but the man with the ugly little automatic was obviously waiting for an answer.

"Clever enough to escape death—this time, Mr. Moore!"

Peter's face had become absolutely expressionless. He could not move a fraction of an inch before that gun could go off.

"This time?" he repeated.

"YOU THINK," Mr. Fung took that up, "that I am resentful because of your interference in my friendship with Miss O'Cilvie. You are mistaken. Wait! I can see in your eyes that you are casting about for some escape. Let me assure you, Mr. Moore, that there is no way of escape. I believe you saw recently what happened to the captain of this ship. He interfered with my plans. I ordered—you saw what I ordered."

"Yes. I saw."

"But Captain Chou was a well-frog. What did he know of the sea? Do you comprehend? I considered him a trifling obstacle—a well-frog whose croaking annoyed me. He was hatching a plan to seize that cargo of opium. He was very foolish. But—but he was a well-frog."

Mr. Fung paused. His mad little eyes roved over Peter's pale face.

"But I do not consider you a well-frog, Mr. Moore. No! I compliment you. Perhaps I may flatter you. I flatter you by calling you a dragon. I see you are puzzled. I will explain. In China, you have a most curious reputation. You are the Man of Bronze—the invulnerable. You have penetrated to parts of China where white men are forbidden. You have crossed swords with the most dangerous and relentless men in this country—

and you have come off unscathed! You are a legend. You are the white man upon whom all the gods have smiled."

The pressure of the ugly little automatic in Peter's side became more perceptible.

"But I am not an ignorant Chinese coolie, Mr. Moore. I know you for what you are. Clever! Clever as the very devil himself! But perhaps I am a shade cleverer. Or perhaps I am a successful opportunist. Shall we merely consider that I have encountered and embraced an opportunity?"

Peter parted his lips to speak. But Mr. Fung anticipated him.

"I could prove how foolish that legend is by pulling the trigger on this automatic pistol, Mr. Moore. Maybe I shall. Certainly, this time you are not going to escape."

Some of the distortion had vanished from the ship-owner's long yellow face. But the madness in his eyes remained. He smiled crookedly.

"A hunter sets up a trap to catch a weasel and—lo! a white dragon is ensnared! I was thinking of Miss O'Gilvie. But she is not a weasel. She is a little, soft, white rabbit. She is incidental. I did not know until a few minutes ago that the great white dragon had fallen into my net. Would it interest you to know how many years I have been hoping our paths might cross?"

"I never," Peter stated, "saw you before this afternoon."

"The reflection of the sun from a mirror might blind a man so that he would fall to his death—but the mirror would never know," the Chinese answered. "It is true. We have never met before, Fate happily threw us together today."

"And," Peter added, "I never heard of you."

"No? That was an oversight. You were sometimes careless, shall we say? Think back, Mr. Moore, to an August night in Hong Kong. Think back seven years, Mr. Moore!"

Peter nodded. "I recall that I was in Hong Kong seven years ago."

"There was a woman," Mr. Fung went on, "the most beautiful woman in southern China! Up and down the rivers her beauty was famous. Her name, among the natives, was Lady of Starry Eyes. Men fell to their death in those eyes. But she was not Chinese. She was Eurasian. Her name was Romola Borria."

Peter nodded with decision. "I remember Romola Borria. Twice she tried to kill me. She was a beautiful—and very dangerous woman."

"She was my wife!"

"Oh, was she?"

MR. FUNG bared his teeth. "Is that all you have to say? 'Oh, was she?' I say, she was my wife! You stole her from me!"

"That," Peter coldly interrupted, "is a lie. I stole Romola Borria from no one."

"She ran away," Mr. Fung said savagely, "to go with you!"

"But she did not go with me!"

"She killed herself! After enticing her away from me, you would not have her, so she killed herself!"

"Wrong again," said Peter. "No man living could persuade Romola Borria to do anything that did not suit her whims. She was a temperamental beauty. What she wanted, she took. She was the kind who would tire of a dozen men—and betray a hundred!"

The little automatic sharply prodded the American.

"Ah, yes; I was forgetting how clever you are—how invulnerable! Seven years ago, I made the vow that I would some day find you—and on that day you would meet death. That day is now, Mr. Moore!"

The door on the opposite side of the smoke-room opened and Randy Nichols came stumbling in. Behind him was Wang, the first officer, his face a death mask. Randy Nichols looked pale.

The ex-pitcher dropped down on a leather bench corresponding to the one on which Peter and Mr. Fung were seated, and Wang dropped down beside him.

Mr. Fung said steadily: "You will not raise your voice, or I will pull this trigger now. You think you have a chance for life, but you have none—absolutely none. And you are going to suffer—just a little—as you made me suffer. Yet any time you wish, you may drink that cocktail. Drink it!"

Peter was gazing past him at Randy Nichols. The face of the wireless operator was in profile. He was as white as death. His red hair was rumpled.

"You won't drink it?" persisted Mr. Fung.

Nichols was lighting a cigarette. Peter watched him wonderingly. He heard Wang's low voice. Nichols looked very unhappy. It flashed into Peter's mind that Randy Nichols, who had sold out once before, might be at the point of selling out again. For a share in that cargo of opium!

"Then," said Mr. Fung, "I will tell you just what is to happen to you. Let me see if you are clever enough to escape! Tonight—within the next hour or two—this ship will be intercepted by a Chinese fishing junk. That junk will be filled with river *fokies*. They will come aboard to take off this cargo of opium."

"Which you sold to Miss O'Gilvie," Peter added.

Mr. Fung ignored this. "If you make any attempt at resistance, you will not live to go aboard that junk."

The Chinese ship-owner smiled, and it was not a pleasant smile.

"Once you were the cat and I was the mouse. Now our parts are reversed. Should I deny that I enjoy this rôle?" He leaned forward, his eyes burning with that seven-year obsession. "You and Miss O'Gilvie and I will be aboard that junk, Mr. Moore. She is so anxious for new thrills, new excitement! She will have her fill. For do you know what is to happen to you on that junk, Mr. Moore?"

He paused. Peter, with murky eyes, was gazing past him at Randy Nichols. The red-head was puffing nervously at his cigarette.

Mr. Fung chuckled. "Look for no help from that quarter, Mr. Moore. Ah, yes; I know that you and Mr. Nichols had a long talk this afternoon. But Mr. Nichols has had a change of heart.

Since you talked to him, I have convinced him of the wisdom of remaining loyal to me. You have heard, perhaps, that the friendships of the day are those of self-interest alone. No, Mr. Moore, you can count on no help from that quarter."

Peter wondered. If Mr. Fung were lying, why was Randy Nichols so engrossed with Wang?

Idly he watched the red-head's cigarette. It glowed and it waned. And suddenly these glowings and wanings took on a sharp and startling intelligence. Three short glows—space— three long glows—space—three short glows!

Definitely, Randy Nichols had turned that cigarette into a visible wireless transmitter! Slowly, painstakingly, over and over, he was sending that most famous and dramatic of all wireless calls:

"S—O—S! S—O—S! S—O—S!"

CHAPTER VI

THE CHINESE SENSE OF HUMOR

THE GRIM HUMOR of it brought a sharp impulse to laughter, which Peter suppressed. Randy Nichols, cornered by the murderous Wang, sending with his glowing cigarette a plea for help to Peter Moore, in whose side an automatic pistol was prodding—a pistol that would be fired the instant he betrayed the slightest inclination toward escape!

He brought himself back to what Mr. Fung was saying with such relish.

"The crew of that junk will attend to you. Perhaps you do not realize with what enthusiasm those half-starved, half-naked yellow devils will handle the job! A well-fed, prosperous white man—one of the race that has been pillaging them, starving them, holding them under the iron heel of military subjugation for how long!

"They will lash you to a mast, Mr. Moore. Would you prefer to drink that cocktail now? No? What a pity! What a mistake! Let me go on."

He paused and stared into Peter's murky, dreamy eyes. Peter had lighted a cigarette. Slowly he spelled the answer to the wireless man's distress call. The answer was the letter K, which meant, "Go ahead. Transmit."

"What," said Mr. Fung, "are you thinking?"

"Of what you are saying," Peter answered.

Randy Nichols lifted his hand to the side of his head and began slowly to scratch his scalp. Slowly and steadily his fingers went up and down in that red thatch. Signals could be formed more quickly that way than with a glowing cigarette. He spelled:

"Wang—took—my—gun. Knife—in—his—hand. What— shall—we—do?"

Peter crushed out his cigarette in the ash tray and began to drum on the table nervously. With drumming finger tips he answered:

"Fung—pointing—gun—at—me. My—pistol—in—cabin. Will—get—if—can."

Mr. Fung was watching him sharply and speaking steadily:

"… and when those starving coolies have you lashed to that mast, Mr. Moore, they will go about their job—an all-night job. Have you ever seen those coolies torture a man to death?"

"Never," Peter said huskily, and drummed out this message to Randy Nichols.

"Where are—other—firearms—aboard?"

"They will burn out your eyes, one at a time," continued Mr. Fung. "They will cut off your nose, they will tear off your ears, and they will rip out your tongue!"

Randy signaled back, *"Automatic—rifle—and—ammuni- tion—in—drawer—beneath—bunk—captain's—cabin."*

"You are sure," Mr. Fung wanted to know, "that you do not prefer to drink that cocktail? Its death would be swifter and much more pleasant."

Peter slowly drummed: *"OK—will—try. If—can—free— you—meet—me—wireless—house. Stand—by."*

"O—K."

"If you won't drink," said Mr. Fung, "perhaps you will smoke. Since this afternoon I have had a particular interest in seeing you smoke one pipe, two pipes, three pipes of opium. I want you to observe how it sharpens the senses, how delicately it will make you feel the tortures those starved devils will inflict on you."

He broke sharply into idiomatic Chinese. Peter caught enough of it to realize that Mr. Fung was ordering the bar boy, who, behind the half door of the tiny bar had been engrossed in the proceedings, to fetch opium implements.

THE BOY came out of his cubicle a moment later with a black lacquer tray on which reposed a pipe, a little brass jar, a wire having the characteristic dipper at one end, and a spirit lamp with a glass hood over it.

He placed the tray on the table and started to remove the cocktail.

"Maskee that cocktail!" Mr. Fung said sharply.

He gave instructions for preparing the pill. The boy removed the glass hood and lighted the lamp. He took the cover from the little brass jar and scooped up a small lump of the brown gum on the end of the wire. Expertly he twisted the lump about in the flame until it began to fizzle.

"It will make you see all things so clearly!" Mr. Fung was saying. "It will make you see the advisability, perhaps, of drinking this cocktail? Do you remember Socrates and the cup of hemlock, Mr. Moore? If you drank this cocktail, you would die far more swiftly than Socrates did!"

The odor of the roasting opium assailed Peter's nostrils.

Mr. Fung's smile was almost charming.

"Another plan has occurred to me, Mr. Moore. This junk that is to intercept us tonight will land my cargo on a wild and lonely beach on Hang-chau Bay between Haining and Song-kiang. When the coolies on that junk have sufficiently mutilated you, your body will be taken ashore to the house of my uncle. If you are still alive, you will be permitted to alleviate your sufferings with—the black smoke. In a few months, I think you will have changed your opinion of opium. You will cherish it as some men cherish love."

He addressed the bar boy in firecracker Chinese. Then:

"Now, Mr. Moore, when I give you this pipe, you will smoke and inhale—or I will shoot."

"I understand," Peter said.

The boy plugged the little fizzling brown lump into the pipe bowl and spun the wire about so that the air could pass through. Mr. Fung seized the pipe; the bar boy held the spirit lamp ready.

Mr. Fung pushed the bit of the pipe into Peter's mouth, and the boy held the wavering blue flame to the bowl.

"Inhale!" Mr. Fung commanded.

Peter sucked the smoke into his mouth. Thereupon he gave a most realistic exhibition of a man strangling. He began to cough. Great convulsive spasms racked him. He bent forward and coughed and coughed.

Mr. Fung laughed. The bar boy mirthfully joined him. The Chinese have a well-advertised sense of humor. They will laugh until they are breathless at a man who is drowning.

Peter's coughing sent Mr. Fung into paroxysms of laughter. The bar boy was holding his hands to his middle, rocking from side to side with merriment at the American's discomfort. The pressure of the ugly little automatic pistol against Peter's side ceased. Peter had not relinquished his hold on the pipe. Now he suddenly grasped it as though it was a club. He swung it smashing down against Mr. Fung's right temple.

CHAPTER VII

YELLOW DEVILS

IF THE OPIUM pipe had been a stout oak club, the ship-owner's skull would have been crushed by that blow. But it was too light a blow. The pipe flew into a dozen splintered fragments. And Mr. Fung was only momentarily dazed.

Peter reached for the gun, but it had evidently slipped to the floor. There was no time now to look for it. Peter leaped up, sent the bar boy flying to the floor with a swinging blow to the jaw, and paused for a moment on the threshold.

Randy Nichols had not moved. Nor had Wang, the first officer. Mr. Fung, recovering from the stunning effects of the blow, was now fumbling about for the pistol.

As Peter opened the door, the pistol appeared above the table in Mr. Fung's shaking hand. And as Peter slammed the door after him, the upper panel suddenly and magically contained five holes in a pattern from which splinters dripped.

A deck hand armed with a knife barred the American's way. Evidently posted there as a guard, the developments of the past ten seconds had taken him completely by surprise. Peter leaped, struck him twice in the face, sprang over him as he fell, and raced for the iron ladder.

As he ran forward on the boat deck toward the master's cabin, the American collided in the darkness with a hot, sweating man who cursed at him in Chinese and fell stumbling over a funnel guy.

Peter ran on. The captain's door was locked. He forced it open, switched on a light over a battered old walnut desk long enough to see the deep drawer under the bunk that Randy Nichols had mentioned, then switched it off.

In the doorway an invisible man uttered a sharp inquiry.

Peter heard his foot fumble over the threshold. He leaped at him, struck him once in the midsection, once again in the jaw, and heard him fall to the deck with a thud.

The big drawer under the bunk was locked. Peter kicked it in. It was necessary to kick the panel completely away. A variety of odds and ends tumbled out onto the floor. Peter's searching fingers found the automatic rifle and two boxes of cartridges.

The rifle was empty. Peter opened one box and dumped the contents into his pockets. As he started aft he loaded the rifle.

He cautiously descended the iron ladder to the promenade deck and peered into a porthole.

The smoke-room seemed to be empty. The porthole was open. Very cautiously Peter put his head through the round opening and looked into the room. No one was there. The bar was closed.

Where was Fung? Where was Wang? Where, especially, was the red-headed ex-baseball pitcher?

He would have killed off Fung and Wang without a moment's hesitation. If he didn't kill them, they'd certainly kill him. With the new developments, he might be anybody's victim.

Peter looked quickly about him. The City of Swatow was lurching along in the rising swell. The air was heavy and hot and breathless. That gale was coming. The first puff of it might blow at any moment.

There was no time to waste looking for Randy. He would get Susan, take her up to the wireless house, and barricade himself there.

AS PETER started down the deck toward Susan's stateroom, the rhythmic clanking of the engines stopped. He recalled what Randy had said: "Just when we get abreast of them junks, that old tin teapot of an engine is gonna sprain an ankle. While we're layin' to, gettin' it fixed, the junks will come up under the bow and the pirates will come swarmin' aboard."

Peter hastened to Susan's stateroom. He wondered whether or not she had recovered from the effects of the opium-smoking lesson he had rudely interrupted.

Anxiously the young man unlocked the door. To his immense relief, Susan was lying in her bunk just as he had left her. He pulled off the blanket with which he had tucked her in and shook the girl by the shoulders.

Her large violet eyes opened dazedly, The pupils were dilated. Her stare was vacant. She mumbled something, then closed her eyes.

"Susan! Wake up!"

But the owner of that cargo of opium would not wake up. She groaned sleepily and mumbled again. Peter picked her up. Susan wrapped her arms trustingly around his neck.

Peter carried her to the forward stairway, and so up to the boat deck and the wireless house. He passed no one, saw no one. Where was Fung? Where was Wang? Where was the wireless operator? Randy Nichols had said he wanted a fight. Well, here was his chance—but where was he? And where were the crew?

A groan came from the wireless room doorway. Peter sat Susan in a chair and arranged her so that she would not topple out of it.

On the floor, with his head lying on his clenched fist, was Randy. Peter flicked on a light.

Stifling a companion to his groan, Peter picked him up; shook him, until his head flopped from side to side.

"What's the matter?" Peter snapped.

"Passed out," the red-head mumbled. "Walloped from behind."

"What's happening? Where's Fung and Wang?"

"Gee, feller, my head is bustin' open! I dunno where anybody is."

Randy Nichols shook his head to try to clear it, then clapped both hands to his temple. "Gee, what a help I've turned out to be. I'll be all right in a minute. Fung? Why, didn't you see him on deck? He followed you out of the smoke-room, and in the excitement I made my get-away from Wang, but as I went out the door somebody clipped me on the dome with something, and I just managed to make this shack when I passed out."

The red-head massaged his forehead and groaned again.

"Say! The engines have stopped! Is there any sign of that junk? You remember what I told you?"

Peter had let go of him and slipped into the seat at the wireless instruments.

That wireless set was antique ten years ago. To Peter it was a wonder that it worked at all. The old motor-generator began to wheeze as Peter threw down the starting lever, then eerily to whine. The old-fashioned spark began singing in its old-fashioned cylindrical glass muffler as his fingers danced on the rubber knob of the key.

"S—O—S! S—O—S! S—O—"

The whine of the old motor-generator abruptly degenerated to a dying moan. It came to a wheezing stop. Nichols exclaimed:

"Ain't that dandy? They've cut off our juice on the engine room switchboard."

"Is your emergency set working?"

"**DAMNED IF** I know! I haven't tested it out in months. It's one of these Marconi six-inch coil sets, run on a storage battery. It shoots about a million volts into that aërial—and has a range of about twenty miles. Say, listen; I think we're all three of us gonna get killed. And I sure do hate to see you and this good-lookin' kid get it. I don't care whether they polish me off or not. What the hell have I got to live for? I've been a dead man for five years, anyhow."

"Snap out of it," Peter said. "Take that rifle and stand in the doorway. Shoot anything that moves."

"Sure, sure—anything but the second mate. He's the only guy on this old hooker I trust, outside of ourselves. But I'm forgettin'. They've got Lou locked up in his cabin. And in a minute they'll get us. And what these Chinks won't do to this girl!"

"Oh, Peter," Susan spoke up, "I'm sick. Everything's going around! What is happening?"

"Believe it or not," Randy Nichols answered, "we're waitin' for a street car, Miss O'Gilvie."

He staggered to the doorway with the automatic rifle gripped in his hands.

"Gee!" he said, "That's funny, Mr. Moore. There's somebody up that after mast! I can just see him. Do you suppose they're gonna pick us off from up there?"

"Shoot him," Peter said.

Working rapidly, he had made the change over to the emergency set. He tapped out a few experimental dots on the key. The old rubber-shelled coil hummed. The points above it crackled weakly a moment later with a blue spark. The storage batteries were weak.

He heard Randy shoot. Then: "Gee. I missed him a mile. My eyes are still fuzzy, and I can't hold the gun steady."

Peter slowly tapped out: "S—O—"

The spark stopped. Simultaneously, something came rattling down on the roof and, high in the air, a man screamed.

Randy Nichols exclaimed: "Gee, there he goes! The minute he cut the aërial, he got all that voltage! He slipped and fell! Stop sending. No use. The aërial's down!"

Peter listened; heard the thud of the hand's body as it struck the deck, and said:

"We'll have to find a better place than this. Where's the second mate's cabin?"

"That's no better than this," answered the red-head. "We would be cornered there like rats. Listen, Mr. Moore—we haven't got a chance. Let's stay here and fight it out."

"We'll try to make the after deck," Peter said. "Susan, pull yourself together."

"How can I? I'm scattered all over the universe. Peter, did I start all this trouble? I'll never forgive myself. It's all my fault."

"It's nobody's fault," Peter disagreed. "Can you walk?"

Susan tried to walk. "I can't!" she wailed. "Everything's going round and round. Oh, why did I smoke that opium!"

"You'll feel better in a few minutes." He picked her up. "Randy," he said, "let's get that second mate. We're going to need help."

"Help!" moaned Randy. "What we need is a destroyer and a flotilla of submarines! And what good would it have done if one of 'em had picked up our S.O.S.? We don't need help a half an hour from now or an hour from now. We need help right now."

"If we reach the after deck," Peter said, "we could hold out against an army. Now, where's that second mate?"

"Right this way, Mr. Moore."

Randy staggered off. At a door under the bridge on the port side he stopped. The door was open. The deck light shone in on a man who lay on the trunk with his hands and feet roped and a gag bound with a towel in his mouth.

Peter undid the gag and cut the ropes.

"Lou don't speak much English," Randy said.

PETER SPOKE to the second mate in river Chinese. Did Lou want to stay here or would he join Peter, Randy and Miss O'Gilvie? The odds were tremendously against them, and when that junk hove up under the bows, they might all be wiped out.

Lou caught his breath and began to talk. He was a wiry little Cantonese. It developed that he was fighting mad and avid for a killing. He was going to get Wang. He was going to get Fung. What he wanted to institute was immediate and wholesale slaughter.

Peter grinned. "Lou says he wants to join us. He wants action."

In the coarse and profane Chinese of the rivers, Peter explained to the infuriated Lou what his plan was. They would barricade themselves on the poop deck. They could stay in the steering-engine house. Its walls were three-eighths-inch steel— bullet-proof.

The mad little second mate agreed that this was the best plan.

Giving an arm to Susan, who was now almost strong enough to walk, Peter led the way aft.

An angry blue-red flame spat out at them from the shadow of a lifeboat. A bullet struck a funnel guy and went screaming off toward heaven. Peter dropped Susan's arm, lifted the automatic rifle and placed two shots in the exact locality where the blue-red flame had spurted. There was no retaliation.

At the top of the ladder he paused to reconnoiter. Voices, angry voices, came up from the deck below.

On the commodious after turn of the promenade a dozen or more armed men were gathered in a thick ring about Mr. Fung and Wang. Fung and Wang were hotly arguing. Their voices, pitched high with anger, went into squeals and yelps.

Peter could not follow the ins and outs of such rapid Chinese, but Lou could. They were quarreling over that cargo of opium. Half the crew seemed to be siding with Mr. Fung, the other half with Wang.

Before Peter could prevent him, Lou had snatched the rifle out of Peter's hands. It was his evident intention to begin firing at the group below.

Then Mr. Fung looked up. His businesslike little automatic pistol was in one hand. Before Lou could place the stock of the rifle into his armpit, Mr. Fung had fired.

Three bullets went wild. The gang of men on the promenade turned, promptly made a concerted rush for the iron ladder. All of them were armed. Some had revolvers. Others had wicked-looking knives.

Peter ordered a retreat. If it had not been for Susan, he would have been willing to stay there and fight it out. But Susan would probably want to fight, too. There was no telling what that girl would decide to do.

Seizing Susan's arm, pushing Randy Nichols ahead of him, and ordering Lou to follow, Peter started briskly toward the forward end of the boat deck.

A bullet glanced off the funnel with the savage sound of canvas being ripped.

"Where," Randy panted, "do we go now? We can't make that steering-engine house!"

When they started down the forward stairway, it became obvious that they could not even attempt to reach the stern. Some of the men who had been gathered aft were surging down the deck toward them.

There was, at least for the moment, no place to escape except the forward deck well.

Peter helped Susan down the ladder. She was laughing hysterically. Randy Nichols, growling, came next. Lou, pouring out Chinese river profanity, brought up the rear, pumping lead from the automatic rifle as he retreated, until the hammer fell on emptiness. His wrinkled yellow forehead was bleeding from a bullet gouge.

SUSAN WAS now thoroughly awake, freeing herself from Peter, she bolted across the hatch and up the ladder into the forepeak, where her fifty cases of opium were stacked.

When Peter reached her she was sitting limply on one of the cases. The glow from the bridge lighted her face. Her eyes were enormous; from either opium or excitement.

She reached up for Peter's hand and pulled him down beside her.

"Peter," inquired Susan, "are we going to get out of this alive?"

"We've managed to stay alive so far," he said cheerfully.

"But what will happen?"

"I'll tell you," put in Randy, "what will happen. Somewhere floating around here there's a junk loaded with bloodthirsty Chinos. They're comin' up under our bows."

"Here?" Susan wailed.

"Yes, ma'am—here. And when they do, you can take your choice. You can be captured by them, or you can be captured by that gang up there. Or we can all jump overboard."

Susan was looking at Peter.

"Is it as bad as that?"

"It's pretty serious," Peter admitted.

"Well," Susan said, "I'm not worrying. You can get us out of it. You've been in tighter corners than this."

"I don't remember them," Peter answered.

She began to weep. She laid her head against his shoulder, snuggled her hand into his—and sobbed.

When this storm had passed, she faltered: "Peter, I've had all the adventure I want."

"That goes," said Randy, "for you and me both, kid. I thought I wanted trouble. I thought I was itchin' for a fight. For years I'd been itchin' to get into some jam and fight side by side with Mr. Moore. Well—he can have his jams."

A bullet from the bridge sang over their heads. Lou popped up with the rifle. Peter firmly took the weapon out of Lou's hand and pulled him down behind the bulwark of opium cases.

Susan sighed. "Peter, I'm cured. If we get out of this alive, I'll never get into another adventure as long as I live. Oh, this is perfectly horrible. And to think it's all my fault!"

"It isn't your fault," Peter answered.

"Sure, it's her fault," put in Randy, "but what the hell? Haven't good-looking skirts been startin' trouble and haven't us men had to finish what they started for the last eleven thousand years?"

Another bullet sang its song, then shrieked as it chipped a lump of wood from the bow mast and ricocheted into the sea. The City of Swatow, having lost all headway, had swung about and was now in the trough. A long puff of wind came from the southeast.

"Look at Helen of Troy and look at Cleopatra," Randy went on. "Look at the trouble they started! Compared to them, kid, you're only a piker."

"Well," Peter took this up dryly, "give her a chance. She's young. She'll learn."

"I think you're perfectly cruel," said Susan. "I am absolutely terrified. We're all apt to be killed at any moment. Peter, I was serious. I mean it. This has taught me a much-needed lesson. I will never go looking for adventure again. I hate adventure! Look! Isn't that a shore light? If only we were ashore!"

Peter looked. As he did so, a blazing spot of white radiance sprang into being on top of the wheelhouse.

The searchlight flooded the forepeak, and it clearly etched the rigging and masts of the junk which had slipped up under the City of Swatow's bows like a gray ghost.

CHAPTER VIII

THE PITCHER'S LAST GAME

WHEN THE SEARCHLIGHT flashed on, the three men crouched down. Then Peter lifted the rifle, squinted along the gleaming barrel—and pulled the trigger. Its report was followed by blackness where the blinding point of white light had been, and the faint tinkling of glass.

He said crisply: "Susan, get down out of the way over by that rail. If they come aboard, they'll climb over the port rail. Randy, you used to be one of the world's greatest pitchers. Have you any of it left?"

"Sure, I have, Mr. Moore; but what's that got to do with these pirates?"

"Rip off the covers of a few of these cases. Those opium balls weigh five or six pounds. They're bigger than baseballs, but if your arm is anywhere near as good as it was cracked up to be, you can throw those balls. Get busy. Your job is to repel the boarding party. I'm going to do what I can to prevent a rush from aft."

Randy Nichols required no further instructions. With his bare fingers he was ripping off the cover of the nearest case. As he worked he chuckled. It may have been from nervous excitement, or it may have been that Randy found the job amusing.

To the second mate Peter issued orders in his halting river Chinese. At first, Lou did not understand; but presently he grasped the idea and he uttered a yelp of delight.

His yelp was answered by others. Chinese cannot work, they cannot fight unless they yell. It is in their blood. The Manchus, centuries ago, sweeping down across the northern plains of China to drive out the last of the Mings from Peking, shrieked as they slaughtered.

A bedlam of yells broke out below the City of Swatow's bows. It was promptly answered by the City of Swatow's crew, and this was, tremendously exaggerated, the *"Hai-hey!"* of the Yangtze river coolie at work.

Above the yells, the oncoming gale expressed itself. A sudden savage puff of wind tore clumps of spray from toppling wave crests and hurled them with a sound like shot against the steamer's side. So strong was this second forewarning of the coming gale that the venerable tramp listed perceptibly.

The tilting side was a distinct advantage to the yelling men aboard the junk. Peter heard the rattling of heavy chains, and presumed that they had grappled onto the anchor chain.

Some one in the wheelhouse was systematically firing down into the opium cases. Bullets sang close to Peter, closer still to Randy.

Peter reloaded the rifle and sprayed the wheelhouse as fast as he could pull the trigger. And he wondered how Mr. Fung and Wang had settled their argument. Or if it had been settled at all.

A head appeared in one of the shattered wheelhouse windows. Nichols picked up a ball of opium, "wound himself up," and let the ball fly.

With startling accuracy the large dark ball sped up. Peter distinctly heard the thump of it as the missile struck that head. In nervous relief, he laughed.

"Watch that rail!" he said.

A Chinese giant with long black hair ran into sight along the promenade deck. He was naked to the waist; his torso was shining with sweat and streaked with black. Evidently he was one of the black gang.

Peter watched him coming. There was a long knife in his teeth and a length of iron pipe in one hand.

THE STOKER reached the ladder leading into the forward deck well. His foot was on the rung before Peter had recovered from his astonishment at the man's daring. Then the long-haired man plunged out of sight.

He reappeared crossing the hatch cover, with the knife still in his teeth.

As he started up the ladder to the forepeak, Randy Nichols climbed upon a case with a ball of opium in each hand. He stood poised, his feet planted widely apart, the ball in his right hand ready to throw.

When the stoker's head appeared, Randy hurled the ball. Swift and true, it shot through the air, struck the man squarely between the eyes with an impact almost as loud as the report of a rifle.

The stoker fell backward. Peter heard the knife clatter to the iron deck below, then the softer but heavier thud of the falling body.

Randy was wildly laughing. And Peter barked: "Randy, watch that port rail. Here they come!"

His attention was diverted by several developments. At the first glimpse of those shaven heads appearing over the rail from the deck of the junk, Susan screamed, disobeyed orders, crawled out of her hiding-place and clutched Peter about the shoulders.

Simultaneously, rifles began blazing from the bridge again. Peter felt a sharp sting in his left shoulder; knew that he had been hit, and wondered if the bullet had wounded Susan also. Evidently it hadn't. Forcibly, he pushed her away, ordered her to crouch down.

The girl was hysterical. "We're going to be killed, Peter!

They'll slaughter us like cattle!" Then another shriek. "You've been shot in the shoulder! I can feel the blood!"

"Get down," Peter groaned.

As he pushed her away again, he saw Randy scooping balls of opium out of the case, hurling them; saw one face after another appear at the rail; heard, even above the yells, the solid impact of the opium balls as they sped to their astonished targets.

The second mate was, meanwhile, carrying out the order Peter had given him. The old donkey engine began to hiss and wheeze and rattle. Lou was at the levers. A cable running from the drum on the engine, through a block on the boom, tightened and hummed. Three cases of opium, looped together at the end of the cable, soared upward and swung outward until they were poised high in the air above the junk.

Lou yelled. Shriller yells from the junk responded. Down the three cases dropped. They vanished. Their disappearance was promptly followed by a splintering crash.

The old donkey engine hissed and wheezed and rattled again. Up came the loop, devoid of the three cases.

The second mate shouted to Peter. Peter looped the end of the cable about three more cases. Again the donkey engine wheezed and whirred. And these three cases were dropped, crashing, upon the deck of the junk.

As rapidly as Peter could loop cases, together and Lou could work the engine, they dumped the heavy cases of opium onto the junk.

The firing from the bridge ended abruptly when Peter emptied the rifle in that direction. Then he devoted himself again to the task of aiding the second mate.

His back was to the starboard rail when Susan screamed a warning. He paid no heed until, out of the corner of his eyes, he saw the glint of light on dull metal. One end of the loop was in his hand; his rifle was out of reach.

A *fokie* had climbed up the anchor chain and come up over the starboard rail with an antique rifle in his hands. He balanced himself against the roll of the ship, his naked feet seeming to clasp the rail like a pair of grotesque hands.

BEFORE PETER could move, he had aimed and fired. The explosion deafened him. But the bullet was not meant for him—it was meant for Randy Nichols. And it struck the baseball star squarely in the back of the head as he was stooping down over an opium chest.

Peter had his rifle now. As the *fokie,* yelling, balanced himself precariously on the rail from the terrific recoil, Peter pressed the trigger. He fired four times before the *fokie,* his yell diminishing to an awful gurgling, fell backward off the rail and into the sea.

Susan had crawled to Peter again. "Peter, they've killed him! That man killed him! Now they'll—"

"Take this rifle," Peter said savagely. "Shoot any one you see climbing over that rail. I'm going to get rid of the rest of this damned opium."

"But how do I work it?" Susan wailed.

"Aim it and pull the trigger. There are four shells left in the magazine."

A moment later, as Peter was shouting at the second mate to haul away, he heard the girl shoot. Then her excited, triumphant cry:

"I got one, Peter; I got one!"

"Watch both rails," he cautioned her.

The firing from the bridge had ceased entirely. And as abruptly, shaven heads ceased appearing at the rail. But the yelling aboard the junk continued.

When only a dozen cases were left, Peter ran to the rail and looked down.

The junk was a smashed and battered wreck. It was hardly afloat. The cases, in crashing down upon it, had battered open the deck and crashed on through to the bottom. It was evident that some of these had plunged clear through the rotten planking into the sea beneath.

Two men were trying to disengage the grappling chain from one of the flukes of the steamer's port anchor.

Peter returned to his job. When only three crates were left, he went to the side and peered over again.

The junk was now hardly awash. Rising seas were swirling over the deck. But it was free of the steamer and was drifting away.

Peter shouted the order to Lou to drop the remaining three crates. He watched them fall through the air to smash down on the wreck. That junk was now scarcely more than driftwood. And the gale would quickly finish it.

Some one was tooting the City of Swatow's whistle.

Peter saw Lee, the deck steward, coming along the deck with his hands above his head. A few feet behind him was the purser and supercargo. There was a bandage around the purser's head, and his hands likewise were in the air.

The deck steward and the purser, still holding their hands high, came to the rail above the deck well. Above the gusts of wind, the purser shouted:

"Don't shoot!"

Peter relieved Susan of the rifle and held it ready, although this precaution was unnecessary. The battle was over. The attack from below had ceased.

Lee and the purser descended into the deck well. Mr. Fung, the purser said, was dead. Wang had knifed him. And Wang had fallen a moment later with a bullet in his back, put there by one of the helmsmen. Three other men in the crew were dead, and five were injured. Those who were fit for duty were back on their jobs.

"Where," the purser meekly interrupted his own recital of these facts, "is Mr. Lou? He is now master of this ship."

There was a faint moan beside Peter—and a soft thud. Susan O'Gilvie had fainted.

CHAPTER XI

PETE'S LAPSE OF MEMORY

PETER MOORE SAT in the smoke-room sipping a dry Martini that he had mixed himself, without a sugar rim. The bar boy was not in evidence.

The old woodwork creaked to the beat of the engines. The smoke-room at intervals rose and fell, rolled to the right, then to the left. But the City of Swatow was not bucking the gale; she was taking it over her stern. Lou's first act as captain had been to put the ship about and lay a course for Shanghai.

Peter contemplated his immediate future somewhat gloomily. The events of tonight would precipitate a tangle in the Shanghai admiralty court that might take months to straighten out. Mutiny! Opium! Murders! Piracy!

As he sipped the Martini, he began slowly to smile. He was not the only witness whose presence would be required indefinitely in Shanghai. Susan, with all her millions, could not escape that witness stand.

Peter's smile was tender and dreamy. He knew that Susan was no longer the spoiled, thrill-seeking girl she had been a few hours ago. That experience in the forepeak, with death showing its ugly face on every hand, had cured her. Certainly, the death of that plucky red-headed exile had spoiled adventuring for her.

And Susan, with the craving for adventure put forever behind her, would make a delightful and charming companion. She appealed to him, certainly, more than any girl he had ever known. And certainly fate had pointed the way. From the moment they had met, on the crossing from San Francisco, there had been some definite and magnetic bond.

Peter's smile grew tenderer. When she wasn't looking for

trouble, Susan was a darling. What a wonderful life they could have together!

His thoughts reached a crisis. At the first opportunity, he would ask Susan to marry him. They would be married in Shanghai. Peter chuckled. And spend most of their honeymoon in the admiralty court!

As if in answer to his thoughts, Susan appeared. The door opened and she walked in, balancing herself against the lurching of the ship. She had powdered her nose and applied scarlet to her lips. Her large violet eyes were still glowing with excitement.

A sudden plunge of the deck almost sent her into Peter's lap. He caught her hands and swung her lightly down to a seat beside him.

Her starry eyes met his and lingered.

"DARLING," SHE said in her sweet, clear voice, "I can't realize yet that some fiend with a knife in his teeth isn't going to pounce on me and carve my heart out! And what a crime it was that we couldn't somehow have saved Randy!"

Peter nodded. He liked her voice, and he loved her hands. They were small but very capable.

She took the cocktail out of his hand and sipped it. Her eyes flirted with him over the rim.

"Loving cup," she said.

"Yes," Peter murmured. He cleared his throat nervously. "Susan—" he began.

"What an experience!" she cried. "Darling, you were wonderful. You were simply superb. You always are. The way you get me out of the most dreadful scrapes is simply unbelievable."

"Susan," Peter tried again, "I've been thinking—"

"Maybe I haven't been thinking! Do you know what I've been thinking?"

"Tell me," Peter said, a little disappointed at this loss of his opportunity.

Susan snuggled against him and clasped his hand in both of hers.

"Peter, I was awfully scared up there. But then I got to thinking. You know, it seems to be—well, written in the stars—that we're to have one exciting adventure after another. Already I can see that what happened tonight was just one of our wonderful adventures! The more I think about it, the surer I am of it! I think it was perfectly fascinating!"

"You do?" Peter murmured.

"I've never had so much fun in my life as in this past month, since I've known you. Oh, Peter, let's go on and on! Let's look for more adventures! With my money and your ideas we can stir up more excitement along this old coast than a revolution! Let's really smuggle opium. Let's really get mixed up with some pirates. I understand that the pirates in southern China are much more ferocious than these northern ones. Let's start a war on them!"

"I don't think that idea is practical," Peter said. "The British might object."

"Then we'll think up some other schemes that are just as thrilling! The more hair-raising adventures I have, the more I want."

She looked at him sweetly. "Peter, what were you going to say when I interrupted you?"

"I don't seem to remember," Peter answered hastily.

"Wasn't it some question or other?"

"Yes," Peter decided. "It was. I was going to ask if you weren't hungry. Shall we go down to the galley and rummage around?"

"I think that would be perfectly grand!" said Susan.

THE HAND OF UNG

Death by oriental magic hangs over the head of
Peter the Brazen, as he decides to defy the high priest
of Ung on that god's gory, orgy-mad birthday

CHAPTER I

A GOD'S RED BIRTHDAY

IT WAS THE birthday of Ung the Unspeakable, and Peter Moore was remaining in Hai-Phang. The American knew that he was inviting trouble. He stood at the balcony rail outside his hotel bedroom and watched the white colony move out. In a little procession they marched down the Street of the Red Lion through mobs of half-naked pilgrims and black-robed priests to the water front, where a wheezy old river steamer was waiting to carry them away to safety.

Shopkeepers, exporters and importers, hotel proprietor and assistant, even the American consul and his clerk—all of them with their wives and children were running away. They were sensible. Wanglat was safe. Wanglat was high in the hills and far removed from the blasphemous doings of the Ungese.

Pride or stubbornness compelled Peter Moore to stay behind. He had come to Hai-Phang on a business errand. He would not leave until he had performed that errand.

His servant, Wan Loo, came noiselessly onto the balcony and said in Cantonese:

"Master, a star, however eager, cannot help the moon. Tigers and deer do not stroll together. The American consul says there is still time. The steamer will wait ten minutes. If you change your mind and will go, you are to wave your sun helmet."

The American smiled. "Wan Loo, you should work for a man who isn't so pig-headed. A wise man in a fool's service is a clear pearl thrown into lacquer."

"You are forgetting," said the Chinese. "I say, master, that the memory of K'ong is amber in which all the insects of past events are clearly visible. I say that K'ong is as cold and deadly as a king cobra, and as cruel as a black leopard."

"K'ong," the white man answered, "will not remember me."

"K'ong never forgets, master. He is not human. He is a devil… Will you wave your sun helmet? If Fong Toy comes in your absence, I will hold him until you return. If necessary, I will bind him to his bed and sit on him with a gun in his ear."

Moore laughed. "Fong Toy is not my enemy. He is a man I want to buy something from. If he returns tonight and I miss him, I may have to chase him all the way to India."

Wan Loo was pale and anxious. "Master, the tongue which is yielding endures—the teeth which are stubborn perish. In the name of Buddha, wave your sun helmet!"

"Mix me a gin rickey," the American laughed, "and shut up."

WAN LOO was a perfect servant. Each time Peter Moore returned to the Far East, Wan Loo learned about it through some kind of oriental grapevine telegraph and offered his services. At Moore's answer he obediently shut up and walked away. If his master was determined to stroll with tigers, if his master was determined to risk recognition by K'ong, nothing was to be gained by tossing jewels of wisdom at him.

Peter Moore, watching, saw a plume of black smoke spout from the river steamer's crazy stack; then he heard her hoarse, wheezy old whistle. She was off for Wanglat and safety, and he was, for the rest of the afternoon and night, a victim of whatever consequences his decision might have in store for him. If he could have seen a little way into the future, Moore would have changed his decision. He would have boarded that steamer if he had had to swim!

A rusty-sided old tramp steamer was coming into the harbor. Moore got his field glasses and read the name on her bows— *Java Bird.* He saw her anchor splash into the jade-green. A moment later the blue peter broke out at her signal halyard and fluttered like a damp handkerchief in the hot offshore breeze.

To the American, the blue flag meant that the *Java Bird* would be steaming off to Saigon and Singapore on the midnight tide.

Through the field glasses he saw a ladder being lowered over-side, A figure in white descended the ladder and entered one of the sampans hovering about in the bright green water like sharks.

Some passenger who had not been warned that today was Ung's birthday was coming ashore. Moore swung his glasses until they bore on the high black steel towers of the Hai-Phang wireless station, and wondered why the wireless operator had not notified the *Java Bird*. Then, swinging his glasses back to bear on the sampan, he made the electrifying discovery that the figure in white was not a man but a girl.

The sampan came fish-tailing toward shore, but when Peter Moore looked again, the girl was hidden from sight by the sampan's cabin.

He watched the pilgrims pouring into Hai-Phang by every road like rivers impounding into a lake. There were copper-colored men from the coastal islands, bronze-colored men from the jungles, brass-colored men from the Himalayan foothills. The city rumbled and roared and buzzed with them; it stank with them.

Tonight, in the mile-square compound of the black malachite temple, the followers of Ung would perform their annual rites—self-torture and hideous forms of blood-letting. They would whip themselves into a state of fanatical frenzy which would make Hai-Phang decidedly unsafe for a white man.

Across red-tile roofs, through the mist of dust rising from naked brown feet, Peter Moore could see the infamous temple. It had always reminded him of a gigantic black fist which had thrust its way up through the earth's crust to poke a stark finger four hundred feet into the hot blue sky of Indo-China.

The disk darted upward, scattering drops of blood.

It stood on an artificial plateau some three hundred feet above the plains of Hai-Phang. This great knoll carried out the illusion. It was as if the hard-baked earth of the delta had resisted; had been forced upward in a large hump through which the black fist had shot up to point its skinny finger at the sky.

In certain lights the great spire of the black pagoda shimmered redly, as though it were smeared with blood. This red shimmering was said to be caused by a crust of rubies. No white man who had been tempted to climb up and investigate had lived long enough to render an authentic report. The black temple, with its blacker mysteries, had been a challenge to white adventurers for centuries.

Five years previously Peter Moore had entered the temple, bent on trouble—and been thankful to escape with his life. The high priest was a Tonkinese called K'ong, a man so powerful, so dangerous, that the French authorities let him strictly alone. K'ong was a mystery, a practitioner, so it was said, of the blackest of oriental arts. His favorite method of putting an enemy to death was disemboweling.

Moore had escaped from K'ong on his previous visit by sheer

luck and the desperation born of danger. He only hoped that this sinister, ruthless Oriental would not remember him.

AT THE balcony railing of the Hotel Europa, Peter Moore watched the river steamer dwindle into the distance and the sampan bearing the *Java Bird's* passenger near the bund.

Wan Loo approached with a tall, frosted glass.

"Master," he said, "I am so much duckweed on the river. I am a worm without a thought fit for utterance. But I am afraid that if K'ong finds you he will cut out your heart, your lungs and your stomach, as he did to that young German a few years ago, who fell in love with the native girl they were about to sacrifice and tried to save her."

"I will not leave this hotel until tomorrow," Moore said.

"Nevertheless," pursued Wan Loo, "I have requested a friend of mine to hide a sampan for you under the Yang Gan dock. If you are in danger, you can use it. With your permission, master, I will go and stay with my friends in the Chinese quarter until this horribleness is over. You are a brave man—I am a coward. The crow does not roost with the phoenix."

"Go when you wish and stay as long as you like, Wan Loo."

"Gin, limes and ice are on the table in your room, master. As Confucius said, one bout of drinking dispels three anxieties. Kindly be good to your faithful servant and worshiper and do not leave this hotel. Without going out of doors, one may know the whole world. I will go after the procession has passed."

"Very well, Wan Loo."

Wan Loo entered the bedroom. Peter heard him moving about in there.

A moment later he heard a knock on the hall door. A girl's excited voice cried:

"Is this Mr. Moore's room?"

Wan Loo said coldly: "Yes, missy."

"Where is Mr. Moore? Peter!"

As Peter's heart sank and cold sweat formed on his forehead, the girl ran out onto the balcony. She was not more than five feet tall. Her eyes were not blue, but deep violet. She was slender and lovely in cool-looking white. A white sun helmet was perched jauntily on the side of her head.

"Peter!" she cried again, and threw her arms about his neck; gave him a wild hug, a wilder kiss on the mouth, and said:

"Thank Heaven, I've found you! Isn't it perfectly wonderful?"

CHAPTER II

THE TORTURE PARADE

PETER MOORE'S SUN helmet came to a rocking rest in the corner where it had been knocked. He looked flustered.

"Susan, you little idiot, what are you doing here?"

"Gee!" she said. "It's hot, isn't it? How can you stand this climate? You look wan, Peter. I didn't think I'd find you here. I mean, I hardly dared hope I would. It's just marvelous luck. Isn't it perfectly marvelous? I've had the vilest trip down from Hong Kong. These little coastwise steamers ought to be towed out to a deep spot and sunk. The food was simply vile."

"Why," Peter asked sternly, "aren't you in Hong Kong?"

She looked reproachful.

"Why? Aren't you simply tickled to death to see me? Aren't you tingling all over with joy? Don't look so grim and haughty, darling. I just got bored, that's all. Now, don't scold. I can't stand a scolding until I cool off. After what I've been through, you ought to get out the brass band and shoot off fireworks."

"What happened to your young Englishman—Cyril?"

"Peter," she wailed, "he was simply impossible. He kept talking about the chawming little home we were going to have in Sussex. There was going to be trailing arbutus or honeysuckle, or maybe it was poison ivy, growing all over everything. And when he wasn't talking about what a wonderful find he was for a lucky girl, he was telling me how fortunate I was in finding a man who would make me such a wonderful husband. I could stand his conceit. What I simply could not abide was his telling me how nobly he would put up with me until he had taken the foolishness out of me. I don't want the foolishness taken out of me. I like being foolish. So I gave him the air."

"I thought he was a fine chap."

"Sorry," Susan said, "but I don't like 'em tame. I kept thinking about the wonderful time you were having down here in Indo-China, stealing diamonds out of Buddhas' foreheads and having knife fights with oily bandits in smelly alleys. I couldn't stand it. I simply had to come and help. What have you been doing? Tell mother everything."

"It's been a wild adventure," Peter said. "I got here a week ago. I had luncheon yesterday with the American consul and spent the afternoon making mud pies with his five-year-old daughter. I've done a lot of reading. The rest of the time I've been waiting for Fong Toy to come back from the jungles.

"As you know, I went to Hong Kong to buy a gadget he is said to have invented which will eliminate the static from radio reception. He came here and is in the jungle trying to find some particular kind of gum arabic to use in some experiment. As soon as I've transacted my business with him, I am returning by the fastest ship to Schenectady, U.S.A."

"And you're staying here, waiting for Fong Toy, in spite of these Ungese celebrations?"

"I might miss him if I left. He may be here tonight."

Susan looked up at him skeptically. "It all sounds logical, Peter, but I somehow suspect you of being up to trouble."

"I am taking a slight risk by remaining. Your coming here so unexpectedly may cause real trouble."

She grinned. "Bawl me out, Peter. I love it when you bawl me out. You're the only man I ever knew who can make me like it."

"When we said good-by in Hong Kong," Peter said, "after that little opium affair aboard the City of Swatow, we agreed that it would be safer for everybody concerned if we didn't see each other again. Unless I am mistaken, that was your own suggestion. You said you were going to find a nice, pleasant young man, marry him, and settle down."

"Ah, yes," Susan said, mocking his seriousness, "but that was before I knew how I would miss the fun we have together. After I gave Cyril the air, I knew that the one thing I wanted in life was to go looking for thrills with you, my dear. What are you going to do about it?"

BY MAKING quite a business of lighting a cigarette, Pater sparred for time; and in the few seconds at his disposal he reviewed his thrills with Susan. He did not know what to do about Susan O'Gilvie. Perhaps another man would not have hesitated. Susan was young, beautiful, generous and very rich. She didn't know how much she was worth, but it was well up in the millions. She loved thrills. The more dangerous they were, the better.

Peter, a veteran of more hair-raising adventures on the China coast and elsewhere than he cared to think about, wanted his hair raised no more. He had met Susan on the trip across from San Francisco; had saved her from a band of scheming, cutthroat Orientals and delivered her safely in Yokohama. Instead of going back to America as he had hoped she would, Susan followed him to Shanghai and plunged him into trouble with a Chinese secret society—trouble from which he had, almost miraculously, saved them both.

Still uncured of her adventurous fever, still thirsting for greater excitement, Susan next defied him by purchasing a cargo of opium which she intended to smuggle past the blockade into Macao. Once again she had been victimized. Once again Peter schemed and fought to save her from trouble and the threat which her greed for excitement had brought against their lives.

Sometimes he thought he was in love with Susan, and sometimes he wished he had never seen her lovely eager face nor heard the sound of her voice, which was clear and sweet and, like the rest of her, curiously suggestive of romance.

She was in one of her demure moods now—sweet and wistful, and doing her utmost to show him that she meant to be a nice, untroublesome girl. In these moods, he had learned, Susan was at her most dangerous. Something was brewing.

But when he looked into her deep violet eyes, so young, so friendly, he was apt to forget all the rest and to tell himself what a great little pal she was.

This meant that a conflict went on within Peter, and the result of the conflict was usually a grouch, which was contrary to Peter Moore's nature, because he was generally the most cheerful and amiable of men. He decided to come to the point at once.

"Susan, if you knew what the conditions are here, you wouldn't have come ashore. The captain should have told you."

"He did," the violet-eyed girl said.

"Did he tell you what's going on here tonight?"

"Why, yes!"

"Don't you realize," Peter asked indignantly, "that this town is so dangerous while these celebrations are going on that all the white men in Hai-Phang have gone to the hills?"

"That's funny," Susan said, wrinkling her lovely brow.

"What's funny?"

"I always thought you were a white man. Don't tell me you've been deceiving me! Don't tell me you're really a Chinaman!"

"I am staying here," Peter said stiffly, "for business reasons. If I went, I might miss Fong Toy."

"Just the same," the beautiful trouble-maker said, "you're here—and there's excitement brewing. I suspected it! I knew I'd find you here, just waiting to start something. Peter, you're wonderful! I've taken a room down the hall. My luggage is being moved in now. If you need help, holler. I won't handicap you as I've done in the past. I've been practicing with my automatic. I am a good shot."

"This town," Peter said firmly, "is dangerous enough for me. If it's risky for me, it's doubly risky for you."

"Why?"

"As you know, I got in hot water here five years ago. I am taking absolutely no part in these birthday celebrations. As for you, you are going aboard that ship—and you're going to be aboard when she pulls out tonight."

"I won't be bullied," Susan declared. "That old hulk is going to Saigon, Bangkok and Singapore. Her speed is six knots an hour. I haven't the slightest interest in Saigon, Bangkok or Singapore. Besides, I am tremendously interested in these Ungese. I've heard Ungism is the most picturesque religion in the Far East."

"It's the most horrible religion in the world," Peter said. "Come over here. Don't go too near the rail. Don't let them see you. Look at their faces."

Susan looked. She saw yellow and bronze and copper faces. They didn't look any more savage to her than the faces she had seen in Shanghai and Hong Kong, and she said so.

"Your marksmanship wouldn't be of much help if that mob took it into their heads to start trouble. I hope you haven't come here to mix into Ungism. You'd be better off if you put your head in a tiger's mouth. Keep back from that rail. Don't let that priest see you."

Susan laughed softly. "You're jealous," she said. "You can't tolerate another man looking at me. You adore me, but you won't say so. You're afraid people would say you were a fortune hunter."

"Listen," Peter commanded; "when this procession is past, you're going back to that ship. You will connect with a Messageries Maritimes liner in Saigon that will land you on the dock at Marseilles. That's your program."

SUSAN DID not argue. She gave him a mischievous smile and sat down on a chair behind the white bars of the grilled balcony. She had learned that the easiest way to deal with Peter was to let him roar at her until he tired of the pastime, then to smother him with one of her demure glances, tilting her head down so that he saw her eyes through their long curving lashes.

"I want you to see this procession," Peter said in a hard voice. "I want you to get the idea."

"Yes, Peter," she answered meekly.

A clashing of cymbals and a hollow booming of gourds came to them from the bund. The ranks of pilgrims in the street parted and a lane was formed.

Susan, peering out between white bars, saw six bronzed men with wild blue-black hair leading the procession in a weirdly oriental dance. Save for breech-clouts, they were naked. Each of them carried in one hand a long thin dagger, red with blood. The six shouted and leaped into the air in time with the booming of the gourds.

At intervals, each of the six would, in turn, pierce the fleshy part of his forearm or upper arm with the dagger, pushing it on through until the point came out the other side. Blood was flowing freely. The men's arms and faces were smeared with blood.

Peter was watching Susan. He saw her sink her teeth into her lower lip. She had turned pale. For a moment he thought she was going to faint.

"Those six," he said, "are priests of the so-called inner temple. Their self-stabbing is a preliminary. It is intended to get the crowd excited. By morning, the big compound of the black temple will be a lake of blood and Ung will be satisfied for another year. You can see the temple, beyond that grove of mahoganies."

"It's horrible. Peter."

The crowds lining the streets were shouting, yelling, screaming. And in these voices was a note of fanatical madness.

"I've watched the Chitties in Singapore drive thin spikes into their arms," Peter was saying. "But this is different. The Chitties don't believe, as these Ungese do, that their god is drinking the blood they draw. Ung is a horrible god; and Ungism is the rottenest of all the degenerate Eastern religions."

"Who was Ung?"

"It's hard to say—so much legend has grown up about him. According to Professor Dowles, at the University of Peking, Ung was a gigantic Abyssinian Negro who somehow found his way to this country. The old legends say he was twenty-two feet tall. He may have been eight. At all events, he was a true giant.

"Because he was black and such a giant, these people took him to be a god. He founded Ungism, which is a religion of sacrifice and wrath. That is, an Ungese makes awful sacrifices to Ung so that he won't incur his wrath. He certainly got a firm hold on these people's imagination. Ungism has been a religion in this part of Indo-China for almost four hundred years. It doesn't seem to spread or shrink.

"I don't believe more than three white men have been inside that black temple. The Ungese are much more savage with white curiosity seekers than the Burmese priests at the Schwe Dagon, in Rangoon."

"You were in it, Peter."

"That was five years ago."

"What did you see?"

PETER NARROWED his eyes. "I don't remember much. It was at night. I went into a black corridor and finally found myself in a room containing an altar. The walls looked like pure gold. There was a dais in the center, a kind of pyramid with steps of carved gold. On the topmost step was a heavily carved gold box. That was what I was after. They say the largest ruby ever mined is in that box. You see, Ung loved rubies. He was mad about them. He didn't care for diamonds, emeralds, sapphires or other precious stones. But he loved fine rubies. You'll find the ruby very prominent in all Ungese rituals and ceremonies. K'ong, the high priest of the inner temple, wears one on his hat.

"The story that came to me was that if that ruby could be stolen, the power of Ung would be broken. I thought it would be a noble idea to steal the great ruby."

"It would be a wonderful idea!" Susan cried.

"So I thought. So I went into the ruby shrine, intending to grab it. As I say, I don't remember clearly what happened. It was very mysterious and very oriental. The atmosphere in that room suddenly seemed to turn black. Not gray. But black—as if blackness were oozing out of the very walls and floor. There were two great gold incense burners, one on either side of the golden box. When I first went in, a pinkish-gray smoke was spiralling up from these burners. Overhead, there were two oil lights—dongs—hanging by fine gold chains from the ceiling. Even that light seemed to be black light. It sounds ridiculous. Some kind of magic."

"Some one crept up behind you and walloped you," Susan suggested.

"No. It wasn't like that. It was really magical and pretty terrifying. I knew that something worse was on the way. And suddenly there were black-robed men all around me."

"Why didn't they kill you?"

"I was lucky. I got away. Later that night, K'ong, the head priest, came down to my ship. I was a wireless operator then. He came aboard at midnight—came right up to the wireless house on the top deck. I can still see those cold yellow eyes of his. He just wanted to look me over. He said very little, but he spoke English as well as you and I do. He stared at me with those yellow eyes and told me that if I ever ventured near that temple again, he would carve my heart and stomach out with his own hands. And he smiled at me all the time he was talking. There were two priests with him—men over six feet tall. They kept their arms folded, and they kept looking at me as if they'd love to help K'ong do that carving job."

"Weren't you absolutely terrified?"

"Yes—and mystified. As you know, these harbors are full of river pirates. My skipper had all the crew on deck, armed, and on the lookout for pirates. There were men on every deck—white men, not Orientals or Eurasians. In spite of their close watch, K'ong and his bodyguard came and went without being seen.

How did they come aboard? How did they get away? I asked
the skipper. He questioned every man in the crew. In the end,
he said I must have been seeing things. I haven't the slightest
desire to cross K'ong's path again."

Susan was looking at him with shining eyes. "But you're going
to, aren't you, darling?"

"Absolutely not."

"But wouldn't you be willing to sacrifice your life for such a
worthy cause?"

"Yes—if I accomplished my object. If there were a real possi-
bility of my securing that ruby and bringing Ungism to an
end—yes. But why throw my life away when I've proved to my
satisfaction that it cannot be done?"

But the light that he had kindled in Susan's eyes did not
die down. And it was destined to flame much brighter before
many minutes had passed. Susan was an idealist—and a born
trouble-maker. It was a dangerous combination to be at large in
Hai-Phang on the birthday of Ung the Unspeakable.

CHAPTER III

THE WHIRLING DEATH

AFTER THE SIX priests of the inner temple followed the
"musicians"—black-robed men furiously clashing cymbals and
beating on gourds with bones.

"Human bones," Peter said, and added: "You have heard of
the horrible practices of Voodooism. They can't compare with
the practices of Ungism."

Susan was looking down. Behind a long line of priests came
a narrow teak platform lashed to two long bamboo poles which
were carried on the shoulders of a dozen coolies. On this platform lay a terrified native girl—naked. She lay on her side,
huddling in a pallet of straw, staring up with wet blurred eyes

at the hot blue afternoon sky. A trickle of blood, flowed down
to the rounded point of her chin from the corner of her mouth.
A wail, strange and terrifying, issued from her parched lips. It
attacked the nerves of the listener like the sustained note of a
violin.

Susan darted a quick glance at Peter.

"Who is she?"

Peter was pale. "An offering to Ung."

"What do you mean?"

"Once a year a young girl is selected as an offering to Ung.
She tops the climax of a night of varied tortures, in which men's
hands and feet are chopped off and their eyes gouged out—men
who have offended K'ong. Ung's mantle has descended from
high priest to high priest, to K'ong. Ung is now K'ong. K'ong is
all powerful. I don't suppose there's a man living in the world
today with unquestioned power of life and death over men and
women, except K'ong.

"Sacrificing this girl carries out a custom established by Ung
four centuries ago. I don't know how they kill her, but I've heard
they cut her heart out—without benefit of anæsthetic—and
squeeze the blood on that great ruby in the inner temple."

"Peter, I simply can't believe it!"

"Quaint little custom, isn't it?" Peter replied. "Their process
of selecting the girl makes it even more interesting. The Ungese
priests of various districts hold a sort of vote. The girl who is said
to be most deeply in love is selected. Ung, you see, was a great
lover. He loved love. They say he ran through three hundred
wives and heaven only knows how many concubines. A god
among gods was Ung—ruthless, destroying, potent."

"I simply can't believe," Susan muttered, "that they're going
to murder that child."

"They will assure her," Peter said, "that it is a great honor
being conferred on her."

"WHY," SUSAN demanded, "doesn't somebody do something

about it? Why don't the French bring gunboats into port and mow them down?"

"There has been a great deal of trouble," Peter said. "When the French first took this province, they tried to wipe out Ungism. They went so far as to bombard the temple. That same night, the French ministers in Peking, Tokyo and Bangkok mysteriously died. French consuls in half a dozen ports along the coast were found dead in bed next morning. How was it done? Ask K'ong!

"The next attempt the French made on Ungism was backed up with five companies of colonial troops. They chased the Ungese army into the jungles. Not one officer, not one soldier, was ever seen again. The jungle mysteriously swallowed them up. So the French authorities decided it would be simpler to let the Ungese alone.

"By a tacit agreement, all the white residents of Hai-Phang go off for a holiday to Wanglat once a year—on Ung's birthday. Perhaps K'ong is a sorcerer. Perhaps he knows how to use some kind of oriental black magic. Since that affair, twenty years ago, he has been let alone. And commerce goes on. This country is rich, prosperous. After all, what's one unknown native girl per year?"

"Peter, you don't mean that?"

"Of course I don't mean it. But what can I do about it? I tried—five years ago. If I could prevent the yearly sacrifice by throwing my life away, I would. But I would only be killed."

"That poor child!"

The brown-skinned girl vanished into the mist of golden dust kicked up by the naked feet of the pilgrims and the sandals of the black-robed priests, but her awful wailing lingered in the air.

A golden palanquin now came into view. It was carried on the shoulders of twenty men dressed in bright red robes. The gilded roof of the palanquin went up to a sharp peak like that of a Cambodian pagoda. At the crest of the peak was mounted a ruby as bright as a drop of fresh blood.

Susan heard Peter say, in a harsh whisper, "That's K'ong! Don't let him see you!"

Reclining on the cushions in the palanquin was a man who looked old, although he might have been any age. His skin was the parched yellow skin of an old war drum, and he had the coldly glowing yellow eyes of the black leopard. They seemed full of curiosity, somehow denying the evil smile which flickered at his cruel thin mouth. He was glancing everywhere—at the faces pressing about him, at the windows of shops and houses along the Street of the Red Lion.

The high priest of Ung fixed his yellow eyes on the barred grille behind which Susan and Peter sat. He could not possibly see beyond those bars, because, to have done so, he must look into the glare of the setting sun and into the darkness of the balcony. But it seemed to Susan that his eyes took on a sudden malignant gleam.

It was as if the wooden bars did not exist, as if K'ong were seeing through them and into her terrified, hating eyes. Then they shifted and glared at the spot where Peter was concealed.

They glared, and the smile became fixed, as if it were carved on a face of yellow marble.

Susan glanced quickly at Peter. He was as pale as death. She whispered: "Is he stopping?"

"I don't know."

"What will he do?"

Peter shook his head. She glanced down again. The palanquin had not stopped. But K'ong was bending out and looking up. What could he see? Susan saw the ruby on top of his hat. It was a strange-looking hat, of varnished brown reeds closely woven, coming up to a peak like the hats of the Japanese shoguns. On its peak the ruby gleamed and glowed like a phial of fresh blood.

AS SHE heard the crash of an over-turning chair in the bedroom behind them, Susan started. Both she and Peter looked into the room. Peter saw Wan Loo pick himself up from the floor and heard, in the distance, the sobbing wail of the girl whose life's blood was to appease the monstrous thirst of Ung.

It was all very confusing to Susan. She saw Wan Loo, the servant, pick himself up, then, glancing back, she saw that K'ong was smiling up at her, as if he saw her clearly by some kind of necromancy through the wooden grille. His teeth were yellow fangs. His yellow eyes seemed to brood on her terrified white face.

Peter saw nothing of this. He was intrigued by Wan Loo's actions. His old and faithful servant was stumbling toward the window at the end of the room. This window gave upon the courtyard in back. Peter saw Wan Loo lean far out and look up, then down, as if to investigate.

Then Wan Loo screamed out: "Master! Here! Quick!"—as if in the throes of mortal terror.

Peter leaped up and hurried into the bedroom. He was crossing the threshold when he was amazed to see what appeared to be a thin, whirling gold or brass disk, like a giant cymbal, float down through the air outside the window. It hovered a moment above Wan Loo like a metallic halo, spinning rapidly and striking glints from the sun, then it dropped before Peter could utter so much as a strangled warning.

Wan Loo gave another short, sharp scream. The disk darted upward like a moon on a string, scattering drops of blood as it spun—vanished! Wan Loo plunged from sight through the window into the courtyard.

Peter snatched his automatic pistol from a suitcase and ran on to the window. He saw his servant's headless body lying on the compound flagging. A half dozen feet from the body lay the head. Flies were buzzing around it. The courtyard was otherwise empty.

A wave of fury swept over Peter. He and Wan Loo had been like brothers. But there was nothing on which to vent his wrath. Below—a dead man in an empty compound. Above—blank white walls and shuttered windows. There was no sign of life. Nothing.

Susan screamed.

Peter ran out to the balcony to find her on her hands and knees, writhing. He would not have been surprised to see her head abruptly leave her body and go rolling into a corner. He felt sick and dazed.

Then he realized that she was struggling with something on the floor. He pulled her roughly aside and saw that the object of her attacks was a jade-handled dagger, similar in shape to the ones the six priests had been using. The blade was still sticky with blood. Four inches of it were embedded in the floor.

CHAPTER IV

GREEDY INVADERS

HE WRENCHED THE dagger free and saw that, close to the handle, it pierced a wad of rice paper. He slid the wad off the dagger and unfolded it. The wad became a long strip of rice paper covered with rows of oriental characters. In the lower right hand corner was a small blood-red seal, an official "chop."

Susan's shoulder was pressed tightly against his. She was shaking. She grasped his wrist and stared at the long columns of ideographs on the slip of paper.

"What does it say?"

"It's Tonkinese," Peter answered. "I can't translate it in so many words, but the gist of it is that K'ong, who knows all, hears all, sees all, knows I am here and that you are here with me. He has just murdered my Chinese boy, he says, as an indication of his disapproval and as a warning of what we may expect if we annoy him in the slightest degree. If either you or I step foot from this hotel, some dreadful thing will happen to us. The rest of it is taken up with assurances that he is the most dangerous, most ruthless, most powerful man in the world, with the power to read men's hearts and minds as if they were pictures under sheets of diamond glass."

Susan huddled closer to him and he was keenly aware of her trembling.

"How," she wanted to know, "did he kill Wan Loo?"

Peter described the mysterious murder, his eyes still blazing.

"But how?" Susan demanded. "How did he do it?"

Peter glared into the street. "I don't know."

"But, Peter, he didn't move from that palanquin. Look?"

The golden palanquin had advanced no more than half a block. Its occupant was leaning outward and looking back and up at the balcony. The ruby flashed. Suddenly, K'ong withdrew into the palanquin. The wail of the doomed native girl came thinly now, but somehow it pierced the other sounds.

"Peter, what are we going to do?"

"What K'ong says. Stay here. We don't leave this hotel on any pretext until tomorrow."

"Can't I go back to the ship?"

"Not now. Perhaps I'll find a way to smuggle you aboard shortly after it gets dark."

"Is it my fault?"

"Certainly not. What have you done? K'ong learned you had come ashore and to me. Not a man in Hai-Phang but is one of his spies."

Susan shivered and cuddled still closer to him.

"There was something in his eyes, Peter. It wasn't madness. He could hypnotize anybody. I believe he does these horrible things by sheer mental power. I say K'ong is a demon."

"I say," Peter suggested with a wan grin, "that we mix ourselves a drink. Wan Loo's last act on earth was to leave gin, limes and ice on the table. He assured me that one bout of drinking dispels three anxieties."

Susan clung to him. "I'm scared, Peter. I have the feeling that something frightful is going to happen to us."

"Don't worry. We won't stir from this building. We'll be perfectly safe. Come on; let's have that drink."

AS THEY started into the room, some one pounded heavily, slowly on the hall door. Three times.

Susan shrieked. "What was that? Did you hear that?"

Peter shook his arm free, slipped his pistol out of his pocket and ran to the door. He flung it open, holding the gun in readiness.

A giant with a black beard loomed in the dusk of the hall. He must have been close to seven feet in height. His white drill suit was wrinkled and baggy and soiled. Greedy, close-set blade eyes peered out from that hairy dark face.

"Your name Peter Moore?"

"Yes."

"I'm Charlie Ling—'Shanghai Charlie.' Put that rod down. I've got a friendly proposition."

Peter considered him a moment, then stepped back to admit him, and dropped the pistol into his pocket. He had heard of the big Eurasian, and little that he had heard was savory. The son of a British sea captain and a Chinese sing-song girl, the half-caste had grown up on the Shanghai water front and had amassed something of a fortune in dark and sinister ways— piracy, opium smuggling, slaving.

Charlie Ling was staring at Susan and licking his lips. His eyes crinkled. He grinned, revealing blackened stubs of teeth. Susan maneuvered to a position behind Peter, where she gazed at the big Eurasian with fascination and terror.

"Excuse me, little lady," the bearded giant rumbled in his thick voice, "but I've got some business to discuss with this gentleman."

Susan said nothing. She had never seen a man so tall nor so dangerous-looking.

"It's nothing we can't all discuss," Peter said.

Shanghai Charlie looked at him thoughtfully, with the air of a man measuring a dangerous antagonist.

"I've heard a lot about you," he remarked. "For the past six, seven years I've been hearin' what a cool, dangerous article Peter Moore is. I've heard that you spit icicles on the Equator." The bearded giant chuckled. "They tell me you're quick on the draw, quick with a knife, and quicker yet with your mitts. It's a pleasure to meet you. You and I could go a long way together. What are you doin' in Hai-Phang?"

"Supposing," Peter said coldly, "we take up the object of your visit."

The bearded man chuckled. He was looking at the table on which stood a bottle of gin, a bowl of limes, another bowl of cracked ice, several bottles of charged water and some drinking glasses. He picked up a lime, sniffed it, and put it down. He looked at Peter and grinned.

"Mind if I have a little drink? It's been a hard day."

"Help yourself."

"Thanks."

Shanghai Charlie uncorked the gin bottle, poured himself a brimming glassful and drank it down neat without blinking. He wiped his mouth with the back of one hairy paw. Then he extracted a long thick black cigar from his pocket, chewed off the end, spat it out on the floor, and struck a match.

"Mind if I set down?"

He selected the strongest-looking chair in the room and seated himself. His beady little black eyes did a kind of dance between Peter and Susan.

"I'M GOING to come clean," he said. "I'm in Hai-Phang on a job. I want your help, Mr. Moore; it's the kind of a job that's right up your street. If I'm interferin' with your caper, just say so. There's a lot of bad joss in this town, and we white men have got to stick together."

He puffed amiably at the cigar.

"Tied up to the Yang Gan dock, Mr, Moore, is my junk—the Smilin' Eye. On board that junk at this minute are twelve of the hardest, toughest fightin' men on the China coast—my gang. Every one of them boys is a dead shot. Every one is an American. Mostly they're gunmen from Chicago and New York. I have things very well organized. I have a Diesel engine in the Smilin' Eye, but you would never suspect it to look at her. Wide open, she can do better than sixteen knots. Each one of my twelve boys is an expert with a sub-machine gun. I have enough ammunition on board the Smilin' Eye to mow down an army. Do you follow me, Mr. Moore? I'm equipped for making a lot of trouble for somebody."

He paused and looked at Susan.

"You needn't look at me like that, little lady. I am not declaring war on you. I am simply spreading my cards. I have been anchored in this harbor for three weeks, sizing things up. I have been learning all I can about a guy named K'ong. Maybe you think I am bluffing. Shanghai Charlie never bluffs. For example, I know that you and your boy-friend here are on a spot. I know that if you step out of this hotel before tomorrow, this guy K'ong is goin' to take you both for a ride."

Susan stared at him incredulously. "How did you find that out?" she gasped.

Shanghai Charlie chuckled. "Lady, I may look like I was born this mornin', but appearances are deceivin'. I have my own personal secret service. Today is my big day. The French authorities think they have turned this town over to K'ong for twenty-four hours. What they don't realize is that they have turned it over to Shanghai Charlie Ling. Until tomorrow, I am the king of Hai-Phang. Got that?"

"I'm beginning to see a design," Peter said.

"It will get clearer as I go along. You know that this guy K'ong has this town on a spot. You know he has these yellow-bellies on a spot. They think, if he lifts a finger, a thousand men drop dead. Maybe that is so. But I'm not afraid of this guy K'ong. I'm not afraid of anybody, white, yellow, or black.

"This religion K'ong heads is a terrible religion. It ought to be stamped out. I'm the man who is goin' to stamp it out. My system is simple. Up there in that big black temple is a gold room. In that gold room is a sort of gold pyramid built against a gold wall. It makes my mouth water to talk about it. On top of that gold pyramid is a gold box. And in that gold box is the biggest ruby in the world. They say it weighs six hundred carats. I don't know. I don't care. I know it is the biggest ruby in the world and I want to get it.

"If that ruby is stolen, Ungism as a religion falls apart like a house made out of cards when you give it a kick. That's my idea. The religion is a terrible religion. It ought to be stamped out. If some one stamps it out, he gets the ruby." And he grinned.

CHAPTER V

STRAINED NERVES

"SUPPOSING," SHANGHAI CHARLIE proposed eagerly, "you and I got that ruby, Mr. Moore. How much is it worth? A cold million? I don't know. Nobody knows, because a ruby that big, that perfect, has never been offered on the market. Supposing you and I got that ruby. It would have to be cut up to be sold anyhow. We would cut it in half. You get half; I get half. What do you say?"

Peter shook his head. "I'm not interested."

"But look at the good you would be doin', Mr. Moore. Do you know that this time every year they take a poor little native girl up to that temple and cut her heart out and squeeze the blood on that ruby as a sacrifice to Ung?"

"I know."

"And you can sit there and not lift a hand while year after year they murder a poor, innocent, helpless girl like that?"

"It's horrible!" Susan exclaimed.

"And it would be so easy to stop," Shanghai Charlie persisted. "You've been there, Mr. Moore. You know the way. That's why I want your help. All you've got to do is to show us the way. My boys with their sub-machine guns will blaze a path for you and me. I'd trust them to blaze a path through hell. It ain't the ruby I want. It's to put an end to this terrible practice of killin' poor, helpless, innocent girls. Ungism is horrible. It ought to be wiped off the face of the earth."

"Indeed it should!" Susan agreed warmly. That adventurous light was shining in her eyes. Peter saw it; saw that she had forgotten her fear of K'ong, forgotten her instant and instinctive distrust of this black-bearded giant. "I'd love to help!" she said impulsively.

"Lady," said Shanghai Charlie, "I don't want to hurt your feelings, but I don't want your help. I've heard about you. I heard about the jam you got into in Shanghai with the Green Circle. I heard about the jam you got into with that load of opium on the City of Swatow. You are one of these ladies who like to smoke cigarettes around dynamite."

"But this is different!" Susan pleaded. "I'm a good shot with a pistol. You could explain a sub-machine gun to me. I'd love to use one and help get that ruby."

Shanghai Charlie looked at her thoughtfully, doubtfully. He looked at her slim, pretty ankles, then ran his eyes up slowly to her slim waist, then up more slowly to her throat and hesitated there. He licked his lips.

"I'd be afraid to trust you," replied Ling. "What do you think, Moore?"

"I think it would be perfectly wonderful!" Susan cried.

"I agree with her," Peter said. "Your idea *is* wonderful."

"Don't kid me," the half-caste snarled. "You think I'm crazy. I am crazy—like a fox. I've got things perfectly organized."

"I want to help," Susan insisted.

"That's the spirit," said Shanghai Charlie. "How are you voting, Mr. Moore?"

"No," Peter said firmly; "and that goes for Miss O'Gilvie and me. To begin with, Ling, I don't trust you. In the second place, your idea is impractical. Thirdly, what possible help could this girl be to you?"

"She can handle a gun, can't she? I can use anybody who can handle a gun. I want you because you know the ins and outs of these people; and I want her to help us in pinches."

"The idea is," Peter said, "we go to the temple, steal the big ruby, then all go aboard the Smiling Eye—Miss O'Gilvie, me, you and your twelve gunmen."

"That's the idea, Mr. Moore. What's wrong with it?"

"Everything," Peter said. "I'm sorry, Ling, but we aren't interested in your proposition."

"Yellow?" Charlie Ling sneered.

Susan was looking at Peter with impatience. The lust for excitement, gunplay, oriental adventure was blazing brightly in her deep violet eyes. She was a changed girl.

"You can count on me, Mr. Ling."

"No," Peter contradicted.

"I'll do what I please," she snapped.

"You'll do what I say," Peter said grimly. "You may go, Ling."

The half-caste, who was looking hopefully at Susan, ignored Peter and said to her:

"You can find the Yang Gan wharf easy, Miss O'Gilvie, if you change your mind. Just wear something black and keep your face shadowed. Here's some stuff you can put on it. It's a kind of powder that actors use—brown." He gave her a small flat tin. "The Smilin' Eye is the only junk in port. There's a red and white striped flag flyin' at the masthead. She's black and shiny. You can't miss her—"

"Get out of here at once!" Peter ordered.

The bearded man backed to the door. He was grinning at Susan as if they shared a secret. With his hand on the knob, he urged:

"If you want the biggest thrill of your life, Miss O'Gilvie, and if you want to help stop this horrible yearly sacrifice of help-less, innocent girls—come down to the Smilin' Eye before ten tonight. We'll be gettin' under way at ten."

He opened the door, went out and slammed it behind him.

ANGRILY SUSAN glared at Peter.

"Why are you so stubborn? You know it wouldn't be half as dangerous as dozens of your stunts."

"You've already seen," Peter replied, "that K'ong is as danger-ous as a mad cobra."

"But Ling's twelve men with those sub-machine guns—"

"How do you know that Ling is telling the truth?"

"What do you mean?"

"Shanghai Charlie is probably the toughest, most dangerous crook on the China coast. He has never hesitated at murder. Supposing he is telling the truth. Supposing the scheme goes through, and we all get to sea on that junk with the ruby. What then?"

"We've crushed Ungism, haven't we? That's what we want to do, isn't it?"

"Ling," Peter answered, "knows you are a rich girl. Once he has you on that junk, then what?"

"I see," Susan laughed, mocking him. " 'Once aboard the lugger and the girl is mine.' You make me furious. I'm certain he doesn't mean the slightest harm to me."

"Did you see him looking you over?"

"Most men look me over. I've managed to take very good care of myself."

She paused. Darkness had fallen suddenly. It was so dark in the room she could not see Peter's face. Over the hubbub in the streets she heard a faint sobbing wail, like the sustained note of a violin.

"Peter!" Susan cried. "I can't stand it. Do you hear it?"

"Yes."

"How can you stand there and not want to do something?"

"Perhaps Ling was right. Perhaps I'm yellow."

"We've got to do something. Peter, why can't just the two of us slip up there and take that ruby? You know the way. I'll go with you. I'm not afraid. Supposing we do get killed. It would be worth it."

"No." Peter refused bluntly.

He knew that Susan was on the verge of hysteria. He knew that the madness of the night was in her veins. In the darkness she crept close to him. Her arms went around his neck.

"Peter, let's do it. We might succeed." He pushed her hands away. Susan began to cry. "I can't stand it!" she repeated. "I'd rather die myself than let them murder that poor child. We're going to do it!"

"Listen," Peter ordered, trying to calm her. "Go to your room. Lie down awhile and try to pull yourself together. I'll call in a couple of hours and we'll have dinner. After dinner I'll try to take you to the *Java Bird*."

"I don't want to go to the *Java Bird*. I want to go to that temple!"

"It's about six now," Peter said. "We'll have dinner at eight."

He heard her heavy breathing in the darkness.

"I hate you!" she cried. "I wish I'd never met you. You're always ruining my plans."

"I've done my best," Peter said dryly.

"But this is different! The others were foolish and—and selfish. If we could crush this horrible religion—"

"Dinner," Peter said, "eight o'clock sharp."

"Very well!" Susan snapped, and went out.

SHE WENT down the hall and into her room and switched on a light. She began to pace up and down between the hall door and the door which gave upon the balcony. She turned out the light, went to the balcony rail and looked out over the city.

In the distance she could see the lights of the *Java Bird*. Below her, in the Street of the Red Lion, mobs were churning. The glare from torches lighted her face. She saw a man pierce the palm of his hand with a long thin knife.

Her nails bit into her own palms and her teeth sank into her lower lip. A group of men went past savagely singing; it was like the cries of animals in the jungle. Far away, over the rooftops, she could see the black spire of the temple silhouetted against the stars.

Then, from the direction of the temple compound, above the babble of voices in the streets, she heard, or imagined she heard, the shrill sobbing wail of the girl who was going to be sacrificed. She saw, in imagination, that girl being led up the steps to the temple; saw K'ong plunge a knife into her bosom while, no doubt, her lover looked on.

Listening to that faint, violin-like wail, Susan saw a procession of such helpless, innocent victims being led up into the temple; saw K'ong plunging a knife into the breast of each; heard the girl's gurgling death cry.

"I can't stand it!" Susan muttered nervously. She returned to her bedroom, turned on the light, and picked up the small flat can that Shanghai Charlie had given her. She removed the lid. In the can was a brown powder.

In something of a frenzy, Susan smeared cold cream on her face, dusted on the brown powder with a powder puff. The effect was strange and wild. Her deep violet eyes stared out from her brown face alarmingly. She looked like an actress. To herself she was a heroine.

She opened a suitcase and removed from it a black coat. It was not what Susan wanted, but it would do. She slipped into the coat, then rummaged about until she found a silk blouse of midnight blue. This she tried draping about her head until it somewhat resembled the black hoods worn by some of the Ungese priests.

The effect, generally, was satisfying. She glanced at her wrist watch. Shanghai Charlie had said ten o'clock. With luck, she would be back here long before then—and wouldn't Peter be proud of her!

If her luck failed, if she lost her life—what of it? What was her life, measured against the lives of all those girls?

Susan hesitated long enough to dash off a note to Peter. She went out, leaving her light burning, her door slightly ajar, after placing the note conspicuously on her dresser. She intended to have in her possession, when she returned, the largest, wickedest ruby in the world!

CHAPTER VI

THE BLACK TEMPLE

DOWN THE HALL Susan tiptoed, and discovered a back stairway. For obvious reasons she did not wish to go through the hotel lobby. With her small automatic pistol comfortingly in her hand, she descended the stairs, opened a door, and found herself outdoors in the semi-darkness of the compound.

A man lying in the compound momentarily terrified her. The man was headless. Some few feet away she saw his head lying. K'ong had, with his black magic, done that to Wan Loo. Susan overcame her fright and hastened out of the compound.

Crowds surging in the streets caught her in their tide, the mass of men and women moving toward the black temple. A copper-colored man with a torch glared at her, then glanced away. Slowly the mobs were milling toward the temple. Susan tried to force her way through them, but they would not let her pass. It took her an hour to go five blocks, and she had still not covered a third of the way.

Finding a side street, she took that and escaped the mob, which was approaching the temple by the main roads. Susan circled about until she was behind the temple. There were no crowds here. She did not know it, but she was now in forbidden territory—streets and lanes reserved for the exclusive use of K'ong and his highest priests.

The great mile-square mound on which the temple stood loomed above her, and above that towered the great four-hundred-foot spire of the infamous pagoda. It was raised above her like a naked black sword held ready to strike.

Susan sought the deepest shadow and glanced at her watch. She was alarmed to find how much time had passed. If Charlie Ling and his gunmen were coming to the temple—if he had not lied—she did not want to be in the vicinity when he staged his attack. But she did not think he intended to stage an attack; she was now convinced that Shanghai Charlie had been lying. There was only one way to secure the ruby—her way, simply and directly and without noise.

She was conscious of danger, of threat on every side. Things were top calm here, too quiet. Above, in the vast courtyard, she heard the screams and shouts of men. Now and then, through the noise, she heard, or imagined she heard, the thin wail of the girl who was to be sacrificed. When? She must reach the temple, secure the ruby, and escape before that sacrifice took place.

A sudden feeling of dismay and discouragement overwhelmed the American girl. Peter Moore had failed. Other men had been afraid to try. They had been afraid of losing their lives. That was where she had the advantage. She would willingly lose her life, if she could only secure that ruby.

A LONG flight of steps confronted Susan. They would lead, she knew, to the back of the temple. What awaited her at the top of these glistening black steps? Susan climbed them cautiously, Every few steps she paused and looked behind, ahead, and to both sides. The steep slope was covered with a rank growth. Odors of flowers assailed her, southern oriental night flowers which she had never smelled before. The air was sickly sweet with the concentrated fragrance.

Halfway up the long flight of steps, she stopped. Almost paralyzed, she had to sit down and recover her strength. Terror welled up within her. Her heart was beating in a panic. Her throat was dry. But she gripped the automatic, found comfort in her knowledge that it would account for nine men if her hand was steady, and climbed on.

The base of the black temple was surrounded with innumerable small shrines, each containing, in black quartz or malachite, an effigy of Ung, a great brooding, black god, low of forehead, thick of jaws—a beast of a man in life, a fiend in his influence since death.

The invader made her way stealthily among these shrines. Candles were burning at some, incense at others. Wherever she looked, she saw the black god Ung staring at her. It was like a nightmare. Narrow lanes led between shrines, and these lanes were full of leaping, threatening black shadows cast by the flickering candles.

The folly of her expedition occurred to her again as she stared at the shining black wall of the malachite temple. There would be dozens, hundreds of doors. Doubtless the temple would be swarming with priests. She only hoped that they would be out in the courtyard.

She reached the temple wall and cowered in deep shadow. Above her the tower rose, shining faintly in the candlelight of the numerous shrines, reaching up and up above her until it tapered into the stars.

Fury at the temple and the horrors it stood for replaced her terror. Her heart quieted. She slid along the wall and came to a bronze door. It was green with erosion. Susan pushed the door, but it did not give. It was as solid as the rock into which it had been set.

She went on fifty feet, and found another door. It similarly was solid and unyielding. On another fifty feet—another door. This one showed evidence of use. It had a heavy bronze handle.

Susan stopped with her hand on the bronze handle. What would she find beyond that door?

SHE PUT her ear against it and listened. She was startled to hear a thumping as of the beating of a giant's heart, and her own heart leaped into a frantic beating. Then she told herself that the beating was nothing but the measured thumping of the great drums in the compound; so penetrating a sound that it reached through the earth and reverberated in the very walls of the black temple.

Susan drew a deep breath, gripped the automatic, and swung the door open. She stifled a scream of terror. A tall man in black stood just within the door with folded arms, staring down at her. Dangling by a thong from his wrist was a long curved sword, red with blood.

The black-hooded man was momentarily as surprised as she. He uttered a sharp, sibilant sentence in an unknown tongue and grasped the bloodstained sword.

Susan aimed at where she thought his heart would be. She heard the echo of the shot come bounding back to her from the far-distant end of the black corridor.

The man in the black hood slipped without a sound to the black stone flagging.

With pounding heart the girl waited. Certainly that shot would summon some one. But no one came. The noise in the compound had evidently swallowed up the single sharp explosion. There was still time to retreat. An odor of stale incense floated out of the corridor. Behind her lay safety—the hotel— the comforting presence of Peter. Should she go on, or should she not?

Susan stepped over the body of the guard and proceeded on tiptoe down the corridor. She passed a flight of steps carved in the black rock. Hesitating, she struck a match and regretted that she had not brought along a flash light

The feeble glare of the match lighted smooth black walls, richly carved. The steps went up into nothingness. Susan extinguished the match under her heel and went on.

The corridor ended abruptly in another bronze door. Again the youthful venturer hesitated. She estimated that the corridor had taken her two hundred feet toward the heart of the temple. But what lay beyond this door? She fumbled for a knob and found it. Gripping the automatic, she pulled the door open. Again she was amazed at what was revealed.

CHAPTER VII

A GRISLY RELIC

CANDLES LIGHTED A room perhaps fifty feet square. There was a round slab of black stone raised ten or twelve inches from the floor in the very center of it. Otherwise, the room was empty.

Susan struck a match and examined the slab. Her heart leaped. It was covered with splashes of fresh blood. Her hand was shaking so that she dropped the match. It fell into a pool of blood and, hissing, expired. Was this a sacrificial room?

Several doors led from it, but only one was set into the wall opposite the door by which she had entered. That door would, presumably, lead on to the heart of the temple.

Cautiously she opened it. Another corridor. It was wider than the first. The black flagging was worn by centuries of passing bare feet. Susan advanced down it, and her fear increased as she progressed. So far, her only confederate had been luck. Beginner's luck, she told herself. Five minutes earlier, five minutes later, she might have encountered a dozen, fifty priests. Where were they?

Faintly through the walls she could hear the beating of drums, the hollow booming of gourds, the clashing of cymbals, and the shouts and screams of men and women. The black walls seemed to press in upon her, to smother her.

She remembered what Peter had said: "The atmosphere suddenly seemed to turn black, as if blackness were oozing out of the very walls and floor."

Susan would not have been surprised at anything. If doors along the corridor had opened and she had been surrounded by howling men in black with bloody knives, if the very walls had closed in on her and crushed her to a boneless pulp, she would not have been surprised.

But she was prepared to shoot the first thing that moved.

The good fortune that had so far attended her took her into custody again at the door at which the corridor ended. Still another impassive bronze door loomed up, beyond which might lay anything. She drew it open as she had the others, with her automatic in readiness. And she knew that she must be close to the heart of the black temple.

Candles set into wall niches dimly illumined a curving passageway. She traversed it for fifty feet and found, about every ten feet, a door. This passageway, she presumed, was circular. Within the circle, no doubt, was the shrine to Ung. At last she had reached the Ungese holy of holies.

Susan paused at one of these doors and removed her shoes. Their high heels clicked on the black flagging. She also stripped off her stockings because, when she walked, they made a whispering sound as her knees passed one another.

She placed the shoes with the stockings on them where they would be handy when she escaped—if she ever did escape. With an effort to calm her frantic heart, she drew a deep breath and, holding the automatic in readiness for what might confront her, she opened the door.

The room she entered was, without question, the inner shrine of the unspeakable Ung.

AGAINST ONE curving wall was the famous gold pyramid, solid shelves of gold, wide at the base, narrower toward the top.

It was built against the wall in an equal curve, and it curved also at the front The pyramid went up until it vanished in black mists.

The atmosphere of the room was golden. Only the floor was black. The walls were slabs of gold. They were inset with rubies. Susan stopped and stared in wonderment. She may have had dreams of lavish oriental magnificence, but none of them could compare with this actuality.

So dazed was she by the golden richness of the shrine that she did not for a moment appreciate that danger was close at hand. She was drinking in details—heavy gold incense burners on the bottom step of the pyramid, heavy gold dongs suspended by fine gold chains and giving off a truly golden light—these she was staring at when she saw, a few feet from the base of the golden pyramid, two men crouched.

Susan's automatic flew up. Then she saw that the two men were priests. The sleeve of one had fallen back, and she saw that the arm was bleeding in a dozen places. And she realized that these two must have been among the priests who, a few hours ago, she had seen stabbing themselves in the street procession. In the posture of Buddhas, they were squatting now and sleeping with exhaustion.

The seeker did not hesitate. On silent bare feet she ran between them to the pyramid. With only one glance behind her, she climbed up the steps of gold toward the black shadows at the summit.

She left the light of the dongs behind her, below her. For that golden flight went up and up and up into the darkness. A new kind of fear possessed her. If she could have seized the golden box and made off with it, her nerves would have stood the strain, but the endlessness of the pyramid plunged her again into terror. The two sleeping priests became two black ants.

But Susan dared not pause. She must reach the top, secure the golden box and the great ruby, and hurry away. Beginner's luck would end some time. With chattering teeth and shaking knees, she climbed on up. Suddenly the pyramid narrowed and ended. Her shaking hands found a box, but it was not the kind of box she had in mind. It was a heavy casket. It was too heavy to lift! Her fingers fumbled at the lid; she was so weak she could not open the lid.

FAR BELOW her a bronze door clanged.

Susan sank her teeth into her lip to stifle a scream. Six or seven men in black seemed to bound into the golden room. One of them was carrying, in each hand, a long wisp of golden silk. Susan waited. She was trapped. There was absolutely no escape for her. She watched the men. They pounced on the two dozing priests. Quickly the man with the wisps of silk bound one about the neck of each priest.

High above, staring, Susan saw the priests writhing on the floor, suffocating. Her vision clearing, she saw metal glinting in the hands of the six men. Doors opened, and the golden room suddenly was filled with priests in black. The six who had first entered backed against the golden pyramid. There was no question now what was in their hands.

As the sub-machine guns began to bark, one of the six started up the pyramid. He had not climbed four steps, when a knife sped through the air and plunged into his back. He collapsed and rolled down the steps to the floor.

Susan, clinging to the golden casket, saw men surging into the room; saw them fall. Then the smoke from the guns formed a mist which quickly grew thicker until it became a curtain through which Susan could see nothing.

In this confusion, she realized, she might escape with the great ruby. Summoning all her strength, she pushed up the heavy lid of the gold casket. It fell back against the wall with a clang. Susan plunged her hand in. Once again she stifled a scream. Her groping fingers had not found a ruby. A shiny claw had seemed to close upon them. She struck a match and held it with trembling hand over the casket. Another scream bubbled up to Susan's lips.

Lying in the bottom of the gold casket was a dead hand, black and shriveled. The dead black skin of that hand was as shiny as though it were varnished.

It was a gigantic hand. It must have been seventeen inches in length, nine in width. The flesh had withered, leaving only the skin sunken between the bones. It had been cut off at the wrist.

Susan stared at the hand with shuddering horror. It stank of blood. But she knew that this horrid relic was far more precious here than the largest ruby ever mined.

She knew that it was the hand of Ung.

CHAPTER VIII

RED CHAOS

THE FIRING BELOW the pyramid was intermittent now. Had Shanghai Charlie and his gunmen succeeded—or were they being wiped out?

Susan did not hesitate. She thrust her grisly souvenir down inside her dress, shuddered as the giant claw scraped her bare flesh, then quickly clambered down the pyramid. The sharp odor of gun-smoke was exhilarating. She felt triumphant and a little giddy. She had succeeded, or was on the verge of success.

The smoke from the native guns which had replied to the *rat-tat-tat* of the sub-machine rifles grew thicker as Susan descended. She heard a man shriek, "Don't! Oh, my God— don't!" Then a bubbling cry as though blood had rushed into his mouth.

Susan hugged her coat about her, drew the dark blouse more closely about her face. The floor of the golden shrine was covered with men and pools of their blood. Priests were coming in and running out. She realized that Shanghai Charlie's raid had been a failure. She counted four white faces on the floor. Then she stumbled and went to her knees.

She almost fell over the body of one of the two priests. And she stared at his throat. One of her silk stockings had been used to strangle him. As Susan got to her feet she was caught in a tide of black-robed men who surged toward a doorway. They paid no heed to her, and Susan was swept along with them into the circular corridor, on out through other rooms, and so to the compound.

Beginner's luck was still holding, miraculously. She saw suddenly before her a sea of copper and bronze upturned faces, gleaming in the light of pitching torches. And she saw blood everywhere. She saw a man without a hand holding a wrist from which blood spurted in spite of his efforts to stem it.

Susan was probably the first white woman—perhaps the first white human—to glimpse the compound of the black temple on the night of sacrifice. The odor of blood made her ill and weak. She heard, or imagined she heard, the thin wail of the doomed girl. She knew that for years to come she would awaken from sleep with that awful cry in her ears. Yet she had triumphed over this horrible form of worship. She had, she was certain, struck it a death blow—if she could now escape.

If these half-mad men and women who pushed her this way and that but knew that she was nursing to her breast their treasured relic of that horrible black god!

Unnoticed, Susan made her way to the edge of the compound. She found her way to the innumerable little shrines in the rear. Breathlessly she descended the steps to the quiet of the forbidden zone and at a run returned to the welcome confines of the business section of the city.

What she had been through was a dream, a horrible dream, an oriental nightmare. Her plans were clear now. Site would stop at the hotel for Peter, would tell him what she had done, and they would go out to the *Java Bird*. Nothing, she was certain, could go wrong now. She could taste the ambrosia of triumph. She could picture Peter's amazement and admiration. After all, she had done this partly to show him that she could, single-handed, manage a great adventure. And she had succeeded.

Susan did not realize that already Hai-Phang was being searched for her; that those wisps of silk stockings had been to K'ong a certain clew. As far as Susan was concerned, beginner's luck had carried her thus far, and she was confident that it would carry her adventure to a triumphant conclusion.

BY WAY of the compound Susan slipped into the hotel and raced up the stairs. Peter's door was closed but not locked. She hurried in without knocking.

He was not there. For the first time since leaving the room of gold, doubts assailed her. Peter had found her note and gone in search of her. Peter had gone to the temple and been murdered!

But she promptly questioned this. Peter was reckless, but he knew the East. He had been through too many close shaves. He was alive; he would be back. But she would not wait for him.

Susan knew that a certain black hand bag of his contained all of his valuable papers. He had once told her he would almost rather lose his life than lose that bag. She rummaged among his bags until she found it. It was, fortunately, not locked. Susan lifted up papers and thrust the hand of Ung under them. Then she wrote a hasty note:

DEAR PETER:
    I am going directly to the *Java Bird,* because I've had nothing but luck. Follow as soon as you get here. Bring your black bag.
                                                                    SUSAN.

It was much better than waiting for him to come back. She could ride her luck, she could escape. But her presence might complicate Peter's escape. Susan slipped out the back way and went down black alleys to the water front. There would be plenty of sampans at the landing stage where she had come ashore this afternoon. She found a sampan. It was empty. As she jumped into it, she was glad she had left the hand of Ung in Peter's black bag. Even if she were caught now, that grisly relic was in safe hands.

Susan pushed out from the shore. The sampan's sweep was

heavy and clumsy, but she did not have far to go. Her hopes rose as the lights of the bund fell astern and sent long quivering knife-blades across the water to her feet. She hoped she would not faint from sheer excitement before she reached the steamer. A wave of exultation swept over the girl. She had come to the Far East looking for thrills, adventure, excitement. Tonight she had found them to her heart's content.

The deck lights of the *Java Bird* were bright and hopeful beacons shining across the waste of water. The starboard running light was a kindly and inviting green eye. Susan saw a deck steward walking forward with a tray covered with a white napkin.

Then a shadow, blacker than the night, seemed to fall across the sampan and the excited girl at the sweep. It was like a gigantic bat. At that moment a hoarse and mournful bellow issued from the whistle of the *Java Bird*. Susan screamed.

CHAPTER IX

DISAPPOINTED

WHEN SUSAN LEFT him to go to her room, Peter shaved, bathed, and changed to fresh white ducks. He was worried. He knew that it was unsafe to leave Susan alone with her thoughts. The fanatical madness of the night had got into her veins, and she was quite apt to do something dangerous.

He did not wait until eight o'clock to go to her room. Less than an hour after she had left he went there. The door, which she had left a few inches ajar, had been blown wide open by a draft. He hastened into the room, looked quickly about, and went out onto the balcony. Returning, he found her note on the dressing table beside the can of brown make-up powder:

DEAR PETER:

I can't stand it. I simply must do something. If they kill me— what of it? I simply can't sit around doing nothing while they murder that poor child. I realize I can't prevent her death, but I may be able to help prevent future sacrifices. Wait in your room for me—and the ruby!

SUSAN.

Peter did not for a moment suppose that she would attempt to enter the temple alone. He thought Susan was going down to the Smiling Eye and join Shanghai Charlie. He did not dream she would take any other course.

Pale with anxiety, Peter charged down the hall and into his room. He secured his pistol, slipped several loaded clips into a hip pocket, and was about to hurry out when he heard distinctly a faint scraping sound on the wall outside the window through which Wan Loo had plunged. Some one softly called, "Moore—quick!"

He wheeled about and turned out the light; but he did not approach the window. Ten feet away from it he waited. The darkness, as his eyes became accustomed to it, took on a luminous glow of its own, of starlight and the golden diffusion of torches in the streets.

The scraping was not repeated. As Peter waited, straining his senses, he saw the outline of what appeared to be an enormous bat—a bat with a belly as large as an entire man—slide down outside the window and hover there. Doubtless, this thing—whatever it was—was some visitant from K'ong on some mysterious and diabolical errand.

Peter fired four times at the center of what would have been, had the phenomenon been real, the greatest bat ever seen on earth, and was relieved when the awful thing collapsed, uttered an animal-like groan and plunged into the compound. There was a ringing metallic clash as the body struck the flagging.

Peter looked out. A thin, frayed rope hung over the window. It had evidently been looped under the man's arms, so that he could be lowered from the roof or some window above. By chance, one of the bullets from Peter's automatic had severed this rope. Peter ran out the door, down the same steps which Susan had used but a little while before, and so out into the compound. He was sure he was under observation from the roof, but he trusted to the dimness of the light to thwart any attempt which might be made by knife-throwers to kill him.

He found the victim of his marksmanship merely an Ungese priest, with the black robes of his order tangled about arms and legs which threshed in death agonies.

PETER'S FUMBLING fingers now encountered a curving, sharp edge. The mystery of Wan Loo's death was explained. Here was the bronze disk which had instantly severed Wan Loo's head. The disk spun on a hardwood bearing. It was a kind of flywheel, which must have weighed thirty pounds. A wooden knob at the end of the bearing set the disk whirling, perhaps with the aid of a rope wound about the knob and pulled, so that it would spin as a top spins. The priest had no doubt been lowered from an upper window or the roof. His purpose was to set the heavy bronze wheel to spinning and to lower it on the neck of the intended victim.

It was a typically oriental machine—elaborate, clumsy, and barbaric. It had failed of its purpose tonight because of a miscalculation. The man's confederates on the roof or in an upper window had misjudged the distance. The man had been lowered too far.

Peter drew these conclusions in a matter of seconds as his hands explored the diabolical device. He had expected some such contraption. It was like K'ong to go to such pains. The fact now stood out sharply that Peter's name was on K'ong's death list.

He could not hesitate now. Rolling the lifeless body over, Peter quickly divested it of robe and cape. He put these on and adjusted them. Then, holding the hood about his face with one hand, his gun in readiness with the other, he hastened out of the compound and to the water front.

He found the junk Shanghai Charlie had described, and a ladder leading up its shining side to the deck. The vessel was

*She took the
grisly souvenir.*

in darkness and it appeared to be deserted, but as Peter started
up the ladder a white face gleamed like a pale moon at the rail
above. A ray of light glinted from a rifle barrel and a harsh whisper said, in English:

"Get off that ladder, or I'll plug you!"

The gleam on the rifle barrel vanished. Peter knew that the
muzzle was bearing on him.

"I'm looking for Shanghai Charlie. Is he aboard?"

"It's none of your damned business. Get down off that ladder,
or I'll shoot you off." Peter heard the click of a cocked hammer.
"Whoever you are, you ain't comin' aboard. I'm gonna count
three. One—two—"

Peter fired twice. The pale moon of a face vanished. The rifle
went twisting end over end to splash into the water between
the junk and the wharf. He clambered up the ladder and found
the owner of the white face seated in the dim light of a lantern.
Ratty eyes glared at him.

"**YOU CREASED** me. Don't shoot again. Who the devil are
you anyway?"

"Where is Charlie Ling?" Peter demanded.

"I know who you are now," said the man. "You're the guy they call Peter the Brazen. Charlie gave me strict orders to keep you off this ship."

"Where is he?" Peter snapped.

"Brother," the man whined, "I don't know. He waited around here for some jane, then he got tired waitin', and barged off with the gang to that temple. I was told to shoot anybody who didn't give the password."

"Was he going to the hotel for Miss O'Gilvie?"

"I don't know nothin'."

"I want to search this ship."

"Go as far as you like!"

"Can you walk?"

"I can try." The rat-eyed man, groaning, struggled to his feet and picked up the lantern.

Peter, with his pistol handy, followed him into the waist and into the cabin under the poop. His escort touched a switch and flooded the cabin with light.

The room was large, decidedly oriental in flavor and lavishly furnished. The walls were of ebony inlaid with mother-of-pearl. The furniture was carved teak and sandalwood. In one corner was a rosewood bed.

"How long has he been gone?" Peter asked.

"Ask me another."

Not satisfied, Peter inspected the junk from stem to stern; then he went ashore and walked slowly back toward the hotel. But he did not enter the hotel. He was certain that Susan would not safely return. He doubted that she had joined forces with Charlie Ling, so he made his way toward the temple, and listened to the voices of pilgrims. He reasoned that if an attempt had been made by any one to raid the inner shrine, the news would have spread and the streets would be buzzing with rumors. But he heard no rumors. He estimated later that at the exact time he was closest to the black temple, Shanghai Charlie and his gang were launching their raid.

In the grip of indecision, Peter returned to the hotel—and found Susan's second note. He read it and cursed. Why hadn't he waited? He went to the black hand bag and opened it. Plunging his hand down under papers and blue prints, he found the hand of Ung.

Peter was inspecting this gruesome relic when he became aware that he was no longer alone. A soft footfall attracted his attention to the door which he had left open. The hall was filled with black-robed men. He looked to the right—and saw three men simultaneously climb over the balcony rail.

Peter thrust the dead giant's hand under his black robe and ran to the window which overlooked the compound. He might break his leg or crack his skull, but this was the only avenue of escape.

A knife buried itself almost to the hilt in the window sill as he poised to leap. He jumped down; landed on the rough flagging catwise, on hands and toes; staggered up and ran back to the wall. Groping his way along this until he reached the alley leading to the bund, he then broke into a run.

He would go to Yang Gan's wharf and follow Susan out to the *Java Bird* in the sampan which Wan Loo had hidden for him there.

But when he reached the wharf, he stopped and groaned with dismay. The *Java Bird* was moving. Her starboard running light vanished as he stared. The mournful blast of her whistle reached him. He could not possibly reach her before she got under way. The question was: was Susan safely aboard, or had she fallen into the hands of K'ong—or Shanghai Charlie—before she could make good her escape?

For a moment, Peter hesitated. Then he started off at a fast walk down the Bund toward the Hai-Phang wireless station. If the station was closed for the night, he would break in and get into communication with the *Java Bird's* operator himself.

CHAPTER X

DREAD SUSPICIONS

THE STATION WAS not closed. Lights glowed yellowly at the windows in the small brick building. He heard the whining of a generator and cast a backward glance to assure himself that K'ong's men had not picked up his trail. Then he opened the door of the wireless station and closed it softly behind him.

A Tonkinese youth with a long yellow face was sitting at the instruments with headphones clamped to his ears. He appeared to be dozing, but when the door closed he looked sharply around. He looked at the black hood and the black robe, and reached quickly into a drawer under the instrument table.

"What do you want?" he asked curtly, in English.

Peter told him. "Get in touch with the *Java Bird*," he said crisply, "and have the operator find out if a Miss Susan O'Gilvie is on board. She would probably have come aboard only a few minutes before they weighed anchor."

"It is impossible," the operator said. "The *Java Bird's* wireless equipment is out of order."

"Try calling them," Peter urged.

"It is useless."

Peter wondered why the man was so antagonistic. Was he, also, one of K'ong's men?

"Let me try," he said. "I used to be a wireless operator."

The Tonkinese sprang up. There was a knife in his hand. He was not clasping it by the hilt but by the blade, in the throwing position.

Peter was not prepared for this. He had dropped his automatic into his hip pocket when he approached the wireless station. It would be impossible for him to reach it under the heavy black gown before the operator threw the knife. But he reached for it as quickly as he could—and saw the knife leave the man's hand.

He heard the twang of the blade slicing the air as it sped past his ear. Although Peter had ducked his head, the knife had missed his face by less than two inches and had sunk into the wood of the door-jamb.

Peter wrenched it out of the wood as the Tonkinese sprang at him. And Peter swung the knife as he would have swung his fist, in an uppercut aimed at the jaw. The very force of the man's rush completed Peter's effort at a reprisal. The knife sank into the operator's throat. He staggered back and blood gushed from his mouth as he crumpled to the floor.

PETER SHOT the heavy iron bolt of the door and pulled down the shades. Then he seated himself at the instrument table, glanced at a typewritten list of call letters pasted to the wall, found the *Java Bird's* letters and flashed out her call.

The *Java Bird* did not answer. He called again, and again there was no answer. He told himself he was a stubborn fool to have let Susan out of his sight; that he should have taken her aboard the *Java Bird* by force if necessary before this trouble started.

He sent out the *Java Bird's* call again. This time, when he threw the switches to the receiving position, there was an answer. The shrill whine of the steamer's transmitter, so close at hand, was like a scream in the phones over Peter's ears. Dash-dot-dash. K—"Go ahead."

Peter's fingers rapped out on the key: "Urgent. Find out if a passenger named Susan O'Gilvie is aboard. Would have come aboard in past few minutes."

The answer came: "O.K. Stand by."

In an agony of suspense Peter waited. If she had not reached the *Java Bird* safely, what chance had he of finding her in Hai-Phang tonight? She had jeopardized her life by stealing the hand of Ung; she had made him a target for the first Ungese who detected him. He recalled those priests swarming into his hotel room.

The *Java Bird* screamed in his headphones: "No such party aboard. Only passengers are a Jap merchant from Osaka, a Chinese trader bound for Christmas Island and an elderly English couple named Bruce. Captain reports Susan O'Gilvie left this ship and went ashore this afternoon about three against his urgent advice and warnings."

Peter tapped off a series of I's—the wireless operator's method of letting his listener know he is thinking. Peter was thinking—thinking faster than ever before in his life. Dot-dot. Dot-dot. Dot-dot. He sent rapidly: "Make sure she is not anywhere aboard. Have search made."

The *Java Bird* promptly answered: "Search has been completed. Ship has been combed from chain locker to steering engine house and from trucks to keelson. Miss O'Gilvie positively not aboard. Aren't you Peter Moore?"

"Yes."

"I knew it. I would recognize that fist of yours anywhere in the world. This is Cy Morton. I punched brass on the old Siberia when you were on the China run six years ago. Are you in more trouble?"

"Plenty. Miss O. is lost somewhere in this man's town. I am going to try to find her. Ask your skipper if he will send me a boatload of men armed with rifles, pistols and cutlasses."

The answer came so quickly that Peter knew the *Java Bird's* skipper must have been in the wireless house all this time.

"Skipper says cannot send anybody ashore as all our crew is white and cannot take risk of their getting murdered by these maniacs. He is not sympathetic. He says you have always managed to get out of your jams without help."

Peter angrily flashed back: "Tell him I am not asking for help to get me out of a jam. I must have help to hunt for Miss O. I am single-handed against this entire city."

A pause. Then the answer: "I would swim ashore myself and help, but the skipper has all hands on deck with orders to permit no one to leave or come aboard. We are under way, just passing the headlands."

Peter was sweating now, and angry. "Ask your skipper if he will stand by an hour or two. Very urgent. If I can find her and get her aboard, it is our only possible way of escape."

The *Java Bird* answered: "Skipper says O.K. Will stand by all night if necessary, but make it snappy."

And Peter tapped back: "Tnx—30. Thanks—all through."

He had signed off with that celebrated numeral so many times. Now he wondered if tonight it might not have some especial significance. All through! He had been in tight corners in his Far East adventuring, but never in a corner so tight as this one. What possible chance had he of finding Susan in this seething city? The news had doubtless flashed from end to end of the city that the American girl had defiled the shrine of Ung by stealing that treasured relic, and that the white man—Peter—was her accomplice. If she was not already captured and dead, she soon would be. And Peter writhed at the thought of their manner of putting her to death. Some horrible torture.

K'ong would attend to that personally. He would tax his fiendish oriental imagination for some method of death by torture which would be hideous, unspeakable.

NOW IT occurred to Peter that Shanghai Charlie might have captured Susan. He dashed sweat from his eyes. That had been Shanghai Charlie's plan—to capture her, take her aboard that black junk… Peter sprang up. He knew well enough what Shanghai Charlie's plans were. He had seen the half-caste looking at Susan, drinking her in with his greedy, lustful eyes. He might hold her for ransom. He might sell her to some wealthy up-country mandarin when he had tired of her.

What course, Peter savagely demanded of himself, should he take? If Shanghai Charlie had her, how could he single-handedly rescue her from that gang armed with sub-machine guns? If K'ong had captured her, she was already dead or dying in K'ong's private room in the black temple. Peter knew that room. He had been there on his previous visit to Hai-Phang. But could he remember how to reach it through that labyrinth of corridors?

His disguise would be useless. It would be quickly penetrated. Wild ideas occurred to him, were discarded. His mind played with the thought that K'ong had worn, that night five years ago, robes of bright jade-green, the costume of the high priest worn only on the night of sacrifice, Ung's birthday.

The unmistakable *rat-tat-tat* of submachine rifles came spattering across the night as Peter arose from the instrument table. He glanced at his watch. It was half past eleven. In another half hour, the native girl whose terrified wailing had aroused Susan to such a hysterical pitch would be put to death. In the glare of torches K'ong would plunge the sacred knife into her bosom and hack out her heart.

Peter glanced at the Tonkinese lying on the floor. He was dead. His fingers were still clutching the handle of the knife buried in his throat. His eyes stared upward glassily.

Peter stepped over him, switched off the light, wrapped his fingers firmly about the butt of his automatic, unbolted the door and opened it.

The savage snarl of a bullet passing close overhead caused Peter to drop down. The firing was occurring somewhere down on the Bund. It seemed to be coming from the direction of the Yang Gan clock.

To answer the question of whether or not Susan was in the hands of Shanghai Charlie Ling, Peter must run the steel gantlet of sub-machine rifle fire. He started down the Bund.

CHAPTER XI

THE MARK OF K'ONG

NEARING THE YANG Gan dock, Peter saw a milling mob of men, mostly natives with old-fashioned rifles, draw away and begin to retreat into the side streets. He wondered why they were retreating. If the Ungese, whipped to their present maniacal state by scenes of torture and blood-letting, wished to board the Smiling Eye, nothing could stop them. They could have been slaughtered by hundreds, but other waves of hundreds and thousands would have carried on the attack. Why were they withdrawing?

The machine rifle fire was lessening. It started up again in a burst, then died down. It stopped entirely.

Peter slipped along warehouse walls toward the Yang Gan dock. He was amazed to see the last of the Ungese withdraw. The Bund, except for the dead, was empty.

Nearing the black junk, he ran to a pile of teak butts, then ahead to a mound of rattan-bound casks. He was now well within the shadow of the Smiling Eye. In the feeble glow from a street lamp he could see that hopeful eye painted in glaring white, blue and red on the junk's bow. The silver pupil glistened like a star.

The odor of spices came down the wind to Peter; spices and the strange smell of the oriental water front, an odor characteristic of Yokohama and Singapore and a hundred ports in between. Somehow, to Peter Moore that odor had always spelled adventure. As he sniffed it now, he wondered if this adventure was to be his last.

With the wind came suddenly the blood-chilling cry of a man in terror or agony. It rose up and up until it became a scream which sent chills down the listener's spine. Peter waited, listened and heard other similar sounds. He heard groans and cursing, the amazing sound of a man sobbing. Then the scream again, followed by a high-pitched babbling in Chinese and coast pidgin.

Crouching by the casks, Peter saw the silhouette of a head at the forward rail. The shoulders of a man with a long, curving knife appeared, and he began to hack away at the forward hawser. Another man appeared, aft, and began hacking away at the after line. Then Peter heard the muffled exhaust of a Diesel motor. The Smiling Eye was preparing to get under way, was slipping out to the refuge of the open sea. Was Susan aboard? Why had the Ungese retreated after putting up so short a fight?

With the automatic in his hand, Peter sprinted across the intervening space to the ladder which still stood against the junk's side.

The scream came again—long-drawn, high-pitched, ending as before in a jumble of Chinese and coast pidgin cursing. And the sobbing of the other man grew louder as Peter scrambled up the ladder. The wailer was drawing in his breath in a series of short, convulsive sobs; expelling it in thin, anguished gasps.

As Peter reached the rail, a lantern swung before his eyes. The glare of it prevented him from seeing the man who wielded it. He was using it as a weapon—was going to bring it smashing down on Peter's skull.

Peter dropped back several rungs. The lantern flashed up and came down with a splintering crash on the rail. The light went out. Peter waited with pistol ready. A face appeared. Peter aimed between the eyes and shot. The face vanished. He climbed back up, poised a moment on the rail and jumped to the deck.

A man with his back to the mast and a rifle in his hands saw him; raised the rifle; fired. Peter felt the scorching slash of the bullet as it ripped across his left shoulder; aimed and deliberately fired. The man toppled face forward to the deck.

Peter ran to him, plucked the rifle from his hands, and saw that it was a sub-machine rifle. The barrel was so hot that it scorched his fingers. He found two disks of ammunition beside the dead man; stowed them under his arm, restored the pistol to his hip pocket, and with the sub-machine rifle ready, advanced cautiously toward the luxurious cabin, aft. It was there that he heard the screaming.

He passed the sobbing man and saw, by the light streaming from the doorway, that his left arm was amputated at the elbow, hacked off, no doubt, by an Ungese sword.

AS THE scream again arose and, as before, ended in a volley of profanity, Peter hastened into the half-caste's cabin. Writhing on the rosewood bed was a man who could be identified as Shanghai Charlie Ling only by his size. He was writhing and squirming from side to side. His face was bound up with bloody bandages. Peter saw, to his horror, that the half-caste's hands had been cut off at the wrists.

Peter went quickly to the bedside. Eyes shivering with torture stared up at him from holes in the bandages. No other part of Shanghai Charlie's face was visible.

"Where's that girl, Charlie?"

The man on the bed began to scream. He must have been more than half delirious with pain.

Peter snapped, "Is she aboard?"

"No!" the half-caste shouted, hoarsely. "She did this. She's the one who started all this. If it hadn't been for her—"

"Where is she?"

"Who knows? Who cares?" The pain-stricken eyes peered at Peter. "Look what they did! Look what they did to me! They cut off my ears! They cut off my nose! They chopped off my hands! Look at me!" His voice rose again to a scream.

Peter was sweating with horror. Shanghai Charlie Ling was a rascal, a thief, a murderer, a scoundrel. The world would be well rid of him. But as Peter watched him suffer and writhe and twist and heard him scream and curse with pain, a fresh hatred for K'ong swelled within him.

"Look at these!" The suffering man thrust out the bandaged stumps where his hands had been.

The man on the bed began to babble incoherently. And Peter pieced together something of what had happened. Susan's stocking in the corridor outside the golden shrine. The raid on the shrine. The fiendish resistance of the Ungese priests, armed with rifles, pistols, knives.

"They never stopped comin' at us. We shot them down until they were lyin' four deep on each other—and still they kept comin'. We pumped lead into 'em until the guns were srnokin'.

And still they came at us with guns and swords and knives. The opium's been stolen. If I only had some opium to dull this pain!"

"How did you escape?"

"We made a wedge and fought our way out." The half-caste began to curse. He screamed and writhed and cursed. "But that grinnin' devil got me. He had on a green robe. He got me and did this to me—and laughed while they held me. I can hear him laughin' now. Cacklin', as they held me and he took his time and sliced off my ears and nose and carved off my hands!"

"Didn't you see Miss O'Gilvie?"

"I'd kill her if I saw her, I would. She got away with the big ruby—or they got her. One of the two. I ain't clapped eyes on her since this afternoon in your room."

PETER BELIEVED that this was the truth. In his present state, Shanghai Charlie would not lie. Susan, then, was somewhere in the city, a prisoner of K'ong. There could no longer be the slightest doubt of it.

His heart was beating dully, heavily, as if it were tired of its work, Peter felt the floor vibrate under him to the slow revolutions of the Diesel, and for a fugitive moment was tempted to stay aboard. On the Smiling Eye was safety—for him. Doubtless, he could muster enough of a crew to handle her. Why should he go back into this mad city and try to rescue that foolish girl? Doubtless, Susan was already dead. Doubtless, K'ong had finished his hideous work of torture.

Peter walked out on deck. There was nothing he could do for Charlie.

There was still time for him to scramble down to the dock. But why should he throw his life away? A breath of the sea came to his nostrils. That saline tang had always meant freedom and peace to him.

He looked down dully at the city from the high stern. A sustained roar of human voices came to him from the compound of the black temple. The orgy would be reaching its height now, the compound would be a reeking lake of human blood.

As he stared, an audacious plan came to Peter, such a plan, as had won for him the name by which the Chinese called him: *"Ren Beh Tung"*—"Man of Bronze."

If Susan were still alive, if he could execute the plan, there was a slim chance of saving her.

As Peter started down the shining black side of the Smiling Eye, the hand of Ung, in the folds of the black robe, seemed to claw at his ribs.

CHAPTER XII

ORIENTAL PERSUASION

A BRAZIER HANGING from the cobalt ceiling by means of a single blackened brass chain filled the small room with murky light. This room contained one small square window, fitted with a bronze grille, and one door which was a slab of bronze.

It was K'ong's private torture chamber. Here were brought the poor devils, men and women, from whom he wished to secure some precious secret. It was seldom that K'ong found it necessary to use his private torture chamber. Such secrets as he wished to know were generally forthcoming from his victims long before that room was mentioned.

But this was an extraordinary case.

An ingenious bamboo rack was built along one wall. There was an adjustable extension at one end to which the feet were bound with thongs. And there was a strange-looking bamboo device above the head of the rack where the hands were bound with thongs. The victim lay on his back, with heavy ropes binding the shoulders to the rack, and could look up and see his hands.

Susan O'Gilvie lay on the rack and stared up at her hands which were draped down and over the horizontal bar above her. The ropes about her chest, holding her back to the rack, were so tight that she could hardly breathe, and the thongs at her ankles so tight that all sensation in her feet had ceased.

K'ong, with the jade-green hood of his robe thrown back, stood looking down at her with his cruel grin. He realized that this helpless girl was only beginning to get back some of her interest in life. She had thought that he would kill her promptly. She should have known that K'ong never killed—promptly.

When that black shadow had been cast over her sampan and she had screamed, she knew that she had been followed and captured. She expected, the next moment, the feel of cold steel for an instant before it plunged into her heart. And even with the horror of that thought, she was relieved. She had delivered the withered hand of Ung the Unspeakable into safe keeping.

Peter would read her note and hasten out to the *Java Bird.* He would spend hours having the ship searched for her, and by the time he was forced to admit that she was not aboard, the steamer would be well at sea. He would be safe. The hand of Ung would forever be disposed of. Ungism would be crushed, never to rise again. And Susan would long since have joined that ghostly procession of fearless women who had died for a cause.

But Susan did not know the East. She did not give K'ong sufficient credit for patience and cunning.

She almost fainted when that plunge of cold steel into her heart did not come. And she was vaguely conscious of being transported rapidly through the city toward the temple. Her senses did not quite organize themselves until she had been strapped, a few minutes ago, onto the rack in K'ong's private torture chamber.

HER FEELING of heroism was gone now. She was a terrified girl at the mercy, she well knew, of one of the most cruel human monsters that had ever lived. She thought of that razor-edged bronze disk slicing down to sever the head of Wan Loo from his body. She thought of the hideous scenes she had witnessed in the great courtyard. And she thought of the brown girl who was to be put to death at midnight.

Susan wanted to scream with fear. Her heart was thumping madly in her breast. Her breath came and went with a faint whistling sound in her parched throat.

What would he do to her?

The high priest was grinning. His face was a skull on which human skin had been pasted. He did not have human feelings. He was a horribly ingenious machine with a brain of brass and a heart of cold steel. These thoughts and others raced madly through the girl's frantic mind.

What would he do to her?

His yellow eyes were roving over her body. They slid down her tattered dress to her bare legs and feet. They roved back to her hands, dangling from the horizontal bar above her.

In a voice as clear and shivery as thin bronze rapped sharply with steel, he said, "So you disregarded my request."

Susan tried to moisten her lips, but her tongue was as dry as chalk.

"I requested you not to leave that building until tomorrow morning."

"What," Susan gasped, "are you going to do to me?"

The yellow eyes glowed and glared, but the death-like grin remained. "You left that hotel against my orders, and you made your way into this temple, knowing what your fate would be, realizing that what you planned to do was the sheerest folly—"

"I succeeded."

"Realizing," he went on in the same brassy voice, "that you would, in the end, fall into my hands. You entered my temple. You entered the forbidden shrine. You climbed the golden pyramid. *Where is the hand of Ung?*"

Susan looked at him fearfully. She compressed her lips. What was he going to do to her? What fiendish torture would he apply to force her to tell? But she would not tell. She recalled Peter's words: "If I could crush Ungism by throwing my life away, I'd throw it away. But I would be killed—and Ungism would continue to flourish."

The words gave her strength. She had crushed Ungism by stealing the hand of that horrible black god. She would throw her life away; but she could not tolerate the thought of her life being stripped from her a little at a time by dreadful torture. Peter was safe on the *Java Bird.* He would throw the hand of Ung into a deep part of the sea. Was she brave enough to play her part?

In a sharper voice K'ong repeated: "Where is the hand of Ung?"

"Gone," she said defiantly.

"Where?"

"Gone—forever!"

The yellow eyes drank in her white face. It seemed to Susan that they were hot, like glowing coals. She could feel their heat in her face. Yet they were cold—cold as ice.

"Where?" K'ong demanded again.

"At the bottom of the harbor."

"That is a lie!"

THEN SHE saw that he held a knife in his hand. Her eyes opened more widely. What was he going to do?

It was a thin, long, curved blade as bright as new silver. At the widest place, it was about a half inch wide. It may have been seven inches long. The blade was set in a handle of kingfisher jade in which jewels sparkled.

K'ong was looking now at the blade. His death-grin had widened. The brazier light glittered on the sharp points of his yellow teeth. They were like the teeth of a fox; fine and sharp, but yellow. He ran the edge of the blade very lightly along his thumb. It looked as sharp as a surgeon's scalpel.

Susan involuntarily shrank from that cruel-looking knife. Her heart went faster. She stilled a scream. What was he going to do with it?

He walked to the window and looked out info the night. There was a steady glare through the bronze grille-work, which may have meant that the window looked down on the compound. The ruddy light would have been the diffused glare of torches. Over his shoulder Susan could see a star. It was blue-white and heavily glittering. It occurred to her that this was the last star she would ever see.

The man in jade-green left the window and slowly paced down the room. He vanished behind her. Again her heart fluttered in a frantic hurst of beating. She could not see him. What was he doing behind her?

She tensed herself; waited. There was no sound. What was he doing? She rolled her eyes back as far as she could, but saw nothing. The faint beginning of a scream forced itself from her lips. She tried to control herself. She would not scream. The martyr to a great cause, she would go to her death courageously. She would not whimper. No matter what he did, she would not say a word.

K'ong reappeared, carrying a low black stool. He placed this beside the bamboo rack and seated himself, so that she could see his hands and his face. He had the knife in his right hand. In his left hand was a block of smooth white wood about six inches long by two inches square.

With the grin flickering at his lips, he whittled a sliver from the block.

"You may imagine," he said, "that this is your wrist, this little block of soft white wood. See?" he said quickly, and touched her nearest wrist with the knife.

Involuntarily, Susan gasped, then bit her lip. The blade had been ice-cold, yet for the past five minutes it had been in the high priest's hand.

He whittled another sliver from the block.

"Your wrist," he repeated. "That is what I am going to do to you—if you do not tell me where you put the hand of Ung. First I will whittle one wrist, down to the bone through the flesh; then I will whittle the other wrist, down to the bone through the flesh. Then, one at a time, I will carve through the bones."

The yellow eyes hovered on hers.

"Ah, no. You are thinking that, with both wrist arteries cut, you will lose so much blood that you will soon die. We will avoid that. The ends of the arteries will be seared and closed with a white-hot iron to prevent that. But perhaps you have changed your mind. Perhaps you wish to avoid these discomforts by telling me where you put the hand of Ung."

"At the bottom of the harbor," Susan got out between clenched teeth, and wondered why she did not faint. But she had never fainted; she was not the fainting kind.

K'ONG WAS busying himself with a small charcoal brazier which he placed on a small table beside the rack. It was smoldering when he picked it up. He fanned the embers with his breath until they were glowing red, then he laid among them several long slender iron rods.

Susan looked at them fearfully. When he had cut off her hands, he would use the white-hot ends of those rods....

"The infidel who touches the hand of Ung dies," K'ong was saying. "You are doomed to die—very slowly, unless you prefer to change your mind and tell me where you hid that sacred relic. If you tell me, I shall be merciful. I shall kill you quickly. It is for you to choose how you are to die. Shall I whittle away your wrists—or shall I plunge this dagger into your heart and let death come swiftly and mercifully?"

Susan, holding her lower lip between her teeth, said nothing. K'ong went on:

"That man, your lover—"

"He is not my lover!"

"—is doomed to die as well. You gave the hand of Ung to him, did you not?"

"No."

"I think you are lying. You gave the hand to him. Supposing he escapes... what then? Under my orders, priests would scour the world until they found him. They would bring him here. But let us see whether or not you are lying. No man, no woman, has yet lied to me and lived."

He shifted his position slightly and picked up Susan's nearest hand. She shrank at the touch of that cold claw. Far more terrifying than the dead hand of Ung was the live hand of K'ong. As the sharp, gleaming blade came closer and closer to her wrist, Susan lost all control.

Susan was no longer a modern Joan of Arc. She was no longer one in the procession of historic women who had laid down their lives for a worthy cause. She was suddenly a limp, terrified girl; her hands were to be cut off, whittled off, a little at a time—a shred of flesh, a sliver of bone.

Death would, in time, mercifully follow, but not until she had suffered agonies such as she had never dreamed. The thought that her hands—beautiful hands of which she had always been proud—were to be hacked away until nothing but bloody stumps remained was more than she could endure.

As she stared into the yellow face of this horrible creature who could conceive and execute such torture, a little scream came from her. She frantically threw herself against the ropes and thongs. She tried to pull her hands away from the bamboo bar.

But she was bound so securely that she could hardly work a muscle. Yet she pulled and twisted.

K'ong watched her hungrily, as if each squirm of her helpless body, each convulsion of her face gave him the greatest delight. His smile widened.

She moaned, "Peter! Oh, Peter!"

Why hadn't she followed Peter's advice? Why hadn't she gone to the *Java Bird* when he had asked her to? He had warned her so many times that her craving for adventure would sometime get her into a situation from which no one could extricate her.

Her eyes suddenly burned with tears. She began to cry, as a small girl cries. She tried to assure herself that she was dreaming all this; that she would wake up, in a steamer chair on the *Java Bird*, perhaps, and find Peter smiling down at her.

Her eyes cleared. K'ong's face was very close now. A new

expression had come over it; an expression so cruel, so terrifying that she screamed again.

The keen edge of the dagger touched her hand just above the wrist. K'ong's eyes were glowing now, balls of yellow fire. Susan set her muscles in anticipation of the first sharp pain of the knife entering her flesh. She whimpered.

CHAPTER XIII

BLACK PASSAGES

ON THE EMBANKMENT, Peter waited in the shadow of the Smiling Eye until he was convinced that no one was watching him. He knew that his escape from the wireless station and his boarding of the black junk had been attended by miraculous luck. He knew that K'ong's men were searching the city for him—knew that the slightest misstep would ruin his daring plan.

The rifle-wound on his left shoulder throbbed painfully. He touched the wound and found that, while it was superficial, it was bleeding badly. Quickly, he smeared blood from the wound over his face. In Hai-Phang tonight, blood itself was the password. But he would not make the mistake of returning to the temple through the streets. He was sure that every man on the streets was being searched.

Peter slid over the side of the Yang Gan dock, found a stringer with his feet and lowered himself down. He listened to the water gurgling against the piles, and heard the sound of wood rubbing wood. He climbed along the stringer until he found the painter of the sampan which Wan Loo had hidden for such an emergency.

Cautiously, he pulled the boat out of its hiding place and climbed aboard. Keeping the sampan close to the shadow of the dock, he maneuvered it to the outshore end just as the Smiling Eye was moving off.

He caught a dangling rope and pulled the sampan close under the high black stern. In this shadow, he was sure no one on shore could see him. And he was sure he knew now why K'ong's men were no longer interested in the owner and crew of the Smiling Eye. Shanghai Charlie and his men had been fitly punished for their raid on the shrine. Shanghai Charlie, as long as he lived, would be a horrible warning to any man who had designs on K'ong or Ungism. He would be a hideous reminder of K'ong's power and ruthlessness.

When the Smiling Eye reached mid-channel, Peter cast off and began to work the sweep. His shoulder pained him so that he could not work it rapidly, but must pause for an occasional rest. The city glided past him. Lights sent shivery reflections along the smooth black water, of the river. The ruddy glare of the temple compound grew brighter.

Peter gave it a wide berth and set his course for a grove of date-palms which, he knew, clustered about one of the secret underground entrances to the black temple.

When the bows of the sampan parted the grass at the river's edge and came to rest on mud, Peter picked up the sub-machine rifle in one hand, firmly gripped the automatic pistol in the other and, with senses alert, stepped ashore. He sank almost to his knees in the mud, and hoped there were no alligators about. The smell of the blood in the compound drew them from miles up and down river. But he encountered no alligators.

Reaching firm ground, under the palms, he made his way carefully toward a yard-square lump of black malachite which lay, he knew, as a random bowlder might lie, at the southern fringe of the palms and near the base of the artificial plateau.

Exactly ten feet west of this lump of black malachite a trap-door was hidden in the sand.

Peter measured off the distance and scooped out sand until he found the slab of bronze and the ringbolt with which it was lifted. Then he hesitated. He knew that this errand on which he was embarked was the most dangerous he had ever undertaken; most likely to fail. How many hours had Susan been in K'ong's possession? What chance was there that she was alive? What chance that his audacious plan of rescue would succeed, even if she were alive?

With his heart beating at double tempo, Peter lifted the heavy bronze door and let it fall back with a soft thud in the sand. Then, drawing a deep, hopeful breath, he picked up the rifle and pistol and started down the stairway into utter, complete blackness.

HE REACHED, at the foot of the stairs, a tunnel which ran, as he remembered it, nearly a quarter of a mile without a turn. He started down the tunnel with both guns in readiness. Did K'ong know that he had once traversed this black tunnel under the temple? Had K'ong set a trap for him?

The uproar of the compound faded as he progressed. There was presently no sound but the echo of his footfalls, the harshness of his breathing. The air in the tunnel was damp and moldy and dead. And the tunnel seemed to go on and on as if he would never come to the end of it.

He reached presently the bronze door at the end of the long passage. Beyond, he knew, was a small room containing three doors: one leading under the compound and probably to another point on the river—a tunnel he had never explored; one leading to a trapdoor set in the black malachite of the temple's entrance from the compound; the third leading directly behind the shrine and so on up to K'ong's private torture chamber.

Peter slipped the automatic under his arm, to open the door. He opened it an inch, and light gleamed through. He peered through the crack. The room seemed empty. He opened the door a little wider and hesitated. Fresh candles had been placed in bronze sockets along the walls. Why had those candles been placed there?

Suspecting an ambush, he waited. Nothing happening, he opened the door wide enough to squeeze through and, looking

sharply about him, advanced to the middle of the three doors—
the door directly across from the one by which he had entered.

There were, he knew, four steps just beyond this door. And,
beyond the steps, a long, straight corridor which led to other
steps. There were doors all along this corridor. At any instant he
might be apprehended.

Holding his breath, Peter opened the door. If K'ong had set a
trap for him, this was the place where it would be sprung.

As he opened the door and stepped into the corridor he saw,
in the dim light of a dong, far in the distance, what appeared to
be a black halo, or the black rim of an empty circle. It dropped
toward him. He struck it aside and dropped to his knees, with
the steps just before him.

The noose was withdrawn swiftly. Men magically appeared.
They had been lying in the corridor beyond the steps. Dimly,
Peter saw them in the light of the distant dong; saw light flicker
on steel; knew that that corridor was full of men who had been
waiting for him if he entered the temple by this route. Behind
him, he heard a door clang.

Evidently, men had been lying in wait for him in the corridor which ran up to the front entrance of the temple. He was
trapped!

A rifle flashed. A bullet flattened with a terrific thump against
the bronze slab behind him. That was evidently the signal for the
attack. It was followed by the rippling crash of a volley.

Peter knelt as if he were in a trench and began pulling the
trigger of the sub-machine rifle, spraying steel-jacketed lead
into the close-packed men ahead of him. Miraculously, he was
not hit.

He could not see his enemies now. The corridor was full of
smoke. He continued to fire, aiming blindly down the corridor,
until the disk was exhausted. Then he emptied his pistol into
the blackness, heard the bullets ricocheting and thumping in
the distance and, as quickly as he could, reloaded both guns.

Listening, he heard men groaning and gasping and cursing.

Then, with a terrific impact, some object struck the door behind him. The door swung against him and almost knocked him off his feet.

Dazed, Peter hastened up the steps and made his way as swiftly as he could through men who had been cut down by the awful barrage of his submachine rifle.

Glancing back, he saw the door open behind him. He dropped down between two dead men and began firing at the opening. Then he felt a knife slash along his leg. He climbed up and backed down the corridor. When the door opened again, he fired a burst at the glowing vertical streak in the smoke.

THANKS TO Shanghai Charlie he was alive so far. Certainly this rifle, which sprayed bullets as a fire hose sprays water, had blocked K'ong's plan to capture or kill him. Perhaps K'ong had issued orders that he was not to be killed, but brought to him alive. The high priest's love for torture might, if Peter's good luck held, result in K'ong's downfall. Peter hoped so. Hope, in fact, was reviving for the first time tonight.

The door he had left behind him remained open. One of the guards had evidently fallen into the opening. But Peter could see nothing. The old-fashioned black gunpowder smoke from the rifles of K'ong's men had created a pale fog through which Peter could see none of his enemies. How many men were back in that room? How many lay ahead?

Had he thwarted K'ong's elaborate plan to capture him? It seemed incredible that he had, yet no more shots were fired. He advanced through the fog, which stung his eyes and smarted in his nostrils; climbed over the bodies of men dead and dying and recalled Shanghai Charlie's description of the wholesale killing in the golden room. "We shot them down until they were lyin' four deep—and still they kept comin'. We pumped lead into 'em until the guns were smokin'. And still they kept comin' at us with guns and swords and knives."

Peter reached the steps at the end of the corridor and glanced back. It was almost a fatal mistake, that pause. A bullet came screaming out of the smoke, struck the wall near his head and went ricocheting on, while sharp splinters of rock spattered his face.

Peter ran up the steps. He wondered if K'ong had laid further ambushes for him; or had K'ong assumed that he would never reach these steps without being captured? There was no doubt in his mind now that K'ong had issued strict orders to capture him; under no circumstances to kill him. How many men had that mistake cost him?

The American climbed up and up without being stopped, without, so far as he knew, being seen.

As he started up the spiral staircase cut into the black mala-chite which ended at K'ong's torture room, a wave of weakness went over Peter. It was like the black spell cast by a magician. He remembered his previous visit to this unholy place, when the atmosphere had seemed suddenly to turn black, as if blackness were oozing out like a thick liquid from the very walls and floor and ceiling.

He fought off a rising tide of faintness. The wound in his shoulder throbbed. The knife wound in his leg was, he knew, bleeding badly. Did he have the strength to carry out his audacious scheme?

A faint, muffled scream sharply cut off his thoughts. He reached the bronze door of Ung's torture chamber, a room which had witnessed the most horrible scenes of suffering.

He leaned against it, panting so heavily that his breath seemed to come and go in sobs. The strength seemed to ooze from his arms and legs. He had hardly the strength to hold the heavy rifle in his hand. He swayed. For a moment he thought he would faint.

Peter caught the wrist of his hand holding the automatic to his mouth and sank his teeth into it. The sharp pain acted as a restorative. It chased the dark, swirling mists from his brain.

Then, from the other side of the bronze slab, he heard again the faint, muffled scream.

CHAPTER XIV

A DESPERATE RUSE

ALL HIS WEIGHT Peter hurled against the door. But it did not give. He put the muzzle of the rifle against the crack where he knew the bolt was, and set the adjusting lever so that the bullets would leave the muzzle in a steady stream. It was dangerous. Bullets might ricochet back and tear him into fragments.

He pulled the trigger, aimed upward, and crouched down. A shattering roar followed. Lumps of rocks came tumbling down on his head.

Suddenly the bronze slab gave. The bullets had bored their way, enlarging the crack until it became a hole, cutting away the bronze bolt on the other side like the teeth of a terrific saw.

Unconscious of pain now, Peter stepped back and brought his injured shoulder smashing against the door. It flew open with a clang. Holding his pistol in readiness, Peter stepped over the threshold.

Swaying, the American stared at the figure in jade-green robes flattened against the grilled window across the room. He dropped his eyes for a moment to the slim figure strapped to the bamboo rack to his left.

Susan's eyes were closed. Her face had the bloodless whiteness of death. He glanced sharply at her hands; saw a tiny thread of blood extending downward from her right wrist to her breast.

He looked up as K'ong threw the knife. Peter dropped to his knees. The handle of the knife struck the wall behind the bamboo rack and dropped with a clatter to the stone floor. Peter threw both his guns to the floor and leaped at K'ong. His fist, in a tremendous uppercut, struck the high priest a glancing blow along the jaw line. K'ong squealed, turned about and clawed at the bronze grille of the window. The grille gave, and K'ong started out. Peter seized his feet, dragged him back and hurled him into a corner.

"Did you kill that girl?" he panted.

The yellow hands of K'ong fluttered. "No, no, no!" he squealed.

Peter picked up the knife and slashed the thongs which bound Susan's hands to the horizontal bar, slashed the thongs which bound her feet, then attended to the ropes binding her to the rack. He lifted her shoulders. They fell back limply when he let her go. Peter arose and grimly shut the door.

"K'ong," he said in a harsh voice, "if this girl is dead, you are going onto that rack. I am going to torture you to death as you have tortured others."

"She is not dead."

Susan now gave a demonstration of this fact. She opened her eyes and groaned. Peter knelt beside her. She looked into his face with unbelief. Then she looked at her gashed wrist.

"Peter!" she whispered. So she was the fainting kind, after all!

"Try to sit up. We've got to get out of here. And there's no time to lose."

"I'll try, Peter." She tried. With Peter's help, she sat up and swayed. Then she saw K'ong. Involuntarily, she whimpered and sagged against Peter's arm.

"Don't worry," he soothed her. "Everything is fine. We're going to get out of here. Try to stand up."

Susan came weakly to her feet and clung to him.

"How can we get out of here?" she wailed. "We'll be killed."

"Try walking around," he urged her.

Susan tried walking around. She stopped and looked at K'ong. "What are you going to do to him?" she asked.

"Plenty. Do you think you can walk as far as the Bund? It's necessary, Susan."

"I could walk from here to Hong Kong!"

"The *Java Bird*," he said, "is standing by for us to come aboard."

"But how can we get through?"

"K'ong," Peter said, "is going to carry me on his shoulders. K'ong, take off those robes."

The high priest hesitated. "Where is the hand of Ung?"

Peter produced the gruesome relic from his robes. K'ong stared at it. He licked his lips.

"You will never leave this temple alive with that hand."

"Take off those robes!"

THE HIGH priest hesitated again, but began divesting himself of the jade-green robes when Peter started toward him. When he stood in his customary black robes, Peter told Susan to put on the green ones.

"But why, Peter?"

"You are K'ong."

"I don't understand."

"Hurry, Susan."

She hastily donned the green robes.

"Pull the hood about your face and keep it there. You are K'ong. Remember?"

"Yes, Peter. Who are you?"

"I am—with K'ong's assistance—Ung."

"These robes are much too long for me."

"No one will notice that." He gave her his automatic. "Take this and keep it handy, but out of sight. K'ong, I am going to ride on your shoulders. We are going to walk out of the temple. I am going to hold this knife at your neck. I will give you directions in English, which none of your people understand. If they do, they'll be too scared to notice. Get down on your hands and knees."

"You will never get out of this temple alive," K'ong repeated.

"Perhaps not. But if I die, you will die one second earlier. Your only chance of life is to carry me, without stumbling, to the Bund. It is a long walk, but you are a strong man. Get down on your knees."

K'ong hesitated, but obeyed. His willingness caused Peter's eyes to narrow.

"K'ong, I will warn you once more. I am the great god Ung, who has been resurrected from the dead. I am going to ride your shoulders, and you are to walk slowly from this temple, through the streets to the Bund. The point of this knife will ride your jugular vein. If you stumble, or disobey orders, if you make the slightest appeal for help, or if you make, in any way, a false move—this knife will slash that vein."

Once again the high priest said: "You and this girl will never leave this temple alive."

Susan's eyes were glittering and her cheeks were flushed with excitement.

Peter was rubbing charcoal from the brazier into his finger tips. This he rubbed over his face with Susan's help, until, from forehead to chest, he was black—as black as Ung.

This detail attended to, Peter seated himself on K'ong's shoulders, with his legs about the high priest's neck.

"Stand up, K'ong."

The high priest of Ungism staggered to his feet. The combined height of the two men was close to nine feet.

Susan looked up with an excited smile.

"You're positively terrifying. Peter."

"How do these robes hang? We must create the illusion of one man—a giant."

"You do. The deception is perfect."

"Give me that hand."

Susan gave him the hand of Ung. Peter gripped it by the wrist bone and held the ugly relic so that the hand was protruding from the robes.

"You," Peter said to Susan, "are to walk behind me, not farther than a yard away, with that gun ready. I will fold this hood about my face to present possible detection. I will lead the way, and you will cover our retreat. Do not fire unless it is absolutely necessary... K'ong, proceed slowly. We are going across the compound and down the steps to the Street of the Red Lion, on down to the water front and to the sampan jetty. If you value your life, do as I tell you. Walk!"

CHAPTER XV

UNG WALKS AGAIN

WITH THAT KNIFE threatening his jugular vein, K'ong obeyed. He proceeded slowly out of the room and down the spiral stairway to the corridor below. Susan followed, a yard behind.

"You will never—" the muffled voice of K'ong began.

"Silence!" Peter snapped.

"I cannot see."

"Keep your voice low. Turn left."

Suddenly the glare of the countless pitch torches in the compound was in Peter's face. And suddenly the shouts of men and the screams of women ended. A hush followed. Men and women stared up at him. For a moment, his heart thumped with fear. Then they threw themselves face downward, and a great moan rose up.

Peter waited, then held out the hand of Ung. When silence fell again, he spoke in Tonkinese. He pitched his voice as low as he could.

"I am Ung!" Another moan from his thousands of listeners followed that startling assertion. "To touch me, to touch so much as a fold of my garments, means instant death. Keep away!"

He looked quickly about him. "That man or woman who looks upon me too closely will be stricken blind. Listen! I have tired of you. I have tired of your needless sacrifices and blood-letting. I am returning to the land from which I came. I am no longer your god. You are to seek a new god. You are to return to your villages, your farms, to the jungles and islands and hills.... Where is the girl who was to have been sacrificed tonight?"

There was a stir in the crowd. Two priests appeared, supporting the girl.

"Give this girl clothing," Peter ordered in a voice of thunder. "See that she is safely returned to her home. There are to be no more human sacrifices. There is to be no more self-torture. There is to be no more bloodletting. All you priests who have been sinning in my name are to seek useful employment. It is Ung who so orders. I am coming among you. Keep back! Death to the man who touches my robes! Blindness to the man who stares!"

Peter dropped his voice to a murmur, and spoke in English.

"Cross the compound to the steps leading into the Street of the Red Lion."

K'ong hesitated. Peter prodded him with the point of the knife; felt a shudder go through the high priest; knew that K'ong saw riches, power, glory vanish forever in the words Peter had thundered.

If K'ong did not collapse, if K'ong did not somehow contrive to gain the upper hand, Peter knew that Ungism was dead— as dead as ashes; knew that he was taking part in a historical moment. If he and Susan could escape, Ungism would be dead. What would happen to this great temple, whose origin was shrouded in the mists of oriental legend? The jungle would reach into it and overrun it and smother it, as the jungle had crept upon and smothered the ruins of the Angkor Wat to the south. Would the black temple present the baffling mysteries to a future civilization that the crumbling Angkor Wat presented to this one?

K'ONG WAS descending the steps into the Street of the Red Lion. Susan, holding the jade-green robes about her and the automatic pistol in readiness, followed three feet behind. Silence continued in the mile-square compound until they reached the beginning of the Street of the Red Lion. Then a babbling arose. Would they suspect? Would they follow?

Some did, but at a respectful distance. Others circled about and were peering out from street crossings. Once, when a mob drew close, K'ong stumbled and all but fell. Peter prodded him with the knife. K'ong recovered himself and went on. He proceeded to the Bund and, under Peter's directions, to the sampan jetty.

The inshore side of the Bund was packed with men and women. Climbing into the sampan was difficult and dangerous. A misstep now would spell disaster. Susan, breathing hard, held the sampan while K'ong stepped aboard. Once on the after deck, their safety was assured. Susan picked up the sweep and, for the second time tonight, made for the deck lights of the *Java Bird*.

As the sampan vanished into the blackness of the harbor, a groan went up from the Bund. It was like the moaning of wind in palm trees. And Peter knew that it was the final moan of a black religion which had seen its last ritual, caused its last poor victim to writhe in agony.

In his relief, Peter all but forgot the venomous nature of the man on whose shoulders he sat. He had unconsciously relaxed the pressure of the knife. And the man under him snatched at what was certainly, to him, the only straw of hope.

If K'ong could regain command of the situation and bring these infidels immediately to shore, the power of Ungism and, with it, the power of K'ong, would be restored.

His hand leaped up and snatched at the knife at his throat. Surprised by the swiftness of the attack, Peter let it be plucked from his hand. With a convulsive heave, K'ong sent him toppling from his shoulders to the deck. Peter fell on his right side.

Peter shouted a warning to Susan as he plunged down. The light from the street lamps on the Bund provided so little illumination here that it was next to darkness. He saw the flash of the knife in K'ong's hand as the high priest leaped on Susan. Peter's breath had been knocked from him by the fall. His clutching fingers closed on a hard, brittle, shiny object—the hand of Ung.

As K'ong raised the knife, Peter struggled up and leaped on

him. He brought the worshiped relic down with all his power on K'ong's head, and both heard and felt the skull of the high priest crush under the blow.

K'ong crumpled to the deck. Peter picked him up and threw him overboard. He threw the hand of Ung after him and saw, for a fleeting instant, a light from one of the lamps on the Bund flicker across the black knuckles before it sank forever from sight into the tidal mud.

Susan was clinging to him, laughing and crying with relief.

"We're safe," he comforted her.

"I'm not afraid," Susan said. She shivered, then cuddled against him.

Peter was swept by a wave of tenderness for this plucky girl, and as she lay for a moment in his arms, it occurred to him that Susan must have had enough thrills, enough excitement, enough danger to last her a lifetime.

He looked down into her face. In the diffused glow of the *Java Bird's* deck lights, it was pale and wistful and somehow yearning. And he knew that, if Susan was cured of her thirst for adventure, Susan was the one girl in the world for him.

"Peter?"

"Yes, Susan?"

"I've been scared tonight as I've never been scared in my life," she said in a husky little voice. "I was closer to death than I've ever been before. Peter, you were perfectly wonderful."

Her deep violet eyes were glowing.

"It's funny," she said, "but I'm not the least bit scared any more. I think I'm growing used to adventure. When you look back upon it, even now—wasn't tonight perfectly marvelous?"

"Marvelous!" Peter dryly agreed, and released her. He picked up the sweep and began vigorously working it. He was wrong again; Susan wasn't cured. But Peter was.

ABOUT THE AUTHOR

THE DECISION TO become a writer of fiction was made for me by fate. In 1914, in Panama, where I spent a week when I was a wireless operator on a little steamer that creaked up and down the Central American coast, I met an author who painted the joys of free-lancing so vividly that I could not resist the call. We were drunk. I was twenty. Since then, I have been trying to catch up with all of those joys he mentioned.

Starting to write stories in 1914 and, four years later selling my first one, marks up, I suppose, a very poor batting average. But in those years I was getting experience, seeing the world, and acquiring knowledge. I "punched brass" as a wireless operator all over the Pacific. I entered Columbia University in 1915, and one year later left because I didn't believe in higher learning. I still don't believe in it. I became a newspaper reporter, later a magazine editor.

Then came the war, which I won practically single-handed by writing high-pressure publicity to induce patriotic Americans to send books to Washington for camp libraries for soldiers and gobs. Books came by the carload, by the ton: McGuffy's readers, old almanacs, spellers, arithmetics, out-dated novels and just trash. The soldiers and sailors who read those books soon hated the war so bitterly, that they promptly got busy and ended it. That's how I won the war.

After the war, I wanted another look at China, and was sent

to the Far East by *Collier's* to write articles on China, the Philippines, India
and Malaya.

The first story I sold was written
while I was editing a motion picture
trade paper. It was bought by the
Argosy, and it was about a wolf named
Murg. Don't ask me why. In the intervening years I have written millions of
words. Perhaps it is Murg who sits so
patiently at my door!

*George F.
Worts*

I started writing fiction under the
pen name of Loring Brent, because it would have annoyed the
owner of the motion picture magazine to learn that I was writing fiction out of hours. He thought I fell asleep at my desk
because I was working so hard for him! When my income from
fiction exceeded my salary, I quit the job. Since then I have been
free-lancing exclusively, except for a two-year period when I
lived in a Florida swamp town and added to my writing the
duties of postmaster, game warden and deputy sheriff. Out of
that experience came a long series of stories about a Florida
town I called Vingo.

I have enjoyed most writing stories about certain established
characters. Apparently the most popular of these have been the
Peter the Brazen, the Vingo and the Gillian Hazeltine stories. I
stopped writing about Peter the Brazen (a swashbuckling wireless operator on ships in the China run) about ten years ago.
He was, incidentally, the subject of the only novel I have had
published in America. I am now starting a new series about him.

When I am not traveling I live in Westport, Connecticut. My
interests are horses, sailing and flying. I took up flying about a
year ago to write some articles on how it feels to learn to fly, and
was badly bitten by the bug. I can make a three-point landing
about five times out of ten.

I like New York, but would prefer to live in Honolulu. I smoke sixty cigarettes a day. I like murder trials. I have never mastered the noble game of poker, although I once wrote a book about it. In my spare time I study law and medicine. I have two young sons and a still younger daughter; an able crew for my sailboat—except that there is usually mutiny aboard the lugger!

Made in the USA
Monee, IL
19 December 2020

54530283R00152